THE MURDER WHEEL

THE MURDER WHEEL

A JOSEPH SPECTOR LOCKED-ROOM MYSTERY

TOM MEAD

THE MYSTERIOUS PRESS
NEW YORK

THE MURDER WHEEL

Mysterious Press
An Imprint of Penzler Publishers
58 Warren Street
New York, N.Y. 10007

First Mysterious Press edition

Interior design by Maria Fernandez
Maps by Eric Timothy Carlson

Library of Congress Control Number: 2023909991

ISBN: 978-1-61316-409-9
eBook ISBN: 978-1-61316-410-5

10 9 8 7 6 5 4 3 2 1

Printed in the United States of America
Distributed by W. W. Norton & Company

To my mum and dad

and

once again, in memory of the maestro

(1906–1977)

If the world will be gulled,
let it be gulled.

—Robert Burton, *The Anatomy of
Melancholy* (1621), Part III, Section IV

CONTENTS

DRAMATIS PERSONAE

At the Pomegranate Theatre:
"Professor Paolini," a magician
Martha, his assistant
Sidney Draper, a stage manager
Kenneth Fabris, a stagehand
Max Toomey, a look-alike
Alf, a doorman
Will Cope, a lighting technician
Andrew Morgan, a journalist
Ned Winchester, a troublemaker

And elsewhere:
Edmund Ibbs, a lawyer
Titus Pilgrim, a criminal
Mr. Keegan   } his men
Mr. Branning
Carla Dean, a widow
Dominic Dean, a bank manager (deceased)

Felix Draven, an acting bank manager
Maudie Cash, a cashier
Miklos Varga, a fairground man
Boyd Remiston, a suspicious character
Inspector George Flint, of Scotland Yard
Sergeant Jerome Hook, of Scotland Yard
Joseph Spector, a professional trickster

THE POMEGRANATE THEATRE

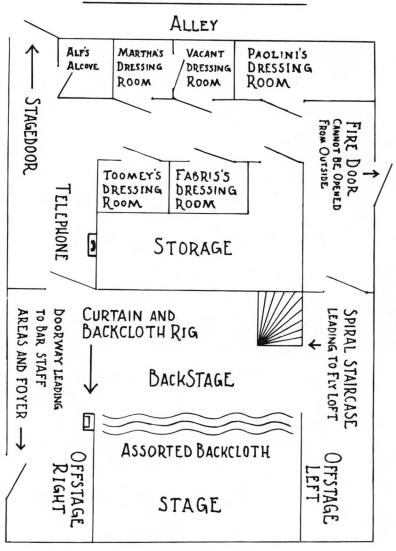

PART ONE

SOME MUST WATCH

No matter how large or small an illusion, there is one thing to remember: your audience is in front of you. Keep them there.

—*The Master of Manipulation*, "Ruminations"

Nothing must be left to chance in a magical performance. Everything conducive to enhancing the mystery of the illusions must be arranged with painstaking care and thought.

—**David Devant**

CHAPTER ONE

"CAN *YOU* SOLVE THE FERRIS WHEEL MURDER CASE?"

I t began with the book. If not for the book, the rest of it would not have happened. At least, that's what Ibbs told himself after the fact. But truthfully, the whole hideous thing—every single facet of the case—slotted together so neatly that it was like an immaculately-timed sleight-of-hand trick. The quickness of the hand deceives the eye. But at the same time it had the kind of mad, surreal logic that is typically found in the most lucid and frenetic of fever dreams.

Ibbs did not believe in magic. And yet the macabre and bloody comedy of errors that occurred at the Pomegranate Theatre that night could not have unfurled more perfectly if it had been planned and executed by some invisible hellion. A puckish trickster, mocking his misfortune at every turn.

That was Friday, September 16, 1938: the day the gods played their wickedest trick on Edmund Ibbs.

But first: the book.

The morning began promisingly enough: a rap on the door of his quarters. He was lodging in upstairs rooms in Chancery Lane, not far from the Inns of Court in central London. Though he had not yet reached his thirtieth birthday, he'd completed his legal studies the previous summer and was now a full-fledged solicitor. Like all greenhorns, he was the object of his colleagues' blade-edged wit, and frequently found himself lumbered with heaps of the most tedious paperwork and monotonous administrative duties. But he didn't let it bother him. In fact, he considered it to be a rite of passage. No doubt they too had gone through it in their time, and now it was his turn.

At the door was the elderly porter Lancaster; stout and stolid as a pint of Guinness. He was holding a parcel.

"Morning Mr. Ibbs, sir."

"How do, Lancaster? Got something for me?"

"Book of some description, sir."

Ibbs took it, feeling its heft on his palm. He had scarcely said a cheery goodbye and closed the door again before he was wrenching the paper away. The scraps drifted lazily to the floor as he examined the book by the window. Its embossed title caught the light: *The Master of Manipulation*.

He could almost feel the book's talismanic power rippling through his fingers and up the length of his arms, like a tangible electrical charge. But it was just a book, he reminded himself. Mere words on paper. What he was actually experiencing was an adrenaline surge; the excitement and anticipation bubbling over.

Ever since he first heard about *The Master of Manipulation*, Ibbs knew that he simply had to have a copy. It was not the sort of item a regular bookseller would stock, but he had a man in Marylebone who tracked down the more outré titles for him, and who had been only too willing to source a copy the day after it was published.

Though a lawyer by trade, Edmund Ibbs was also an enthusiastic amateur magician. Or, to use the appropriate term, *illusionist*. And when he first heard rumours of the book at a meeting of the London Occult Practice Collective (a trade organisation which was surprisingly welcoming when it came to amateurs) it had seemed like the answer to a prayer. Needless to say, the professionals were utterly scandalised. But for dilettantes like Ibbs, *The Master of Manipulation* was the book they had all been waiting for.

A magician lives and dies by the strength of his illusions. Drawing back the curtain to show the innermost workings of stage magic is a risk most conjurors would never take. There is an unspoken code concerning such things. But Ibbs was little more than a curious layman, and so the book (which was due to be published by a second-tier and not altogether reputable publishing house) was little short of a miracle. A single book containing a panoply of magical secrets—all the mysteries and wonders of the stage dispelled at a stroke!

The book was published under a foolish pseudonym—the sort of thing you'd usually find in the pages of *Punch*: Dr. Anne L. Surazal. Ibbs had been puzzling over just who the wicked lady might be ever since he heard of the book's existence. It took an embarrassingly long time to spot that "Dr. Anne L. Surazal" is "Lazarus Lennard" spelled backward. But that information was little use without knowing who Lazarus Lennard might be. Some insider, perhaps, who knew the tricks of the trade.

Ibbs checked the clock on his mantle and judged he had enough time to get to grips with chapter one—which was tantalisingly titled "Cards from Nowhere"—before heading out into the damp and miserable September morning. He opened a drawer in his bureau and grabbed his own dog-eared Bicycle deck. He gave the cards a quick riffle shuffle and set them down on the table (a little messy, but all right otherwise). Then he focused on the text.

The frontispiece bore a minutely detailed pen-and-ink illustration of a Mephistophelean man (complete with goatee and curled moustache). He was one of the Acetabularii, history's first recorded illusionists; the cup-and-ball specialists of Ancient Rome. Ibbs was too excited to notice at the time, but a close examination of the drawing would have told him all he needed to know about how the cup-and-ball trick was done. You see, in the picture the conjuror is holding the ball between index finger and thumb of his right hand, presenting it to the observer. But look closely enough and you'll see reflected in the fellow's eyes the second ball, hidden from the audience in what's called a "Tenkai Palm," sandwiched between thumb and palm of his unobtrusive left hand. *The Master of Manipulation* was one of those books: all the answers were there if you knew how to look for them.

The art of magic, he read, *lies in the manipulation of perception. Most people will look exactly where you want them to; all you have to do is tell them. It is simply a matter of guiding their attention in the correct direction, so that they are never looking at the trick as it is being worked.*

Hardly earth-shattering, but it was enough to ensnare Ibbs's attention that morning, to the point where he was almost late for work. He soared through the first few chapters while eating a breakfast of porridge and dry toast, and it was with a heavy heart that he finally dragged himself away and readied himself to earn a day's pay. There was now the pesky business of the day job to be got out of the way. But it's safe to say that magic was at the forefront of his mind as he headed out to Holloway Prison that morning.

It was hard to leave the book behind, but Ibbs told himself that it would be much worse if he were to bring it with him and somehow lose it, or drop it in a puddle while shouldering his way through the rush-hour crowds. Instead he bought a newspaper from a seller on the corner, and boarded the omnibus. *The Master of Manipulation* would be waiting at his bedside when he got home.

It was difficult to concentrate on the tediously innuendo-laden headlines about Chamberlain's flight to Berchtesgaden and other such abstract political matters. The only flutter of interest he managed to muster was for a prize the *Chronicle* was offering:

CAN YOU SOLVE THE FERRIS WHEEL MURDER CASE?
THE DAILY CHRONICLE IS OFFERING A REWARD OF
TWO THOUSAND POUNDS TO ANYONE WHO
CAN DEMONSTRATE A SOLUTION TO
THE *IMPOSSIBLE* FERRIS WHEEL CRIME!

He folded the newspaper and slipped it under his arm with a sigh. At least the press was on his side. In the *Chronicle*, at least, she was innocent. But the court of public opinion and the court of law are two very different things.

While the omnibus trundled its way out to Parkhurst Road, his attention was caught by a boy of about six sitting across from him. The lad looked miserable and clung to his mother's skirts with palpable despondency. Ibbs took a coin out of his pocket, a sovereign. Then, very carefully as the bus traversed bumps and wove in and out of traffic, he began twirling the coin from knuckle to knuckle, showing off the practiced dexterity of his hands.

The boy watched for a little while, unsmiling and deathly serious. Ibbs placed the coin in the palm of his hand, snaring it in a tight fist. Then he held up two closed fists side by side, glancing at the boy expectantly. After some serious thought, the boy pointed to the right hand, the original hand which had held the coin. Ibbs spread his fingers, showing that the palm was empty. The coin had leapt to his other hand.

The boy's expression did not change, but Ibbs convinced himself there was a sparkle of enthusiasm in his eyes. Taking that as encouragement, he continued. He made the coin leap back and forth invisibly between his hands. It's a simple enough illusion, close in principle to the cup-and-ball trick. You just need another coin your audience doesn't know about. You always keep it just out of sight between the fingers of whichever hand is *not* flamboyantly demonstrating the trick. He had spent countless hours practicing in front of his mirror, just watching his reflection for the slightest hint of the second coin. If *he* couldn't see it, neither could his audience.

The coup de theatre: Ibbs lay flat both palms to show that they were empty. Then he clapped once, loudly enough to wake a woman sitting beside him from a snorting snooze. The boy watched in confusion. He looked up and down the bus to see if there was something he had missed. As he did so, the coin slipped from the dome of his young head and tumbled to the floor. Ibbs stretched out a leg and caught it on his shoe.

"That's yours," he said. The boy pounced on it and held it aloft as though it were some pirate's booty. Then he slipped it into the pocket of his shorts and got back to playing with his mother's skirts.

The next stop was Ibbs's. He stepped off the bus energised, if a sovereign lighter, and strode along Parkhurst Road toward the immense wooden gates of Holloway.

From the outside, Holloway Prison is a kind of palace of brown brick—immense and awe-inspiring, covering untold acres of land, but snared by high walls and discreetly razor-lined wire. A guard saluted as he stepped through the gate. Ibbs wasn't sure how to respond, so he saluted back. Then he kicked himself all the way up the path to the double doors—he should have simply looked at the fellow with steely disdain and then looked away. *That* is how a fellow commands respect.

An older uniformed man was waiting at the main entrance. "Ibbs?"

"That's me, sir."

"Very good. Warden Matthews." They shook hands. "You're here to see the 'lady of the moment,' I understand."

"Carla Dean."

"That's the one. Been keeping us busy, she has."

"Is she a troublesome prisoner then?"

"Not at all. Quiet as a mouse and very subdued. Reads her Bible a lot. But people are curious about her. Many's the time I've had to personally stop a reporter from sneaking in through our doors to try and snag an interview. They try all sorts of disguises. It can get quite comical."

"Seems counterintuitive to sneak into a prison," Ibbs observed.

Matthews laughed. "You're telling me."

The pair strode along drab corridors that reminded Ibbs eerily of his old boarding school. They shared that same conscious absence of ornament. Décor as a psychological weapon.

"You've visited Mrs. Dean before have you?"

"I met her once while she was in police custody. But that was with Sir Cecil. He did most of the talking."

"I see. And now they're trusting you to interview her solo?"

"Well, yes. Truth be told, we're all rather stretched." Ibbs had been roped in to assist the illustrious Sir Cecil Bullivant, QC, who would be acting for the defence. Bullivant had promptly come down with an acute case of copropraxia for which his bemused physician had prescribed bed rest. This left Ibbs with a considerable amount of work to do in the matter of the Crown versus Carla Dean. Currently, the case to be presented before Justice Sir Giles Drury was far from watertight.

The warden threw him a sideways smile: "Well, good luck."

What was that supposed to mean?

There was no denying the case had caused a sensation. Fleet Street christened its new baby the "Ferris Wheel Murder Case," which was an efficient summary of the key features. But the name did not convey the feeling of almost supernatural mystery which permeated the sequence of events. Two people went up on that Ferris wheel, and only one came down alive.

Ibbs had met Carla Dean once before, all too briefly. Not long enough to generate a lasting impression, at least. The newspaper photographs showed a young woman alive with intelligence and excitement. There was a glow about the face which seemed to seep from the photo paper. In prison she had aged decades. There were lines about her eyes and mouth that had grown shadowed, and her hair plumed messily. It was hard to believe this woman was not yet thirty. She wore a shapeless grey dress that looked to be fashioned out of sackcloth. Her thin, pianist's hands were threaded in her lap and she sat patiently, waiting for Ibbs to begin. Her eyes were deep; that is to say there was much in them he could not quite fathom. Like peering into twin chasms whose dimensions are beyond understanding. Like so much in this case, it only occurred to him after the fact, when he tried to picture Carla Dean again. But at that moment, as they faced each other across the cell, his only thought was how feeble he felt in her presence. How inadequate.

Did she look like a killer? It was a question which would need to be looked into seriously sooner or later. But there was undeniably something of the coiled spring in her knotted muscles and the feline uprightness with which she perched on the bed. The stillness too; the stillness meant something.

"Good morning, Mrs. Dean."

"Good morning, Mr. Ibbs. How nice to see you again." When she spoke, she might have been any other high-society hostess.

There was a smoky hush to her voice—the sort of voice one leans in to listen to. But her face was expressionless.

"I hope you don't mind if I get straight down to business. I have a lot to get through today."

"Not at all. Please sit down."

Ibbs perched on the cold wooden chair beside the bed. Mrs. Dean remained on the mattress. She had lost weight.

"If you don't mind, I'd like you to repeat the story you have already told many times. The story of what happened to your husband on the night of August 19th. Will you do that for me?"

She inclined her head. "I'll do what I can."

"Good. Please begin." He had his notebook and pen in hand. This was purely about pinpointing inconsistencies in her account. Of course he knew the story inside out but, like a magic trick, the key was in the repetition. With each new version the nuances and idiosyncrasies came to the fore.

"He took me to the fair. It was supposed to be a little treat for me. He bought me candy floss and we danced and had a jolly time."

"What time did you arrive?"

"I would say six o'clock. My husband works. Worked." She blinked a little, but evidently she had done all the crying she intended to do.

"Whilst you were at the fair, did you encounter anybody you knew or recognised?"

"Certainly. There were a number of people from our street."

"And did you notice anybody or anything that seemed unusual or out of the ordinary?"

"Well, it's hard to say. The place was a cavalcade of clowns and jugglers and magicians."

"Did you recognise anybody among the performers?"

"No."

"Did your husband?"

She paused, considering her response. "He was looking over his shoulder. As though someone were following him."

"And *was* anyone following him?"

"Possibly. The thought didn't occur to me at the time, but afterward . . . I began to convince myself that there *was* someone. A man with a limp, I glimpsed him once or twice as we made our way round the fair . . ."

"Let's stick to the facts for the moment. Was your husband in the habit of carrying a firearm with him when he went out?"

This was the first difficult question. Ibbs wanted to see how she would react. She seemed to take it with aplomb. There was the briefest flicker of concentration on her face, and then she answered: "No."

"How do you know?"

"I think I would have known, don't you? It's true that my husband *owned* a firearm. It was a revolver, an ugly grey thing, I had no interest in it whatsoever. But it never left the house if I had any say in the matter, I can tell you that much. It was purely for personal protection, in the event of a burglar for instance. He had no reason to take it to the fair."

"Ah, yes . . ." Ibbs flipped through a few pages in his notebook. "A 'Nagant M1895.' A Bolshevik weapon, I believe?"

She shrugged.

"How did he come by it?"

"I've no idea."

Ibbs changed tack. "You seem to think that he was being followed that night. Wouldn't it make sense for him to carry a firearm? How can you be so positive that he was unarmed?"

She sighed, clearly growing weary of repeating herself. "Because the evening was a little chilly and he gave me his jacket. You know, draped it around my shoulders. Chivalrous sort of thing. If the revolver was on his person, I should have seen it. And if it were in his jacket, I should have felt it."

"What about his trousers? He might have tucked it down the back of his trousers, perhaps, or concealed it in a pocket?"

"No, no. It was too big to hide in a pocket. And if it were tucked into his trousers, it would have been clearly visible."

"What about his ankles?"

"Stowed in his sock, you mean? No. Again, it would have been plain to see. My husband was wearing a linen suit, so the outline of a revolver anywhere on his person would have been plain to see."

"And what about you, Mrs. Dean? Were you armed?"

"No. I was not. I hate guns with every fibre of my being. It was a great source of annoyance to me that Dominic felt the need to keep one in the house."

"You were carrying a handbag, correct?"

"Yes, but no gun. I most certainly would *not* have left the house with a revolver in my handbag."

"I see. Perhaps you'd better tell me about the pistol. What prompted your husband to buy it?"

She sighed. "He wasn't himself after what happened at the bank. He was . . . out of sorts. Scared of his own shadow. He got the foolish idea that a gun would keep him safe."

"But you disagreed."

"Well, it should be obvious that a bank manager with a loaded gun in his desk is an accident waiting to happen."

"He always kept it loaded?"

"I've no idea."

"Did you ever *see* him load it?"

"Never."

"So you never felt inclined to use the weapon yourself? Or even to look at it?"

She shrugged. "Why should I? The revolver was always in his study. So were the bullets. And I never had cause to venture in there. It simply didn't interest me."

"I see." Ibbs finished scribbling a few notes, then looked back up at the prisoner. "So neither you nor your husband were armed that night. In that case, where did the gun come from?"

This was the key question. The question which both the defence and the prosecution would need to answer.

"I don't know," said Carla Dean. "I heard it clatter to the floor and the next moment it was in my hand. . . ."

"Let's take things chronologically. At what time did you go on the Ferris wheel?"

"I should say around nine, though I can't be sure."

"And whose suggestion was it?"

"Dominic's. He was always fond of them."

"Were you reluctant?"

"No. I'm game for most things."

"But not gunplay," Ibbs observed without looking up. "What did he say to you? Tell me in as much detail as you can."

"We just talked about the ordinary everyday things that couples talk about. We bickered about our finances. We made plans. I honestly don't remember in detail. It was absent-minded folderol. Of course I had no idea it was the last conversation I would ever have with my husband."

"Did he have money problems?"

She was careful in her answer. "He was too generous with his spending. I often had to warn him about tightening his belt, but he never listened."

"I see. Now please tell me precisely. You got onto the Ferris wheel. You had a passenger car to yourselves."

"Yes. Just the two of us."

"Who purchased the ticket?"

"Dominic. When you get onto the Ferris wheel, you have to pass by the small ticket booth. Dominic stopped and bought the ticket. He exchanged a few words with whoever was inside the booth, but I didn't see who it was. I wasn't concentrating."

"And then you climbed into the carriage?"

"Yes." She trailed off into silence, her gaze drifting toward the barred window.

"Please," Ibbs prompted, "what next?"

"It was so cold up there. I wrapped his jacket tighter around me. He was talking ten-to-the-dozen about something he was going to do tomorrow."

"Saying what?"

"I don't remember. All I remember is the shot. I was looking the other way. I was looking down. I didn't see where the gun came from."

"But you believe your husband was the one who pulled the trigger?"

"Well, who else could it have been?"

His pen nib hovered over the notepad. "And it was just a single shot?"

"Yes. It echoed, but all the same I could tell it was just one shot. Then there was a loud clang as the gun dropped to the floor of the car. And poor Dominic was clutching his stomach, crying and yelling."

"How high up were you at this point?"

"We were at the very top. Beginning our descent."

"And what did you do then?"

"I said 'Dominic, what is it, what's happened?' It was a silly question of course. I could see just what had happened. But all he said was 'Please, I'm hurt.' Oh, it was so pitiful, Mr. Ibbs. It broke my heart. So, as the car moved down, I popped my head over the side and called out: 'Help, it's my husband, he's hurt.'"

"And then?"

"Well, naturally a lot of people heard the commotion. A crowd gathered, there was a great deal of pushing and shoving."

"And?"

"There was a doctor on hand, off duty, he just happened to be attending the fair with his wife. He took a quick look at my husband, but of course there was nothing he could do. So an ambulance was called. My husband had been shot in the stomach."

"He was in great pain?"

"Yes. Very much so. He died before the ambulance could get to him."

"And before he could say a word about what happened."

"He made some indistinct mumblings. That was all."

"Let me ask you this, Mrs. Dean," Ibbs said, laying his pen and pad to one side and steepling his fingers, "what do *you* think happened to your husband?"

"Somebody shot him, I know that much. But who it was, I couldn't possibly say."

"The powder burns on your husband's clothes and body indicated that the pistol had been fired at very close range. The two of you were alone in the carriage on the Ferris wheel. Your fingerprints were all over the weapon."

"Because I picked it up from the floor," she protested. "It was instinctive. I know now I shouldn't have done it."

"The weapon was your husband's."

"So I've been told. But they all look the same to me."

"There's little doubt the revolver was the murder weapon. It had been fired, and there were two empty chambers in the cylinder—it seems likely your husband left one empty, to prevent an accidental misfire. He must have been a cautious man. And it would appear he *was* armed that evening."

"He wasn't, I'm sure of it."

"Then where did the weapon come from?"

She was getting frustrated. It was useful to get that sort of thing out of the way now, to give an idea of how she would perform in court. "I don't know where it came from."

"Then who fired the shot?"

"I don't know, Mr. Ibbs! I just don't know!" She quickly lapsed into silence again. Her bony shoulders heaved up and down with each agitated breath, and she could no longer meet his gaze. This was taxing her patience as much as it was Ibbs's.

He paused for a moment, letting this brief surge of petulance subside. Then he said, "Could it have been the limping man?"

She looked up, like a startled squirrel. "Well, I . . ." then the enthusiasm waned. "No. It couldn't have been."

"Why not?"

"Because the limping man never stepped on the Ferris wheel."

"How can you be sure of that? You yourself said you hardly paid any attention to the limping man. It was your *husband* who was looking over his shoulder, and seemed to be wary of this elusive fellow."

"Well . . . that's . . . true," she conceded. "But I still don't see how . . ."

"Never mind that," Ibbs said, aping Sir Cecil's jocular demeanor. "The fact is that he *could* have. We don't know how, but if it comes down to it I shall do my damnedest to find *out* how."

"All right," she said with a fresh sense of resolve.

"Good." Much like a magic trick, the facts in a court case are of less significance than what an audience can be made to believe. If there was any way, any way at all, that somebody other than Mrs. Carla Dean could have killed her husband on top of that Ferris wheel, then it was Ibbs's duty to pursue every possible angle. Anything whatsoever that might exonerate this young woman.

"There's one other thing I'd like to ask," he said, somewhat coyly. It was another difficult question, and he didn't know how she'd react.

"Please do."

"Are you telling me the truth, Mrs. Dean?"

She twitched an eyebrow, but otherwise her face was expressionless. "What do you mean?"

"What you've told me—how you looked away for an instant, then you heard the shot and saw the revolver lying there. How you instinctively grabbed the murder weapon. Is it true?"

"Yes," she said firmly. "Besides, why would any woman be dense enough to murder her husband when she was the *only possible culprit*? You don't think I'm silly enough for something like that, do you?"

Silly enough to pick up the gun, Ibbs thought. "Not at all. But if it's the truth, you'd better tell me. There's ways out of these things, you know. All you need do is be honest. If it happened as I described, we've got a good case for an insanity plea. A few years in an asylum is greatly preferable to the noose, believe me."

"I'll take your word for it, Mr. Ibbs. I have no intention of going to an asylum or to the noose. I am an innocent woman, and I am convinced a jury will find me so."

"All right," Ibbs slapped his thighs and made to stand, "I think I've got what I came here for."

"Is that all? Don't you want to ask me anything more about my husband?"

"Well, I can see you've given me all the answers you're going to give me. I'll leave you to your bed and your Bible."

20

"No, wait! Please, I'm sorry. I don't want you to think I don't appreciate the hard work you and Sir Cecil are doing for me, Mr. Ibbs. But you must understand that I've been through this story so many times now. I know how ludicrous it sounds. They don't let me have the newspapers in here, but I'm sure the press are having a wonderful time making fun of me. The only reason I'm sticking to this story," she said pointedly, "is because it's true."

She was certainly convincing. But being convincing and being honest are not the same thing. Ibbs may have been a young green-horn, but even he was aware of that fact. He studied her carefully—he had given up on making notes. "Was your husband suicidal?"

"You think he shot himself?"

"Well, what other explanation is there? You didn't shoot him—very well. Nobody else could have shot him—very well. So where does that leave us?"

"I . . ." she seemed lost in thought. "I suppose he *could* . . ."

It was a trick question; the suicide angle had been largely ruled out. Men simply don't shoot themselves in the stomach—it's such a messy, painful, drawn-out way to die. But the fact that Carla Dean had not ruled it out herself was . . . interesting.

"If he thought the limping man was after him, then perhaps he *would* have brought a gun with him," she continued. It was as if she were trying to reason with herself. "But I just can't see Dominic emptying six bullets into another man. It wouldn't be his style. And of course, as I have said numerous times, when we went out that night *he was not armed.*"

Ibbs left her not long after that. There was little else to discuss. She had answered the salient questions, after a fashion, and it was now up to him to collate her strange patchwork story into something cohesive. Something which might be presented to a jury.

Had she done it? He couldn't say. Really, it wasn't his place to draw conclusions. She was certainly not a stupid woman. He could tell that by the calculated nature of her speech—even her outbursts. If she were planning to murder her husband, surely she would have come up with a less cartoonish method?

Unless it really *was* a fit of passion. Such things were not unheard of. But then there was the question of the revolver—how did it get there? If Dean himself had brought it, why? And if Carla had brought it, surely that indicated premeditation? And besides, what could there be in poor, middle-aged, bookish bank manager Dominic Dean's life to evince such homicidal fury?

When Ibbs boarded the omnibus again, he was no longer thinking about magic. Now he was wondering what dreadful secrets might be lurking behind the Deans' veneer of civility. And he was thinking about the limping man.

CHAPTER TWO

THE GOLDERS GREEN JOB

T ruth be told, there was a flutter of childlike anticipation in Ibbs's belly as he stepped off the omnibus in Golders Green. He wasn't far from the Dean residence—a neat, terraced home that had featured in several newspaper photographs. That wasn't his destination though. He was heading for the scene of the crime: the fairground.

In a patch of civilised, suburban outer-London, the fair was especially incongruous. But even though the amusements were not yet up and running (that would come later in the day) there was a pleasant buzz in the air. A tangy scent of frying dough and candy floss. He strode through the dried-up mud between merry-go-rounds and helter-skelters and dodgems which looked somehow eerie and menacing, untenanted in broad daylight. The dodgem cars were lined up neatly side by side, as though waiting to pounce.

He could feel eyes on him; the eyes of those brass merry-go-round horses, white and staring. As he passed it, a large ornate fairground organ burst into life, playing "Oh I Do Like to Be beside the Seaside." It made him jump.

He slowed his pace to a hypnotic trudge. Was it really as desolate as this? There was the smell of food and the sound of the organ to convince him there must be fairground folk lurking somewhere behind the scenes. He was heading toward the immense and dominating presence of the Ferris wheel at the far end of the fairground. It was deathly still and unlit at the moment, but somehow that made it all the more awe-inspiring. He looked up at the little metal cars, which would hold no more than two or three people at a time and seemed to dangle and swing slightly in the breeze, and he felt a profound sense of disquiet. In one of those cars, Dominic Dean had been shot dead. He had died there. Perhaps the floor still bore traces of his blood.

Emerging from a duck-shoot stall was a man in a garish chequered suit and pastel-blue bowler hat. He spoke with some sort of accent Ibbs couldn't quite place: something European. "Help you?"

"I hope so," said Ibbs. "I'm here about the Dean case."

"We said what we want to say to the press about that. You got your story already, no more."

"My name is Edmund Ibbs," the young lawyer persisted. "I'm a solicitor, I'm working on the Dean case."

"You're defending her?" He inched toward Ibbs. A silver crucifix around his neck caught the sunlight.

"I am working for the defence, yes."

"Then what do you want to know?"

"I want to speak to the gentleman who was manning the Ferris wheel ticket booth the night Dominic Dean was killed."

"Well, you're looking at him."

"Am I indeed? What is your name, sir?"

"Varga. Miklos Varga."

"Very well, Mr. Varga." Ibbs held out a hand and Varga shook it warily. A few other fairground operators had begun to appear now. Slowly, very slowly, the place was coming to life. "Is there somewhere we can talk?"

"I like to talk in the open," he said.

"All right. My questions are simple enough. All I want to know is whether anything unusual happened during the hour or so before the murder."

"Like what?"

"You tell me. Any kind of disturbance."

"No. We run a tight ship here."

"Carla Dean claims she and her husband got onto the Ferris wheel at approximately nine o'clock. Is that right?"

"Yes."

"Whilst they were up there on the Ferris wheel, did anything unusual occur? Anything even slightly out of the ordinary?"

Varga thought about this. "Your ticket buys you sixteen spins of the wheel. They were about halfway through; seven or eight revolutions. And they were right at the top when I heard the shot."

"So it *was* a shot then?"

Varga looked confused. "Well, of course it was a shot. . . ."

"Yes, but did you think so *at the time*? Or was it just because of all the chatter after the fact about gunshots that you made that assumption?"

"Well, now you mention it, there are other things it might have been. At the fair you get all kinds of sounds."

"Good. What then?"

"Well, Mrs. Dean popped her head over the side of the car as it came down. She was screaming and yelling 'help, help.'"

"All right. Thank you, Miklos, you're doing well. Now, can you tell me about the people on the ground?"

"Well, there was a queue of people waiting to board the wheel. Young couples. Children. People like that."

"Anybody out of the ordinary?"

Varga gave a little smile. "Oh there's *always* someone out the ordinary. What you have in mind?"

Ibbs decided to take a risk. "How about a man with a limp?"

The smile became fixed on Varga's face. He scrutinised Ibbs closely. "Yes. There was a man with a limp. Hanging about with his hat pulled over his face. He wasn't in line for the wheel, but he was waiting for something."

"Waiting for Dean, do you think?"

"I wouldn't know." Varga's body language had changed; now his arms were folded and he looked distinctly guarded.

"Had you ever seen him before?"

"No."

"Why didn't you tell the police about him?"

Varga hitched up his shoulders: "They didn't ask. I think he headed off in the other direction when the trouble started. He had a limp—I remember that much."

"Did you see what happened to him afterward?"

"No."

"All right. What about the other people, the ones that surged forward to get a look at Dean?"

Varga seemed to relax slightly. His arms fell slackly to his sides. "Well, there was a doctor and his wife. Man named . . ." Varga thought about it. "Ransome. Doctor Ransome. He went over and checked Dean's pulse. He was the one who told us Dean was dead. Lord above," Varga took hold of the crucifix, "I will pray for him," he said. He was still looking at Ibbs very strangely, as though he were not sure he could entirely trust him.

By the time Ibbs left the fair, the place was at last beginning to show a bit of life. The organ music had picked up speed and the merry-go-round had begun to spin. He felt Miklos Varga's gaze boring into his back as he left the Golders Green fairground behind.

It was almost lunchtime. The visits to Holloway and the fair had taken the whole morning. Ibbs judged it an opportune moment to catch Dr. Hugh Ransome between patients. Of course, Ransome had been interviewed extensively as soon as the police arrived on the scene, but had mentioned nothing about a limping man. It would be interesting if that was still the case.

The limping man was a clue, there could be no doubt about it. A limping man, lurking as though he were waiting for someone, who had disappeared as soon as the shot was fired.

Ibbs disembarked from his third omnibus of the day, whistling the song the organ had been blasting, and strode along the street toward Ransome's surgery. Ransome was by all accounts a perfectly respectable physician, if rather unimpressive (and, like

Ibbs himself, a little young). This notion was not dispelled by the sight of the pleasant but slightly drab waiting room.

After a wait of perhaps five minutes, during which time Ibbs lit himself a cigarette and studied the paisley pattern in the wallpaper, the doctor himself emerged from his office.

"Hugh Ransome," he announced, "how'd you do?" They shook hands. He was plainly no older than Ibbs, but he had an avuncular nature which bespoke of aging beyond his years.

"Doctor Ransome, my name is Ibbs. I'm a solicitor in the employ of Mrs. Carla Dean. I wonder if you have the time to answer a question or two about her late husband Dominic?"

"Ah, the Ferris wheel fellow. Most unfortunate. Well, there isn't much I can tell you. When I examined him, he was dying from a bullet wound to the stomach. Got a light?" He had produced a cigarette from a silver case.

"He was bleeding?" Ibbs said, striking a match for him.

"Oh yes, profusely. Quite a horror show."

"And what was your initial assessment of the scene? What did you understand to have taken place?"

"Not my business to speculate, Ibbs. All I know—and all I knew at the time—is that a man was shot."

"Did he say anything to you?"

"Who, Dean? No, he was in too much agony."

"What about Mrs. Dean?"

"Oh, she babbled a few hysterical nothings. I managed to calm her down while we waited for the police. Dean was long dead by the time they arrived, of course."

Ibbs thought about this, then nodded. He had decided that he did not like Dr. Ransome, who seemed altogether too sure of himself. "May I ask, had you ever met Dominic Dean before?"

"Well certainly. He was my bank manager. I knew him by sight. Though I must say, I never dealt with him as a patient."

"And did you notice anything out of the ordinary about the other people waiting on the ground? Anybody among them who didn't seem to belong?"

Ransome narrowed his eyes, considering the question carefully. Almost too carefully. "You're talking about the man with the limp." He took a long drag from his cigarette.

"Maybe I am. What can you tell me about him?"

"Not much. When the screaming started, he headed off in the other direction."

"What did he look like?"

The doctor turned away abruptly and headed for the door. "Sorry, Ibbs. I really must get on. Can't dawdle here all day. My next patient will be waiting."

"Hold on!" said Ibbs. "You're the one who mentioned the limping man. What have you got to say about him?"

Ransome jabbed his cigarette out in an ashtray on the side. "Nothing. I have nothing to say about him. Good day." And he held open the door for Ibbs.

"Doctor Ransome . . . has somebody been speaking to you already?"

"No," came the answer. "If you'll excuse me, Mr. Ibbs."

"Did you tell the police what you saw?"

He examined his pocket watch. "I really must be getting on," he said again, fixing Ibbs with a steady glare.

Ibbs didn't have much choice. He headed out the way he had come, through the conspicuously empty waiting room. Both Varga and Ransome had seen the limping man.

Outside the surgery he paused for a minute or two, seriously debating whether to head back inside and ambush the obstinate Dr. Ransome. But the doctor had clearly said all that he was willing to.

Ibbs took stock of the tight-knit little neighbourhood. He wasn't too far from the Dean family home—now tragically unoccupied—but he didn't feel any particular need to pay the place a visit. No doubt the house had its own story to tell, but there simply wasn't time. He checked his watch—it was now close to two P.M. He had another appointment to get to.

He rounded a corner and headed toward the bank where Dominic Dean had earned the money that he spent so prodigiously. Like many banks, there was something church-like about it. The white marble, the pillars. The feeling that one ought to speak in hushed or reverential tones. He had previously arranged an appointment with Felix Draven, acting manager in the wake of Dean's death.

Draven was portly with protuberant incisors and a nonexistent dash of moustache. He met Ibbs in the cavernous foyer, greeting him efficiently and officiously before leading him through to the manager's office, which he had now appropriated. He looked to be still in the process of clearing out Dean's personal belongings. The whole thing was quite gruesome.

"Thank you for agreeing to see me, Mr. Draven."

"Not at all," his voice was clipped. "Whatever I can do to help."

"Mrs. Dean has led me to believe there was a significant change in her husband's behaviour recently. That he appeared to be distressed or frightened about something."

"Far be it from me to speak ill of the dead, but I should be inclined to concur with Mrs. Dean. The late Mr. Dean was always the most fastidious of gentlemen. But in the last fortnight or so, his demeanour underwent something of an alteration."

"Why do you think that was?"

"I would attribute it to the robbery that occurred just over two weeks prior to Mr. Dean's murder. Our vault was broken into and ransacked one night. Perhaps you heard about it?"

Ibbs had, but he merely looked at Draven blankly in the hopes of eliciting something useful.

"It was a horrible thing. And poor Arthur . . ."

Arthur Morrison was the night watchman at the bank who had been coshed by the gang of thieves. Had they left it at a single blow, he would have been merely unfortunate. But they continued to beat him until his face was pulp and the blood poured from his ears. He died in the early hours of the morning.

"Such a vicious thing to do," Draven concluded. "It's not surprising Mr. Dean was upset by it. Particularly as *he* was the one who asked Morrison to spend the night."

"Really?" said Ibbs. "Why did he do that?"

Draven just shrugged. He seemed to be doing all he could to tarnish his predecessor's reputation. But maybe he had a point; Dean was manager at the bank, so ultimately what happened to the elderly watchman was his responsibility. The robbery must have taken a toll on him. He must have felt considerable guilt.

Unless . . .

The fact that Dean's dramatic change in behaviour came so close to his murder could not be mere chance, could it? He had *known* someone was out to get him. Various friends and neighbours had attested to his newfound sense of caution, and now there were these stories of a limping man pursuing him. A man who was on the scene the moment he died. Could there be a connection between the robbery and Dean's death?

For all Draven's ostensible eagerness to help, he was surprisingly tight-lipped when it came to his personal relationship with Dean. There was an unacknowledged frostiness lurking beneath the cordiality. Ibbs would not have wanted to be around when both men were working together, side by side. No doubt it could get pretty fractious.

Next, he procured a quick interview with the aptly named Miss Cash, one of the cashiers. She was not only the eldest but the most senior among them, and she began by treating Ibbs as brusquely as she no doubt treated her subordinates. But all the same, she agreed to answer some questions.

"What is it you're after? Is it the robbery? Or is it what happened to Mr. Dean?"

Ibbs smiled disarmingly. "A little of both, I think."

"You're not with the other gentleman, are you?"

"Other gentleman?"

"Well, we had the police here when it happened. The robbery, I mean. And of course Inspector Flint was in charge and he was asking everybody questions and working out what went on. And then we had some reporters. Next thing we knew, Mr. Dean was dead and all those same reporters were back again. But after that, we had another person come out to see us asking questions."

"Who was he? What was his name?"

"Oh, now let me think. . . ." she screwed up her face. "Remiston," she eventually said. "Mr. Boyd Remiston."

"What makes you think he wasn't a reporter?"

"He asked for Mr. Dean. But when I broke the news to him—you know, about Mr. Dean's passing—he didn't seem in the least surprised."

"Did he say anything else to you?"

"Nothing. He left shortly after that. But I didn't like him, Mr. Ibbs. I can tell you that much."

"What did he look like?"

"All right now let me see. He was stocky. Rather gruff. I should have said he came from up north somewhere, judging by the accent."

"Aha. And what did he look like? Can you describe his facial features?"

"He had a very normal face, Mr. Ibbs. The sort you might encounter in the bank any day of the week."

"What about his clothing? Anything distinctive?"

"He had a black suit and a bowler hat. He also had a slight limp, as I recall."

"On which side?"

"I think he tended to favour his right foot."

"Any moustaches?"

"No. He was clean-shaven."

"And what age would you put him at?"

"Oh, Mr. Ibbs, I'm hopeless when it comes to ages. Perhaps around forty."

"And now the most important question: had you ever seen him before?"

She was surprisingly coy. "I might have bumped into him a hundred times over the years and not remembered a single one. He was just one of those ordinary-looking people."

"I see. Thank you, Miss Cash. That's very helpful all the same. Now, if you don't mind changing the subject for a moment, what were your impressions of Mr. Dean in himself? That is, as a bank manager?"

She seemed mildly affronted by the question—which was no surprise. "He was a model employer," she said with a haughty, puffed-up mien, "and a perfect gentleman."

Ibbs scribbled the word '*affair?*' in his notebook. It was more than likely. But did it really matter if Dean and one of his cashiers were having a liaison? Perhaps, if Carla had found out. . . . "Did you ever meet Mrs. Dean?"

"Naturally. But I hope I never do so again. She's a wicked woman for what she did to poor Mr. Dean." Evidently she had misinterpreted Ibbs's purpose here. She most likely thought he was working for the prosecution. Ibbs decided to change the subject once more.

"A fortnight prior to Mr. Dean's death, you had a robbery here didn't you? Can you tell me about that?"

"Oh." Tears welled. "Oh, that was so dreadful. Poor Mr. Morrison. A lovely old gentleman he was. And it was such a violent, terrible thing they did to him."

"You knew Arthur Morrison?"

"Well of course! He worked at this bank some thirty years. Everybody knew and liked him immensely."

"And do you know *why* he was at the bank the night of the robbery? I understand that was unusual. At least, that's the impression Mr. Draven gave me."

For the first time she seemed unsure of herself. "Well . . . I can't say I do. I know it was Mr. Dean who asked him to spend the night here. But I couldn't tell you why."

So: the robbery again. When it happened, Ibbs came across it in the news as one of those messy, unpleasant stories that briefly snags the attention and then is whipped away again, as though by a stiff breeze. He had scarcely made the connection that the unfortunate bank manager was the same Dominic Dean who died by gunshot wound scarcely a fortnight later. Now, the idea of a connection between the two crimes was beginning to seem less fanciful. It was his job to look into these things, starting with Mr. Boyd Remiston.

When it became clear that Miss Cash had imparted all the information she felt inclined to share, Ibbs thanked her for her time and left.

Outside the bank he hailed a cab. "Scotland Yard," he told the driver thoughtfully, settling back in his seat.

CHAPTER THREE

THE SENSATIONAL MISTER SPECTOR

When he got to Scotland Yard, Ibbs strode up to the desk and asked for Inspector Flint. The sergeant looked up from his paper—the *Chronicle*—distinctly unimpressed. "He's not here," he said.

"Well, when will he be back?"

" 'Fraid I can't say. You'll have to try again tomorrow."

Tomorrow being Saturday, Ibbs doubted he would have much luck then either. "Do you know where he's gone?"

"I do." The sergeant was letting nothing slip.

"Well, will you tell me?"

"No. I won't."

Ibbs sighed, and slipped him five bob. He would retrieve it later from the petty cash.

Pocketing the note, the sergeant said: "He's at the Old Bailey for the Pilgrim trial."

"Pilgrim, eh?" Ibbs tried not to let the surprise show in his voice. Titus Pilgrim was one of the most notorious criminals to emerge from London since Saucy Jack himself. But Pilgrim's methods were somewhat different. He had more in common with the gangsters making a name for themselves over in the United States. He'd set himself up as a "legitimate businessman," to use that hoary phrase. Though it was widely known that he ran protection rackets and heroin rackets and illegal gambling and prostitution and . . . well. The list might readily continue.

Ibbs had never met Pilgrim (lucky him), but the fact that he was making a court appearance that day was no surprise. Ironically, despite concerted efforts by Scotland Yard, Titus Pilgrim had yet to be convicted. Not even once. Today's courtroom action turned out to be a petty financial matter that had taken on especial tabloid significance purely because of Pilgrim's involvement. He always gave good copy.

The desk sergeant, who was suddenly feeling loquacious, told Ibbs that Flint was not even expected to give evidence in today's court proceedings. He had simply gone along to watch the show. "He's got a bee in his bonnet about Titus Pilgrim," the sergeant confided.

Ibbs thanked him and left the building, hailing another cab, which snaked through the London traffic and transported him the mile and a half or so from Whitehall Place to the Old Bailey. A clutch of reporters lingered on the stone steps of the courthouse. Ibbs approached them and called out: "Any sign of him yet?"

Naturally they knew who he was talking about, and answered with a collective shake of the head. He lit a cigarette and waited. The afternoon was drawing on, but he had already achieved a considerable amount today. He'd begun to formulate a theory. Now he deserved the chance to satisfy his own morbid curiosity.

"Hey!" someone cried out. "There he goes!"

And sure enough, there he went. Pilgrim was striding away from the Old Bailey with a swagger in his step, a fur collar about his shoulders, and a black homburg nestled on his lion's mane of white hair. He chewed a cigar and plumed smoke into the air.

Trailing behind him at a distance was Inspector George Flint. Ibbs didn't know it at the time, but Flint was recovering from a summer cold and his throat was still scratchy and hoarse. His moustache, though bushy, was listless. He was pale, paunchy, and generally sickly looking. Ibbs quickly fell into step with the inspector, who evidently only had eyes for Titus Pilgrim. Unencumbered by camera equipment, they beat the reporters to the punch and managed to catch up to Pilgrim.

"Oh, Mister Pilgrim . . ." Flint said coaxingly.

Pilgrim halted in his tracks, and turned to look at the policeman with an expression of mild amusement. "Oh, Flint. I didn't know it was you," he said, forming the words around his cigar. "Come to congratulate me?"

"No," Flint said sternly. "I wanted you to know that I'll be watching you."

"I expect nothing less from Scotland Yard's finest inspector." He was evidently feeling very pleased with himself, and enjoyed preening in front of a crowd. No doubt he had put on quite a show in court.

At that moment, a sleek black limousine coasted to a halt beside him, and Titus Pilgrim quickly clambered inside. As the vehicle whisked him away, only the lingering tang of his cigar smoke remained to indicate he had ever been there at all.

Inspector Flint stood in silence for a moment, watching the limousine as it rounded the corner. Pilgrim had slipped out of his grasp once more. But soon enough he was surrounded by reporters. He gave a frustrated groan and began to walk away in the opposite direction. Ibbs jogged to catch up with him. "Inspector Flint. Inspector Flint!"

"No comment," he said.

"You don't understand. I'm not a reporter."

"Oh no?" For the first time, Flint slowed his pace to let Ibbs catch up to him.

"No. My name is Edmund Ibbs. I'm a solicitor. I wanted to talk to you about the Dean case."

"Dean case? You mean Dominic Dean?"

"Precisely."

"Well, why didn't you say so? Come on, let's get away from this rabble." They made for a nearby tearoom. The reporters had already begun to lose interest, but Ibbs was for the first time beginning to comprehend the true scope of this case. Ideas were running backward and forward through his mind when he glimpsed a pastel-blue bowler bobbing toward him through the crowd. Miklos Varga, the fairground man. Ibbs stepped forward to get a closer look, but the brief flash of color had vanished.

When he and Flint were safely ensconced at the corner table in a pleasant, glass-fronted tearoom, Ibbs decided to launch his first sally. "I'm defending Carla Dean," he said.

One of Flint's eyebrows twitched. "Little young for that, aren't you Mr. Ibbs?"

"Well, perhaps I should say I'm *working* for the defence."

"Ah. Well, in that case you've got your work cut out for you. The whole thing is open and shut."

"Are you sure about that? You sound dubious."

At that moment a young waitress arrived to take their order. Ibbs made do with a pot of Earl Grey, but Flint seemed keen to push the boat out. "Afternoon tea," he said. "Sandwiches, cakes, the whole shebang. My friend Ibbs here is paying."

While she scribbled the order, Ibbs practised a little trick with a coin, rolling it across his knuckles and back again.

"Very neat," said Flint. "You a magic man, are you?"

Ibbs placed the coin in his palm, then balled a fist to make it vanish. But the pressure of an audience flummoxed him and the coin slipped from his grasp. It dropped to the plush, carpeted floor. "Um, yes, actually," he said, leaning down to pick up the coin.

"Never saw the appeal myself," Flint went on, taking his pipe from his pocket and chewing it thoughtfully. "There's far too much strangeness in the everyday to bother with making things up. Take the Ferris wheel for instance. If I sound dubious about it, it's because it was a very literal-minded crime. That means one weapon, one victim, and one suspect. And the crime scene is what you might describe as 'hermetically sealed.' So it's a ready-made collar. A little too good to be true, don't you think? And I have a friend who favours the lateral rather than the literal approach to problem-solving. He's taught me that when something seems too good to be true, it usually is."

"Does this mean you don't think Carla Dean killed her husband?"

He chuckled. "You won't catch me out so easily, Mr. Ibbs. After all, there was sufficient evidence to take the case to trial. All it means is that I'm keen to ensure justice is done. Whatever," he added cryptically, "that might entail. Let's leave it at that for now."

"You were also involved with the investigation into the robbery at Dean's bank, weren't you?"

"The Morrison murder, I prefer to call it. Let's not forget the poor old night watchman was wilfully battered to death."

"Do you have any leads?"

"Just one, and you can probably guess what it is. Titus Pilgrim."

"You think *Pilgrim* was behind the robbery at the Dean bank?"

Flint sat back in his chair and sighed. "My colleagues—*some* of my colleagues, anyway—think I have a vendetta against Pilgrim. Perhaps I do. That doesn't change what I know, and I know for a fact that Titus Pilgrim has orchestrated other robberies in the past which were all but identical to the Golders Green job. Of course he's clever, so he knows how to get away with these things. We've never managed to convict him of a single thing. That's why he walks the streets of London as free as a bird. But I'll get him one of these days, don't you worry about that."

"This robbery seems to be a botch-job though, doesn't it?" Ibbs asked. "After all, the night watchman was killed. Seems a little unnecessary, don't you think?"

At that moment, the teas arrived. The waitress unloaded an immense pyramid of sandwiches in front of Flint; he examined it with undisguised pleasure. Ibbs poured out a cup of Earl Grey and helped himself to a couple of sugar lumps.

"Why are you asking about the robbery?" Flint said through a mouthful of egg and cress. "You think there's some kind of connection between the bank job and Dean's death?"

"That's exactly what I think," Ibbs said. "Of course, my function is to defend Carla Dean; nothing more. But if we can prove that Dominic Dean was involved in the bank job, then we may be able to establish reasonable doubt."

"I see . . . so you think Dean was the inside man? That he colluded in the robbery of his own bank?"

"Inside man! That's it! Exactly! I've been trying for ages but couldn't come up with the term. Yes, it looks to me as though Dominic Dean was paid by Titus Pilgrim to provide details which enabled his gang to crack the safe and rob the bank. But nobody predicted that the poor guard would end up getting killed. Dominic Dean must have been so terribly guilty about that. I doubt he would ever recover."

"And you think he was intending to spill the beans? That's quite an elaborate scheme you've come up with there, Mr. Ibbs. And presumably Pilgrim had him killed. But you've yet to explain how he managed to do it while Dean was on a Ferris wheel with his wife."

"That's just incidental. There's a chain of logic here, Inspector. That's the important thing. *That* is how we'll convince a jury. Incidentally, I don't suppose you've encountered a fellow named Remiston have you? Boyd Remiston?"

"Remiston?" Flint frowned. "How are you spelling that?"

"R-E-M-I-S-T-O-N, I believe."

He shook his head. "No, can't say the name means anything. Where did you hear it?"

"It's my belief that Remiston was present when Dean was killed. And he beat a pretty hasty retreat once the shot was fired."

"Interesting. Very interesting. You may be onto something there, Mr. Ibbs. And there's certainly something fishy about the Dean murder, I can't deny it. But you can't get away from the practical side of the problem, can you? There's a fellow I know with a certain affinity for that sort of thing. Perhaps you should speak with him. His name is Joseph Spector."

"Spector? The conjuror?"

"Yes, once upon a time he was a music hall conjuror. But he's retired. And these days he has a knack for explaining impossible situations. I've used him plenty of times."

"Well fancy that," Ibbs heard himself say, "Spector the conjuror, solving crimes . . ."

"Don't let on that you're a fan. If he finds out, he'll start strutting like a peacock."

"Where can I find him?"

"He typically spends his days at the Black Pig alehouse in Putney. You could probably follow the stench of his god-awful cigarillo smoke, but to be on the safe side perhaps I'd better give you the address."

Ibbs finished his tea and the two men shook hands. "Thank you for your help, Inspector."

"You know," Flint said, still chewing, "I've put a lot of hours into trying to bring down Titus Pilgrim. If you can connect him to the Dean case somehow, I'll assist you in any way I can."

And be sure to take the credit, Ibbs thought but managed to refrain from saying out loud. Then they parted ways and Ibbs boarded his umpteenth omnibus of the day. This time he was heading back to Chancery Lane, feeling satisfied with the day's progress. Tragedians might call it hubris.

By the time he got home, he didn't have long to run a bath and eat a quick supper before it was time to go out again. He had a ticket for the Pomegranate Theatre that night: a rare performance from the stupefying "Professor Paolini." But all the same, Ibbs took a moment to look at the age-worn poster pasted to his bedroom wall, which he had clamoured so hard through an adoring crowd to obtain. It showed a dashing fellow in a silk-lined cloak, fanning out a deck of cards. "THE SENSATIONAL MISTER SPECTOR," it read.

CHAPTER FOUR

THE CRATE ILLUSION

That evening Ibbs resolved to extricate the Deans and Titus Pilgrim from his mind. He spent a little while flipping dreamily through *The Master of Manipulation*, but it wasn't long until show time. It was a show he'd been waiting for: Paolini's comeback.

Professor Paolini was stout and moustachioed and frequently (though not always) spoke with a phony Italian accent. Despite these deficiencies, Ibbs had a real affection for the man's work. The tricks were never quite what you expected them to be. For instance, there was a neat variant on the "Assistant's Revenge" illusion which had always stuck in his memory.

Typically, what happens is that the assistant is strapped to a chair, or else sealed in a box with their head showing through an aperture. They are then covered with a sheet. The magician walks around the back of said box or chair, briefly disappearing from the audience's view, only for the assistant to reappear in his place, whisk way the sheet and reveal the *magician* now bound by the restraints. This was one of Ibbs's favourites because of the alacrity and precision required to pull it off; the switch really was just a matter of seconds.

But Paolini's version was slightly different. In it, the assistant was not simply restrained, but secured upside-down by her feet from what looked to be a steel meat-hook, all while wearing a straitjacket. A shroud-like sheet was then lowered, shielding her from the audience's view, and Paolini stepped behind her. And within seconds—*seconds!*—the assistant emerged from the other side and whisked the sheet away, revealing Paolini himself now hanging upside down in the straitjacket.

During the applause the chain was hoisted up, hauling Paolini up into the gods to be untethered. Ibbs managed to suss out how part of the trick was done (at least, he thought he had). When the girl was hung upside down and the sheet lowered, her outline was very vague save for the shadowed definition surrounding her feet. So Ibbs reckoned her feet must be snared in some detachable model which retained a foot shape when her real feet were extricated from their bindings. That would enable her to slip out as soon as the sheet was lowered, though it would look as though she were still hanging there. But that did *not* explain how Paolini himself ended up in the bindings in a matter of perhaps two seconds. He simply stepped behind the sheet and then . . . out stepped the assistant. She whisked away said sheet with a single motion, to reveal him hanging there.

Of course, the straitjacket would have to be pre-stitched to Paolini's clothing, then covered by an outer layer that he could tear away. That would explain how he was so quickly bound. But it *didn't* explain how he came to be suspended in midair in less than three seconds.

Ibbs hadn't yet stumbled across this trick in his perusals of *The Master of Manipulation*, though he was sure it would not escape the notice of the elusive "Dr. Anne L. Surazal." Just who *was* it? Was it perhaps Paolini himself, on a suicide mission to obliterate his own career along with those of his rivals? Perhaps he was ill. Dying even. Maybe he wanted his mastery to be preserved for the ages. Or perhaps the book was the work of some enemy of his, out to destroy his reputation?

The show was at the Pomegranate Theatre in the West End, and as Ibbs had predicted the brief resurgence of a legend like Paolini had coaxed a host of stars out of their hiding places. Ibbs stood in the street outside the theatre, clutching a program and waiting for the door to open. Paolini had not performed on a London stage for almost five years. He had been on a world tour throughout that time, playing stages from Australia to Utrecht. His return to English shores was quite an event, and had attracted a host of magicians. Ibbs gazed around at them all, starstruck.

There was P. T. Selbit with his lizard-like mouth and sinister side part. *He* was the first one to perform the "sawing the woman in half" trick which had now become a staple of the magic scene. But he was unassuming to look at for one who had the reputation of an innovator. Then there was Bartok the Bamboozler, Rouclere and Mildred, Will Goldston, even the great David Devant—all standing around chatting amiably as though this were the most ordinary thing in the world. Ibbs was agog. And yet at the same time, there was an almost predatory air to this influx of illusionists. Like baying wolves, waiting to pounce.

Somewhere in that crowd, Ibbs spotted another face that he recognised. A creased, kindly face with pale blue eyes. It was none other than Joseph Spector. His heart leapt at the sight of the old music hall conjuror, but he resolved not to trouble him. Discussion of the Dean case could wait until another day. After all, tonight was Paolini's night.

Somewhere in that crowd, Ibbs spotted another face that he recognised. A creased, kindly face with pale blue eyes. It was none other than Joseph Spector. His heart leapt at the sight of the old music hall conjuror, but he resolved not to trouble him. Discussion of the Dean case could wait until another day. After all, tonight was Paolini's night.

A magic audience is unlike any other. There is an atmosphere of sheer boisterousness that pervades, and the crowd outside the Pomegranate was no different. It was all part of the appeal for Edmund Ibbs, overgrown adolescent that he was. His fascination was not merely confined to the realm of intricate legerdemain. It was also a very human intrigue at the impact such things had on a crowd. How the brain computed the impossible. "The thing about Paolini," somebody once said, "is that he does everything a little bit *different*. For instance, he'll do the bullet catch, but he won't just *do* the bullet catch, he'll have the bullet fired by a member of the audience, through a pane of glass. He toys with the idea of risk. It creates a marvellous effect."

It's a paradoxical state of mind that afflicts the magician's audience—they both want and do not want to be fooled. Perhaps they are like juries in that respect—they want to submit themselves to it, but they want to retain their own personal conception of a status quo. Ibbs was thinking about this when the house doors opened and a sea of shoulders began jostling him toward the foyer. It wasn't long until the audience was permitted to enter the auditorium. He filed in along with the rest and took his seat.

In many ways, Paolini was the consummate magician. He was always accoutred as such, with top hat, tails, silk-lined cloak, plus silver-topped cane (except of course during the mentalism acts, when he eschewed the top hat in favour of a turban). He had the delicate, almost effete manner of an accomplished sleight-of-hand man, punctuating even the most inconsequential movements with a flourish. His eyebrows were notable in that he had three of them; two over the eyes and another on his upper lip. Beneath the top hat was a bald dome plastered with thin strands of black hair; in this department he was fooling no one. Paolini was everything you could want from a magician, just the way he looked on the posters. His eyes had a hypnotic, Svengali-like bulge to them, and he seemed to blink considerably less than humanly possible. But his paunch pressed at the inside of his shirt, and caused the buttons to poke outward as though they might fly off into the crowd at an inopportune moment. Ibbs might catch one, he thought whimsically, and it would be another treasure for his meagre collection of magical memorabilia.

Paolini emerged onstage in a puff of blue smoke, to the sound of raucous applause. He silenced the audience with a wave of his hand, and spoke. "Ladies and gentlemen, recently a book was published which claims to expose all the secrets of prestidigitators such as myself. To give away the little gimmicks and sleights-of-hand which I and my colleagues utilise in the name of entertainment. Such endeavours are always folly, my dear ladies and gentlemen, because they neglect to mention the single component which makes the whole affair work. Namely, *magic*. For my first trick of the evening, I will show you something which nobody anywhere has managed to 'explain.' Martha, if you please."

From the wings emerged his assistant, Martha. Her glittering costume was a one-piece, a slim sheaf of fabric covering her from collarbone to thigh. It was threaded with sequins to catch the light and occlude the audience's vision—this was something Ibbs knew about. But her stockinged legs also helped to occlude *his* vision. All part of the show, all part of the show. Her hair was short—scarcely reached her shoulders—but it curled and frizzed outward in a great mad halo. She was even-featured; her face had an uncanny symmetry, and her skin was china-white. Her narrow mouth was ringed with blood red and her dark eyes were dramatically circled by grey-black pencil lines. Her shoes were high-heeled and made a reverberant thump on the stage with each step. Ibbs couldn't decide if the shoes were purely aesthetic or if they served a purpose. Perhaps the sound of her thumping heels would cover some mechanical noise behind the scenes; a winch being lowered or some such. That was how his mind was working that evening.

Martha approached Paolini with a silver tray covered by a cloth. Paolini whisked away the cloth with a flourish. Underneath was a .38 revolver. Ibbs thought of Dominic Dean, and an unanticipated chill ran down his spine.

"A revolver," said Paolini, seizing it. "And fully loaded." He cracked it open and showed the crowd the cylinder, complete with six bullets. "Many great magicians—greater even than I—have perished in the performance of this next illusion. Take for instance the magnificent Madame DeLinsky, executed by an unwitting firing squad in front of the royal court of Germany! Or, scarcely two decades ago, my esteemed colleague Chung Ling Soo, who died on a stage a few miles away from this very theatre. Then there are the imitators and the charlatans; the foolish amateurs like Rusell Zanandra or the 'Black Wizard of the West,' a snake oil salesman shot dead in front of an audience by a scheming wife in the town of Deadwood, South Dakota."

He reeled off this litany of dead magicians with palpable relish, but Ibbs was thinking about Chung Ling Soo. He had been nine years old when the magician died, and it had left him devastated. Dr. Epstein and Michael Hatal were two others. The list of conjurors shot dead onstage was well-populated, and seemed to be growing longer all the time. Ibbs began to sweat. If you had asked him at that moment, he would have told you it was the sheer anticipation and anxiety in watching a magician handle a loaded revolver. But if you asked him afterward, when it was all over, he would have told you that he had experienced a premonition. That he knew something was going to happen that night.

"Now, I know what you are thinking. You are thinking: 'Paolini is a professional trickster! Surely that is merely a prop weapon, which is not capable of firing live ammunition!' Well, let me allay your uncertainty. You, sir!" Paolini leaned forward, holding the weapon out to a man in the front row. "Will you take the revolver, and check that it is the genuine article?"

The man mumbled something and took the pistol, turning it over in his hands.

"Good. Are you satisfied?"

A mumbled response.

"Excellent. Then will you please pass the weapon to the man seated directly behind you?"

The man did. Gradually, the revolver made its way along the length and breadth of the first three rows. Just as the audience was beginning to grumble, Paolini retrieved the weapon. "And so!" he exclaimed. "The weapon is real. The ammunition is real. And the target," he patted his fulsome belly, "is very real.

"Now, for this trick, I will require the participation of a willing audience member. I must warn you, though, that there is a very real risk of death for those who dare to perform this dazzling feat. I would like to assure you that, in the event of my demise, the Pomegranate Theatre will absolve you of any legal responsibility. Well? Who's willing?"

Paolini snapped his fingers and the house lights came on. Ibbs hunkered down in his seat. A foolish move—he caught Paolini's eye.

"You sir! The gentleman in the third row! Will you oblige?"

His face burning red, Ibbs got to his feet. To the sound of nervous applause, he made his way onstage. Martha the assistant beamed at him and handed over the revolver.

It was heavy. Somehow Ibbs had not expected it to be a real weapon. But it was. A revolver loaded with six live rounds. Again he thought of Dominic Dean and his wife Carla. And he began to formulate an idea.

Paolini waved his hand once more and the audience fell silent. Martha was wheeling a large pane of glass onstage. She positioned it carefully between Ibbs and Paolini.

"And what is your name, sir?"

"Edmund."

"And have you ever handled a weapon before, Edmund?"

Ibbs shook his head.

"Very well. I can tell you that it's quite simple. All you need to do is to take careful aim. Here—this should be a big enough target for you." Paolini opened his mouth wide. Cue nervous laughter from the audience.

Ibbs did as he was told, though his hand quivered slightly. His aim was far from steady. It occurred to him what a neat method of murder this would be: a perfect way to kill a troublesome magician.

"Now," said Paolini, "fire!"

Ibbs squeezed the trigger. The blast was deafening, and the kickback sent him reeling backward a few steps. There were gasps from the audience as the pane of glass shattered and Paolini staggered to the apron of the stage.

Martha sprang forward, seizing the revolver from his shaking hand. Paolini dropped to his knees.

The gasps from the crowd gave way to astonished murmurs. Ibbs looked at Martha, who was stone-faced. She stood, silent and statuesque, as Paolini twitched hideously.

Ibbs had never seen a man die before. It was not the way he had pictured it. There was no blood. None. He frowned and, less than a second later, Paolini was on his feet, grinning, flashing the spent bullet between his teeth. He removed it between gloved fingers and handed it to Ibbs.

"You may keep that, Edmund, as a souvenir of the night Paolini cheated death! And you will please return to your seat."

The tension in the auditorium broke. The applause was spontaneous. What an opening to the show!

Ibbs all but staggered back to his seat, slipping the bullet into his pocket.

The rest of the show passed in a blur. His eyelids began to grow heavy. The day's travails catching up with him, no doubt. He blinked several times and sat upright in his seat. Paolini's act was as slick and professional as ever. He did the Assistant's Revenge, but it was all too quick for Ibbs to spot the gimmick.

Now a tall crate was being wheeled onstage by Martha. It was perhaps seven feet in height. When the crate was positioned centre stage, Martha opened a rear door, which swung out to the right, then the front door, which swung out to the left, so the audience could see all the way through the crate and out the other side.

"Now," said Paolini, producing a small square trunk, "for my next trick, I should like to delve deep into England's glorious past. We present to you a piece of history. Or rather, *five* pieces." From the trunk he removed a set of leg armour, which stood upright like a pair of disembodied limbs. "This is a part of a suit of armour worn by Sir Lancelot himself, England's great knight. And legend tells it that when his suit of armour is reassembled once more, his spirit will be summoned forth, and he will walk this green and pleasant land once more!" Then from the trunk he removed a breastplate, followed by arm gauntlets, and finally a helmet. He hooked these together so that the disparate pieces formed a hollow mannequin.

With the mannequin upright inside the tall crate, the front door was closed, then the rear door. With Paolini on one side and Martha on the other, the crate was rotated on the spot. A few hushed incantations were spoken and then Paolini poised to open the door.

"The spell has been cast," he intoned, "now behold as Sir Lancelot steps forth. . . ." With typical flair, he flung open the door on the front of the crate. As before, the suit of armour stood upright. Paolini and Martha were either side of the crate, their faces masks of awe and wonderment. But the reveal went on a beat too long. Ibbs spotted a slightly awkward sideways glance passing between them. Something had gone wrong.

"Watch," Paolini said, "as he emerges from the depths of history. . . ."

And then the suit of armour toppled forward. It collapsed into pieces with an almighty *clang*, and the crowd gasped as one. The helmet spilled off and rolled into the lap of a woman in the front row, who shrieked. From the crate, where it had been positioned *behind* the hollow suit of armour, another figure spilled out. This one was recognisably human, and wore a distinctive suit.

Paolini dropped to his haunches beside the body. "Christ," he said. Any semblance of an Italian accent was gone. The body was not moving.

"Grab his legs," Paolini instructed Martha. The pair of them turned the insensate man over onto his back. When Ibbs got a look at his face, he knew that his initial, seemingly impossible instinct had been correct. It's safe to say it was truly the last person he would have expected to be produced from the magic crate that evening.

It was Miklos Varga. The fairground man in the chequered suit.

"Is there a doctor in the house?" said Paolini.

"Please," Ibbs called out, leaving his seat and advancing toward the stage. "Please, nobody touch anything."

"Are you police?" Martha demanded.

"No. I'm a lawyer. But please, listen to me. I know this man."

"Well, who the hell is he?"

There were now a few dismayed cries as the audience realised the trick had not only gone wrong, but turned deadly. Varga's eyes were closed. His body lolled worryingly in Paolini's arms.

Ibbs managed to get on stage just before the curtain was lowered. He shoved the empty crate aside and it rolled offstage, its wooden doors swinging shut. He dropped to his knees and touched Varga's forehead. Stone cold. He had been dead for some time.

"How did this happen?"

"I don't know. Honest to God I don't know."

The theatre manager was quick to restore order. Ushers were placed at each exit to ensure nobody left the theatre before the police arrived. The houselights came up and Paolini rushed from the stage looking queasy.

Meanwhile, Martha sidled up to Ibbs. "What's all this? What's happened?"

"I don't see how . . ."

"You said you knew this bloke?"

"I don't *know* him. . . . I met him today for the first time. . . ."

"Then what's he doing here?"

"I . . ." Ibbs thought about it. "No, it can't be. Surely it's too much of a coincidence."

"Well, Paolini's right about one thing," Martha said slyly. "Before the show he was ranting and raving about how his career was over. It is now."

PART TWO

'TWILL SOON BE DARK

Part of the appeal of magic is its propensity to reverse the irreversible. Thus severed ropes may be restored, burned notes reconfigured, and the dead revivified.

—*The Master of Manipulation*, "Why Magic?"

Always leave them wanting more.

—**Show business aphorism frequently attributed to P. T. Barnum**

CHAPTER FIVE

THIS IS ALL
VERY UNPLEASANT

The audience was quickly and efficiently escorted from the auditorium by a fleet of ushers. Somebody—Ibbs never found out who—must have called the police. In a matter of minutes the place was swamped by uniformed constables.

"Where's Fabris?" Martha was saying. "I don't understand it. Where's he gone?"

"Check the crate," said Paolini, "I can't fathom it."

Ibbs headed into the wings after them, where they had begun to examine the magic crate offstage right. "But surely it's empty. . . ." he heard himself say. They ignored him. Martha pulled open the flimsy wooden door in the crate. To Ibbs's astonishment, this revealed another suit of armour. This time, however, it stepped out of the crate and removed its helmet. *This* was the way the trick should have played out. Beneath the helmet was a nondescript-looking man, panting like a dog.

"What the bloody hell's going on?" he demanded. "You know full well I can hardly breathe in there. What's the game, you trying to suffocate me or something?"

"Fabris!" said Paolini. "Just what exactly happened?"

"What happened?" The knight in armour laughed bitterly. "What do you *think* happened? Draper put me in the crate as usual. I can't see or hear a bloody thing in there. What happened after that, your guess is as good as mine."

"Ken, this is really bad," said Martha.

"You're telling me!"

"No. Really. A man's dead. He was in the crate."

The knight—Ken Fabris—looked at them for a moment, still panting, trying to gauge whether they were serious. "Well, he wasn't in there with me, I can tell you that much."

Martha stepped aside, revealing Miklos Varga dead on the stage where he had fallen. He was still surrounded by scattered bits of armour.

Fabris's face sagged. "Who . . . who is he?"

"His name is Miklos Varga," Ibbs supplied.

"And who are *you?*"

"My name is Ibbs. Edmund Ibbs."

"Ibbs was in the crowd," Paolini explained. "I just can't fathom this at all. Fabris was supposed to be the one in the crate."

"I *was* in the crate. . . ."

"Not on that stage you weren't. When I opened that crate a corpse fell out of it. Where the hell is Draper? Maybe he can shed some light on this."

"Wish I could, Paolini," rasped a hoarse voice. An old man in shirtsleeves emerged from the shadows of some backstage alcove. "But I can tell you this for a fact: when I wheeled that crate into position, Fabris was inside. And only Fabris."

"He's right," said Fabris. "Draper strapped me in himself."

"Then," Ibbs piped up, "where did Varga come from?"

"Hullo there?" called a voice from the other side of the curtain. "Hullo?"

"Just a minute," answered the old man, Draper. Wincing slightly, he gave a nearby rope an almighty tug and the curtain inched upward.

The auditorium was empty now, and the houselights were up. Striding down the central aisle was none other than Inspector George Flint.

"Well, well," he said. "Young Mr. Ibbs. We must stop meeting like this." He hauled himself cumbersomely up onto the stage. "Ladies and gentlemen, my name is George Flint, Scotland Yard. Everybody please remain in the backstage area. My officers are conducting a search, and I shall be questioning all of you as quickly as possible so that we can get to the bottom of this." He focused his attention on Ibbs, taking him by the elbow and drawing him to one side. "Well this is a lovely coincidence isn't it. And may I ask what brought you here this evening?"

"Well, I came to see the magic."

"I see. You know who the dead man is, of course?"

"Yes. I'm afraid so."

Flint shook his head ruminatively. "This is all very unpleasant. I don't like it, Mr. Ibbs, when unconnected events and persons suddenly and violently connect."

"I'm struggling to comprehend it myself. . . ."

"As far as I can tell there is only one factor which links the Dean case and this present atrocity, Mr. Ibbs, and that's you."

"I . . ." Ibbs began stumbling out a response, but lost track partway. He felt suddenly and inexplicably guilty.

"Well? What's it all about?" Flint demanded.

"I . . . I don't know. I just came here to watch the show. I swear that's all."

"Are you here alone?"

"Yes, I . . ."

"What?"

"Nothing. I, I'm here alone."

"Did you meet someone? Or recognise someone? Did you see Varga before the show? Or during?"

"No, no, I didn't. I just came to watch the magic."

"Well. This is a pretty little mess isn't it?" Flint's demeanour was resigned. Obviously this was not the first time he had tackled the inexplicable.

"Am I under arrest?"

"Oh, don't be stupid young man. Even if you *were* involved somehow, I don't see how you could have pulled that stunt with the corpse in front of the whole audience like that. And you've never been backstage before, have you? You're as much of a stranger here as I am."

"Well, I . . . I see what you mean. But how do you explain it then?"

"That's just the problem," Flint sighed. "I can't."

"It has to be something to do with the Dean case, don't you think?"

He shrugged. "At the moment, I don't know what to think. We'll have to let the audience go soon, since it's unlikely any of them saw anything. I'll be focusing my attention on the backstage personnel. Though I have to say,"—he threw a glance in their direction—"they're surprisingly cagey so far. Almost as if there's some perverse code of silence here at the Pomegranate. I tried to speak with Benjamin Teasel, who owns the place, but apparently he's out of the country."

That's when a thought struck Ibbs. "Joseph Spector," he said.

"Spector? What about him?"

"He's here. In the audience. He was watching the show."

"Spector? Nobody told me that."

"I saw him before the doors opened. I wanted to talk to him, to introduce myself, but there wasn't time."

"Hook!" Flint yelled, and a younger man, presumably Flint's second, appeared discreetly from behind a pillar. "Apparently Spector's here. Have you seen him?"

"Out in the foyer, sir."

"Well what are you waiting for? Fetch him immediately!" As Hook scurried off in search of the old conjuror, Flint murmured: "Is it any wonder nothing gets done around here . . . ?"

Then he was struck by a thought. "Hook! Come back here a moment."

Hook doubled back.

"What about the roof?" said Flint. The question was directed at Paolini and the others. "Could anyone have got in that way?"

"I suppose they could," the old man in shirtsleeves, Draper, chipped in. "There's skylight access. But of course Cope, the lighting man, would have seen them. And then again, you've only got one way to get up to the skylight in the first place. There's a ladder bolted to the wall out in the alley. It's how workmen and what have you get up when something needs doing."

"So even if the lighting man wasn't around, somebody on the street would have spotted an intruder climbing up the outside of the building?"

"Put it this way, Inspector—in theory, somebody could enter or exit via the skylight without anyone seeing them. But that's only *if* they managed to do it so quietly they didn't alert Cope up on the lighting rig. But if they went via that ladder, somebody would most certainly have seen them."

"What if they brought their own ladder and set it up somewhere else? Against one of the other walls, I mean?"

"Possible. But then again, what are you thinking? That this fellow, this 'Varga,' came in under his own steam and one of *us* killed him? If that's so, what happened to the ladder? Or, if you're thinking maybe somebody killed him elsewhere, brought him here, clambered up to the roof with the corpse, and deposited him through the skylight, I find it hard to believe nobody saw it."

"He's right, sir," put in Sergeant Hook. "I saw the ladder myself when we arrived."

"Hmm. I don't doubt it," Flint acknowledged. "But all the same, I want a couple of men up there giving it a once-over. And of course you'll have to question the lighting man, what was his name . . . ?"

"Cope," repeated Draper. "Will Cope."

"Very good. See to that, will you Hook, once you've tracked down Spector."

"Right you are, sir," and Hook vanished.

"And so it begins," said a soft voice, making Ibbs jump. He spun round to find himself face to face with the subject of their discussion, Joseph Spector himself. The old man must have stowed himself somewhere in the auditorium while his fellow magicians and the remainder of the audience were beating a hasty retreat.

"Spector," said Flint, "thank God. I never thought I'd be so glad to see you."

The two men shook hands and there was an instant cordiality between them. They knew each other well, evidently.

"This is Edwin Ibbs," said Flint.

"Edmund," Ibbs corrected. "I'm a great admirer of yours, Mr. Spector."

"A pleasure, Mr. Ibbs," said the old conjuror, and they shook hands.

Spector was thin—wiry might be a better word. There was a certain spiderlike angularness to him. And he dressed much as he had in his performing days: a black suit and a velvet, silk-lined cloak. He carried a silver-topped cane. Ibbs noted that the silver head atop the cane was that of a grinning skull.

"Ibbs is a lawyer," Flint explained, "who's working on the Dean case. You know, the Ferris wheel affair."

"I know it well," said Spector. "I've been following it assiduously in the papers."

"I'm working for the defence," Ibbs told him.

"I imagine that is a complex job," said Spector. "But may I ask, what brings you here tonight?"

"I'm a fan of Paolini's. Of you as well, I must say."

"Most kind. But surely you're not old enough to have seen me perform?"

"When I was a child my father took me. The old Hippodrome. What a treat that was."

"The Hippodrome! God, I remember it well. We must talk further, you and I. I do love to wax nostalgic these days."

"No time for that now," said Flint irritably. "We need to get to the bottom of this mess posthaste, Spector."

"Very well," said Spector, striding toward the fallen Varga. "Begin at the beginning. Who is the victim?"

"Miklos Varga," Ibbs said. "I interviewed him earlier today at the funfair over in Golders Green."

"Interviewed him? About the Dean case?"

Ibbs nodded.

"That's what I can't understand," said Flint. "The whole thing makes no sense. And yet Ibbs here is involved in both crimes."

"Two crimes with more than a hint of *Grand Guignol* about them," Spector observed. "What's Varga's connection to the Dean case?"

"He runs . . . or *ran* . . . the Ferris wheel where Dominic Dean was killed."

"Hmm. And may I ask, when you interviewed Mr. Varga earlier today, did you notice how many arms he had?"

The question caught Ibbs so off guard that he almost failed to answer. "Arms?" he finally asked.

"Yes. Usually attached to shoulders."

"Well, he had two arms. Both arms, I mean, were present and correct."

Spector smiled. "Not three, then?"

Ibbs shook his head.

"The only reason I pose such an unlikely question is that when Mr. Varga tumbled out of the crate during the performance, he was accompanied by not two but *three* armoured gauntlets. One for the left arm, and two for the right."

Immediately, Flint was at his side examining the debris which surrounded the corpse. "By God, you're right. Why didn't I notice that?"

"I should have thought it was very easy to miss," said Spector. "And maybe—just maybe—the killer was counting on us missing it."

"Come on, Spector," said Flint, "this kind of thing is your bread and butter. I know you love explaining away secrets and making the rest of us look like damned fools. So how about it, eh?"

"As it's you, Inspector Flint, I'll do what I can. First we had better enumerate the backstage retinue. Who's here?"

"I got a list from the front-of-house manager," said Flint, consulting a slip of paper. "Well, there's the stage-door keeper. Alf is his name. He's got a little booth out back. Apparently he hasn't moved from his spot since about four o'clock this afternoon."

"And did he glimpse the unfortunate Mr. Varga at all?"

"I'll let you know once I've questioned him," Flint said a little huffily.

"Right you are. No use jumping the gun. Who else is back there?"

As Flint mentioned them by name, they each looked up at Spector one by one. "We've got Kenneth Fabris, the man in armour. He's part of the show of course, so he was backstage the whole time, up until around quarter past nine, when he got into his armour getup and was rigged in the crate. We've also got Max Toomey, he's part of the show too—haven't managed to track him down yet, but he was playing cards with Fabris, Sidney Draper, and Martha the assistant. Sidney Draper is the stage manager. He's the one responsible for all the props and devices being in place. Then there's Will Cope, the lighting man. . . ."

"I was up on the rig the whole time," said a man's voice, and a fat, rubicund fellow in a peaked cap approached the group.

"Don't be daft, Cope," said Sidney Draper. "You were playing cards with us."

"Well," Cope coughed, "I mean, yes, I know that. But when it was show time, I was up on the rig. I didn't move while the show was on. I had to man the lights, you see. Nobody could have done that but me."

Martha the assistant laughed; it was a husky, warming sound. "Stop acting so guilty, Cope. Nobody suspects you of anything."

"Well, I mean, I . . ." Cope blushed.

"All right, Mr. Cope," said Flint. "So you went up to the lighting rigs just before show time and you remained up there throughout. Duly noted. And that just leaves Paolini himself, the main attraction."

"I was in my dressing room up until showtime," said Paolini.

"You didn't play cards with the others?"

He gave his assembled subordinates an unpleasant sideways glance. "No," he said, "I didn't."

"And," Flint raised his voice, addressing the whole group, "none of you caught so much as a glimpse of the dead man anywhere backstage?" There was a collective shaking of the head. "The whole thing is quite bizarre," Flint murmured to himself. "How does a corpse appear from nowhere . . . ?"

Ignoring Flint, Paolini breezed up to Spector. "Joseph, thank God you're here. This is a terrible mess. These Scotland Yard buffoons are trampling all over everything, ransacking my props. I'm counting on you to talk some sense into them."

"Well," Spector said with a shrug, "they have their jobs to do. And from what I saw onstage this evening, it looks to be an unenviable task."

"I just can't get my head around it. I mean, where did he *come* from?"

"He came from the crate," said Spector. "How he got *into* the crate is a different matter altogether. Tell me, what sort of setup do you have for this trick?"

Paolini gave a dismissive flap of his hand. "Draper. Talk to Draper. He's in charge of the equipment. Everything was in order before show time, I can tell you that much. There were no corpses lurking backstage *then*."

"Do you recognise the dead man?"

"Certainly not."

"Really? You've never seen him before?"

"No. But what if I had? Would that make the problem any easier to explain?"

Spector gave an involuntary smile. "Probably not."

While Flint and Spector were having their tête-à-tête with Paolini, Ibbs realised for the first time that the rest of the cast and crew had dispersed, leaving him alone onstage. Moments like that do not come along every day. Gingerly, he peeked out into the now gaping, empty auditorium. He felt around in his pocket for a coin, flipped it high into the rafters, and then—as it began its descent—clicked his fingers and it vanished. He beamed out at the invisible audience, who burst into rapturous silent applause. It was a trick of his own devising, but stage fright meant he had never managed to perform it with anyone watching.

"I wouldn't let Paolini see you do that if I were you," said a voice.

Ibbs jumped, dropped the coin, and whirled round. Standing directly behind him was Martha. She was looking him up and down sardonically. Her head was cocked to one side and she had a hand on her hip. She was still in her show garb, which somehow made her admonition all the more crippling. For the first time he looked at her as something more than a piece of set dressing: she was perhaps a couple years older than he was (early thirties?), and it was evident from her expression that she possessed a wicked sense of humour.

"Uh—yes, so sorry, don't know what I was thinking . . ." Ibbs tried to mask his embarrassment with bluster.

Now she laughed, which made it even worse. "Come on," she said, "let's have a cup of tea."

She led him offstage, into the wings and through a tangle of backstage corridors. The area directly behind the stage—separated from the auditorium by a thin backcloth—was a jumble of props, costumes, and other accoutrements from the Pomegranate's illustrious past. There was a battle-scarred piano on casters, a penny farthing, tiki torches for fire-eaters, a shepherd's crook for the unceremonious removal of performers, a jawless ventriloquist's dummy glaring menacingly, an assortment of swords both real and replica, plus all manner of relics left behind by the various stilt-walkers, shadow-puppeteers, jugglers, musicians, escapologists, and others who had walked these hallowed halls in years gone by.

They eventually reached a row of dressing rooms. "Here we are," she said, unlocking a door, "make yourself at home."

Her dressing room was tiny—scarcely larger than a cupboard—but she seemed to have settled in quite nicely. She boiled up a kettle on a small portable stove, and while she waited for the tea to brew she turned her attention back to Ibbs.

"Now" she said pleasantly, "perhaps you can tell me what the hell's going on."

"I wish I could," Ibbs answered. "Truth is I haven't a clue. I just came here to watch the magic. Honestly."

"But you knew the dead fellow."

"I met him earlier today. I've no idea what he was doing *here.* Or how he got into that crate."

"Quite a mystery," she said. "And it would be tonight of all nights, when the ghost walks."

"Ghost? You mean there's a ghost here?"

"Oh, *every* theatre has its ghosts. But that's not what I meant. 'The ghost walks' is magician's slang. It means payday. Which I doubt will be forthcoming now."

"How long have you worked for Paolini?"

She smiled thinly, and a melancholy look came into her eyes. "A long time," she said, pouring the tea. "You know quite a lot about magic, don't you?"

"I've been studying it for a while. As an amateur, you understand."

"You a fan of Paolini?"

"Yes."

"And what's your favourite Paolini trick?"

"I like the Assistant's Revenge."

"Mm," she chuckled, "that makes two of us."

"But I must confess, I never quite worked out how it's done."

"No? You must not have reached that chapter in *Master of Manipulation*." This last comment was dappled in acid.

"Not yet," Ibbs conceded. "Maybe you can enlighten me?"

Her smile grew sly. "Maybe I can." Then she glanced up and down, as though checking they were not being observed. "That's *not* Paolini hanging upside down in the Assistant's Revenge."

"What?"

She giggled. "It's a double. He clambers into place and hooks his feet up while the real Paolini is still centre stage delivering the patter. Then, when Paolini disappears behind the sheet, he simply steps offstage, leaving me to unveil the double."

Ibbs was aghast. "But I . . ."

"Don't forget that the audience never sees Paolini freed from his bindings. He gets lifted up and out of view. The only real sight the audience has of him is when he's upside down. And I defy anyone, under those blazing stage lights, to identify a double when he's hanging upside down. So you see, the aspect of the trick that *seemed* to make it impossible—namely, the hanging upside down—is the very aspect that makes the trick work. The whole thing is over in seconds, so you never get the chance to think about it too deeply."

"But I *have* thought about it deeply," Ibbs said, "and I still never managed to get it."

"Well," she shrugged, "some people's brains just don't work that way." And she began removing her makeup with a damp cloth. Ibbs just watched her in awe.

There came a noise out in the corridor.

"Ah!" said Martha. "Speak of the devil. May I present Max Toomey." And Paolini entered the cramped dressing room. But it was not Paolini at all—after a startled moment, Ibbs realised there was something a little off about this apparition. The fellow whisked off his top hat and peeled away his moustache.

"How d'you do?" he said affably, if unenthusiastically. He was thinner than Paolini, and bald, and by the cold light of day there would be not even the slightest risk of his being mistaken for the great conjuror. Ibbs could have kicked himself for how easily he had been duped.

He looked on in creeping horror as Toomey sidled up to Martha and with grim inevitability slipped an arm around her waist. He averted his gaze, but the physical closeness of the two people, coupled with the stuffy low-ceilinged room itself, sent a shudder snaking down his spine.

Scarcely missing a beat, Martha slapped Toomey's hand away. "Where were you anyway?" she inquired absently. "The rest of us were onstage. Even Cope managed to drag himself down from his lighting rig."

"I was outside in the alley," said Toomey, "smoking a cigarette."

"Well, the police will want a word with you."

"Wouldn't be the first time," Toomey sighed. Then he looked at Ibbs with a smirk. "Women," he said.

Feeling a sudden pathological desire to change the subject, Ibbs said, "Congratulations on a very convincing performance."

"Thanks awfully," said an unenthusiastic Toomey, heading for the mirror. Ibbs watched as he began to remove his makeup, carelessly disassembling the elaborate illusion before his eyes. He removed the bald dome to reveal a head of silver hair. It had been smoothed down and covered with a flesh-colored cap which, in turn, had thin strands of jet-black hair plastered across it in a neat approximation of Paolini's own somewhat desperate resistance to encroaching baldness.

"See?" Toomey said to the mirror. "Two Paolinis! When I think you'll agree one is more than enough."

"What are you doing in *here* Toomey?" Martha asked vaguely. "Have you or have you not got your own dressing room?"

"I prefer yours," he said. "After all, it's got you in it."

Ibbs cleared his throat. "Fascinating," he said. "You know, you really don't look anything like Paolini."

Toomey gave a boisterous laugh. "Well thank God for that! No, seriously, it's wonderful isn't it? Many's the time I'll go out and mingle in the bar after the show, and nobody has even the slightest idea they're dealing with 'Paolini.'"

"That's because you're *not* Paolini," said the real Paolini, bustling into the already cramped dressing room. "No one is Paolini but Paolini."

"Oh, don't be a spoilsport," said Martha. "I'm just showing Mr. Ibbs a few of our backstage secrets."

Paolini gave her a dangerous look, and for a moment Ibbs was afraid he was about to witness yet more unpleasantness. But at the last minute, the magician restrained himself. He spoke through clenched jaws. "And why not? Why not let in the whole world, now that I'm utterly ruined? This corpse is the last nail in my coffin."

"Don't be so dramatic," Toomey counselled. "You're the one who's always complaining you don't get enough publicity. And as for the book, well I think it's going to help you if anything . . ."

"I don't care. If I find out which of those *vultures* it was that did it . . ."

Book? "Are you talking about *The Master of Manipulation*?" Ibbs put in. Suddenly all eyes were on him.

"As a neophyte, this may not be something you have come across previously," said Paolini with considerable gravity, "but giving away a magician's secrets is a crime of the utmost seriousness."

"Worse than murder?"

"Don't be fatuous. I have lost a career because of tonight's events. That fool merely lost his life."

"Ah, Paolini," said Max Toomey, "sympathetic as ever. It's that warmth and charisma that charms your audiences from here to Timbuktu."

"Shut up. Now please, all of you, leave me alone."

Martha, who had been uncharacteristically quiet since the real Paolini entered the room finally spoke up: "But this is *my* dressing room!"

"Mine is being ripped apart by those brutes from Scotland Yard. Now please: out."

Toomey, Martha, and Ibbs vacated the dressing room. What choice did they have? "You have to forgive him," said Martha when they were out in the corridor. "He's just so upset by what's happened. He's got it into his head that the book is going to ruin him. It's not, though. I think if anything it's going to get even more bums on seats, just to see if they can spot the workings for themselves."

"The artistic temperament," said Ibbs.

"If you want to call it that," said Toomey, and cackled. Then he disappeared through another door across the way—obviously his own dressing room.

Ibbs leaned close to Martha so that he could speak confidentially. "How long has Mr. Toomey been a part of the act?"

"Oh, as long as I can remember. He's . . . all right."

"Does he always treat you like that?"

"Like what?"

"Like . . ." Ibbs made an awkward sort of gesture with his hands, "*that*."

"Ha! I see what you mean. Yes, I suppose he does. I tend not to notice it these days."

"He's a charmer," Ibbs persisted. "And what about Paolini?"

She turned to him with a smile. "Let's drop it shall we Edmund? It's not my favourite subject."

"Of course! Of course. I'm sorry." He steeled himself. "Martha," he said.

"Mm?"

"What do *you* think happened here this evening?"

She shrugged. "Wish I knew. But I can tell you what *didn't* happen."

"Go on then."

"Well, for one thing that fellow Varga certainly *didn't* come backstage before the show. I was here from about five o'clock, that's around three hours until showtime. I was in my dressing room getting ready for a bit, but I spent most of the time out playing cards with the others. I'd have seen him."

"So you think Varga came backstage *after* the start of the show?"

"I don't see how else he could have got in here without one of us spotting him."

He nodded. "And I saw Varga at the Old Bailey at around five o'clock."

"What?"

"I was at the Old Bailey this afternoon. I swear I caught a glimpse of Varga. Here's another question, Martha: Have you ever heard the name Boyd Remiston?"

"Boyd Rem-is-ton," she sounded it out. "No. Definitely not. It's a funny name, so I'd have remembered it."

"What about Dominic Dean?"

"Dominic Dean. Isn't he that bank manager who got killed on a Ferris wheel? I remember Paolini talking about him."

"That's the one. So you never met him?"

She laughed at the absurdity of it. "No. Honestly, I haven't a clue what line of thought you're taking."

"Then you never met his wife either? Carla Dean?"

"She's the one who shot him, isn't she? No, I didn't know her."

"And what about Titus Pilgrim?"

This silenced her.

"Martha? Are you all right?"

"You don't want to be messing about with Titus Pilgrim."

"Do you know him?"

"I know *of* him. That's more than enough, thank you very much."

"Have you met him? Has he ever been here at the Pomegranate?"

"I'm going for a cigarette," Martha said sharply, heading for the stage door. She did not invite Ibbs to join her.

CHAPTER SIX

THE MAGIC ENDURES

Adrift backstage, Ibbs followed the sound of voices. He passed Sidney Draper and Ken Fabris, who were engaged in hushed conversation. Draper looked considerably wound up, with his shoulders bunched around his ears. And Fabris, out of his suit of armour, was far from heroic. Ibbs decided not to disturb them, and instead headed back toward the stage door. But before he reached it he found Spector and Flint conversing with an old man seated in a booth.

"All right then, Alf," said Flint convivially, "we're starting with you. I'll try my best to keep it brief. Where were you the moment the body was discovered?"

"Here. Where I always am."

"So you were here throughout the show?"

"Yep. And beforehand too. I can tell you for a fact that nobody comes through that stage door without my say-so."

"What about objects?" Spector asked. "I'm thinking particularly of crates or boxes. Anything that might be used to hide a body."

Alf was adamant. "I'd get a good look at anything like that. I prefer to know exactly what I'm letting into the building. Mr. Teasel himself gave me that authority."

At the mention of Teasel, Spector's face creased into a narrow smile. "Benjamin Teasel. Haven't heard that name for a little while. You remember him of course, Flint?"

"Yes. The Rees business.* Apparently he's out of the country."

"South of France, I understand," said Spector, still smiling. "For his health, poor lamb. Still, I'm sure he'll be utterly *delighted* to see the Pomegranate doing so well in his absence. He does work so very hard." Spector's words dripped with sarcasm.

"Wouldn't have anything to do with the complaints made against him by a couple of chorus girls, would it?"

"I couldn't possibly comment."

"Hmm—well, I've heard all kinds of rumours about Mister Benjamin Teasel. Apparently he likes to keep a close eye on his performers. A *very* close eye, if you know what I mean."

"People like Benjamin are simply a fact of life in the theatre. Old lechers with more money than sense. And yet paradoxically petrified of scandal."

"Well, I have it on good authority that he's a Peeping Tom. Unfortunately, nothing was proved. But the ladies in his company steer very clear of him."

"Wise," said Spector. "To be honest, I wouldn't have come here tonight if I had thought he'd be in attendance."

"All right," said Flint, returning his attention to Alf the doorman, "is there any other way a person could get backstage unseen?"

"There are two other ways backstage. One is through the bar, where the audience is, so nobody can go that way without being

---

* For details of "the Rees business" see *Death and the Conjuror*.

spotted. The other is the fire door. But the fire door can't be opened from the outside—only the inside. So nobody could have got in that way without at least one person seeing them."

Flint nodded, scribbling all this down. "All right, this is very useful, Alf. So you didn't see Varga backstage at all. Now, can you tell me who you *did* see?"

"Well, before the show Paolini was in his dressing room. Draper, Fabris, Toomey, Martha, and Cope were all playing cards together most of the time."

"Did any of them leave for any substantial amount of time?"

Alf thought about this. "Draper went to answer a telephone call. That was about five minutes. Maybe ten. Martha was getting ready for the show. Fabris, Toomey, and Cope were there more or less the whole time."

"And what about *during* the show?"

"Well, Toomey helps Draper with some of the props, then he goes onstage for the Assistant's Revenge business. After that, his time's his own, so he came over to keep me company. We played whist."

"And what about Fabris?"

"He went to get into his armour for the crate illusion. Draper was around. I didn't see him too much. Cope headed up to man the lighting rig."

"And Toomey was with you when the body was found?"

"That he was."

"Excellent. Thank you, Alf, I won't take up any more of your time. A-*ha*," said Flint, spotting Ibbs, "come to tag along have you, Mr. Ibbs? Well, what do you make of it?"

"Nothing whatsoever. My head is spinning."

"Nevertheless," put in Spector, "I think your observations may prove valuable. You're a witness. I tend to view a crime like this one—a complex network of deceptions—rather like a magic trick. And unlike our mutual friend Paolini, I have no compunction about letting out the secret to how the trick was done. *If* it serves my purpose," he added parenthetically. "Don't misunderstand, secrecy is the greatest tool at a magician's disposal. Well, that and a silk handkerchief. But a finely turned magic trick is like a work of art. It *is* a work of art. And sometimes it takes a shrewd analysis of the method for an audience to fully appreciate the magician's mastery of his craft."

"Mr. Spector," said Ibbs, suddenly inspired, "are you Doctor Anne L. Surazal?"

Spector threw back his head and roared with laughter. "I'm afraid not," he said when the hilarity had subsided. "I doubt I'd have the patience to write a book."

"What's this about a book?" Flint wanted to know.

"*The Master of Manipulation.* A Bible for young conjurors like Mr. Ibbs. It's about the history of magic, but it's also a guide to recreating illusions. And it deconstructs virtually all Paolini's oeuvre. To add to the mystique, nobody knows who wrote it."

Flint had an idea. "Do you think that book can tell us anything about the crate illusion?"

"Excellent question. Wish I knew."

"Well, do you have a copy?"

Spector nodded. "It arrived this morning, I've not yet had chance to crack its spine. The book is newly published, you see. I imagine Paolini has a copy lying around the place. We could check his dressing room, if you think it worthwhile?"

"Well, it's better than nothing. Which is what we've got so far."

They doubled back on themselves, heading past Martha's and Toomey's dressing rooms to the other end of the corridor. In fact, Paolini's dressing room was two doors away from Martha's. It was distinguished by a crudely painted silver star.

"Ah," Spector observed, "trust Paolini to pick out the largest dressing room."

The two "brutes" (as Paolini had referred to them) were just finishing up their search when we arrived.

"Well done, boys," said Flint. "Anything?"

"No, sir."

"All right then. Why not go and take a look at that walkway above the stage? Must be about the only place we've yet to check."

Sidney Draper, who had been hovering outside the doorway, observed, "We call that the fly loft."

Flint ignored the interruption. "And what about the roof? Find anything up there?"

"Afraid not, sir. We tried for ten minutes and couldn't get in. The skylight is rusted shut."

"So the roof's out."

"Looks that way, sir."

"All right. Off you go."

The two constables obediently disappeared.

The star dressing room was roughly double the size of Martha's, square and choked with clutter, boxes and baskets, a large mirror, a sink in the corner, and a wide wardrobe. Its walls were painted a rich crimson. The room itself was stuffy and airless, and, like the skylight, its frosted glass windows were caked with rust. They were also (somewhat incongruously) barred on the outside. The ceiling was uncomfortably low, meaning that the tall, wiry Spector almost banged his head when he entered.

"Such a large dressing room . . ." Ibbs observed.

"It ought to be," said Spector. "I understand it was designed with no fewer than eight chorus girls in mind."

"Ah," said Flint, spotting a small shelf lined with a few books. Before he reached it, though, Paolini himself exploded into the room.

"Thank God!" he said. "Sanctuary at last. When I was abroad, I dreamed of coming home to England. All I had were the English newspapers to remind me there was still civilisation on this sceptred isle. And now that I'm back, I find the place is overrun with bloody murderers!" He was gripping the doorframe as though for dear life. "Water. Please, water," he said. He looked fit to collapse. When the water was not forthcoming, he grumbled quietly to himself and headed for the sink, carelessly filling a glass so that it overflowed and splashed his cuff. Cue more grumbling. "This is without doubt," he proclaimed, "the worst night of my life. It's times like this I could really do with a spot of fresh air. But don't bother trying the window—rusted shut."

"Barred *and* rusted shut?" Spector observed quizzically. "Honestly, my dear Professor, somebody really doesn't want you to leave this room."

Ken Fabris hovered in the doorway. In the dingy dressing room light he looked particularly sickly. "Oh, pull yourself together," he said to Paolini.

"Shut up! A conspiracy, that's what it is. Someone's got it in for me."

"If that were the case," Fabris continued, "don't you think it would be *you* and not some other poor sod lying dead on the stage?"

Paolini had no answer for that. He sipped his water with a conspicuously quivering hand.

"Those bars," said Flint, studying the windows. "Almost as if this were a prison of some kind."

"All theatres are prisons," said Spector. "Just ask an actor."

"They're all the same," put in Fabris. "Every window barred. There's an old story that Lester Lyon, the fellow who built the Pomegranate, was staging a performance by the famous actor Sir Ichabod Vernon. This would be around the end of the eighteenth century. Anyway, Vernon was a notorious drunkard, and Lester Lyon wasn't willing to risk his running out before the show and getting sloshed. Hence the bars on all the dressing-room windows."

"But as I recall," said Spector, "Ichabod Vernon found a way to get drunk anyway."

"Right—it was quite a mystery at the time. Vernon was playing Hamlet—this was at the age of sixty-four. And Lester Lyon was determined that he shouldn't be allowed to get drunk before the performance. So he placed him in the star dressing room (complete with the bars on the window), and dispatched a couple of heavies to guard the door. He wasn't taking chances. Anyway, as they were getting near to showtime, Lester himself toddled along to pay a visit to his star. And found him flat on his back, barely conscious from all the booze in his system. And no one could work out how he managed it."

"Yes!" Spector grinned. "An excellent story of old theatre-land. No one had gone into or out of the dressing room—a veritable locked-room mystery, albeit of a less deadly sort. And ultimately the solution is a disappointment. You see, Lester Lyon was so preoccupied with preventing Ichabod Vernon from going *out* in search of the demon alcohol that he neglected to consider the possibility of it being brought *in*. So there were guards on the door, but none out in the alley. And that's where the great man's cronies simply handed him bottle after bottle through the bars."

The dressing room was beginning to feel pretty cramped by the time Martha and Sidney Draper arrived. Ibbs was no good with ages, but he put Draper at about seventy. He had a face that was so off-kilter and ugly that it almost came back around again to looking beautiful. The community Ibbs grew up in was run by old men like this—men who worked hard and would work hard until the day they died. Thick black eyebrows plumed from his forehead like twin twists of smoke, but otherwise his face was sunken and grey. He had cheekbones like razors, and low-slung jowls swinging about his chin. His eyes were dark and deep-set. He was like a gnarled tree trunk that has withstood a thousand winters and might withstand a thousand more. His handshake was tight, and a knobbly bone protruding from his thumb felt particularly uncomfortable to the touch—it almost made Ibbs shudder. His nose was bulbous and his ears wide and protuberant. Everything about him seemed slightly oversized and exaggerated, given his small stature. His head was too big, and his face bigger still. His voice rasped like a buzz saw when he greeted them. "I need a word with Paolini."

"Good God," Paolini bellowed, "is there no escape? Speak, man, speak."

"We need to know about tomorrow."

"In what sense?"

"You've got a packed house. Are you going to cancel?"

"Cancel? Certainly not. Corpse or no corpse, the magic endures. In some ways, this is the best thing that could have happened to draw attention away from that wretched book."

"Right," said Draper, making to leave. "Should have guessed it would take a murder to up the ante on your act. I'll let front of house know."

"Ah! Just a moment!" cried Paolini. "Don't go anywhere. Inspector Flint, have you questioned this man yet? I have reason to believe *he* is the one responsible for this whole tragedy of errors."

Draper was appalled. "You're off your rocker. I never saw that dead fellow before in my life."

"Don't lie to me, Draper."

"I don't take kindly to being called a liar. I'm an old man, but don't think for a second I couldn't give you a bloody good hiding. So you show a little respect. Understand?"

"Well," said Paolini, summoning up the last vestiges of his battered dignity, "I have matters to attend to." And he left the room, grumbling to himself.

"So, Martha," put in Spector, "would you be so kind as to tell us how the crate trick was *supposed* to have worked?"

"You're asking the wrong person, you know," she said with a smile. "I'm just the assistant. We're ten a penny."

Spector returned her smile. "You and I both know that's not true. A magician is nothing without his assistant."

"Well, I'll do my best," she said, clearing her throat. "The trick is all to do with the crate itself. Paolini opens the rear door first and then the front door so the audience can see right through. What the audience *doesn't* see is that the rear door has a small ledge on the inside, which is hidden from view because the rear door is *always* opened and swung out first—even if only by a fraction of a second. Ken Fabris stands on the ledge in his armour. Sidney straps his legs into position, so there's no danger of him losing his balance when the door opens. Then, when the *other* suit of armour is positioned upright in the crate, Paolini closes the front door followed by the rear door, so the audience never catches so much as a glimpse of Ken. The idea is for Ken to switch places with the complete suit of armour so that when the doors are opened again, he emerges from the crate, alive and kicking. That way, it looks to the crowd as though the suit of armour has come alive inside the crate.

"Of course, what *actually* happened was that the act of spinning the crate caused the mannequin to fall apart and the body to come loose. Then, when Paolini opened the crate again, the whole mess just spilled out onto the stage—including the dead man."

Spector steepled his fingers thoughtfully. "That makes the appearance of the corpse all the more difficult to explain. So you and Paolini had no idea that Fabris wasn't in the crate?"

She shook her head. "Well, I can't speak for Paolini, but from where I stood onstage I couldn't see the ledge inside the crate. I just took it for granted that Ken was in there."

"I don't know what to tell you," said Draper. "I put Fabris in there myself. Then I wheeled the crate into position. Then Martha came into the wings and took it from me. It was never out of my sight in the meantime."

Flint seemed to be getting an idea. "But you were alone back here with the crate?"

Draper scowled. "What's that supposed to mean?"

Flint smirked. "Nothing at all. Just that if anyone was going to tamper with the crate before it went onstage . . ."

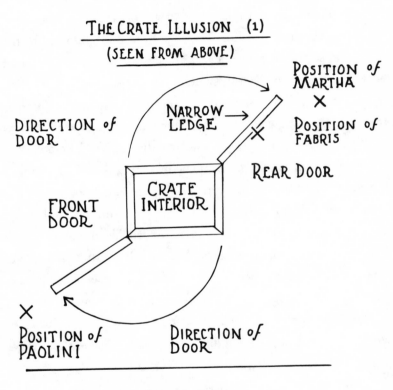

THE CRATE ILLUSION (1)

(SEEN FROM ABOVE)

POSITION of MARTHA

NARROW LEDGE →

DIRECTION of DOOR

POSITION of FABRIS

REAR DOOR

CRATE INTERIOR

FRONT DOOR

POSITION of PAOLINI

DIRECTION of DOOR

AUDIENCE

"It could only have been me or Fabris. Well, all I can tell you is that it wasn't me. And don't go getting any ideas about Fabris either. He can hardly move in that suit of armour, let alone do any jiggery-pokery shifting bodies about."

"There is also," Spector observed, "the matter of the three gauntlets." He clasped his hands behind his back and began to pace. "Mr. Draper, did you know Miklos Varga?"

"Never seen him before in my life."

"What about you, Martha?"

She shook her head.

"And Mr. Draper, you are Paolini's stage manager here at the Pomegranate. What exactly does your role entail?"

Draper shrugged. "Sandbag man is what they call me. I'm an old man now, so I don't have any illusions. I call a spade a spade. It's a messy job but somebody has to do it."

"I'll bet."

"Oh there's chaps half my age they've brought in to help me, and you know what? I've never had one last more than a month."

"Where were you when Varga was found?" Spector inquired pointedly. There was no expression on his thin, creased face.

"Backstage."

"Where?"

"I have a little nook offstage right, where I have my tea. There's a table where we play cards and a little lamp."

"So it's safe to say you would have seen if anybody snuck into the theatre during the show?"

"I'd say the odds were pretty good, yes."

"So how did the corpse get in there?"

"Well, I reckon the crates were switched. Paolini has duplicates for all his props, and I think the crate I put Ken Fabris in was rolled out of the way and the duplicate with the corpse was wheeled onstage."

Flint frowned. "How could that have happened without you noticing?"

Draper shrugged again. "It couldn't."

Spector was thoughtful. "All right, thank you Mr. Draper."

Draper nodded and withdrew.

"What do you reckon, Spector?" said Flint.

"I reckon," the old conjuror began, "that we have so far neglected one of the key players in this little drama. Namely, the victim. What do we *know* about Miklos Varga?"

"We-ell," Flint flipped through his notebook, "the doc had a look at him, so I can tell you the cause of death. He was incapacitated with a blunt instrument, then strangled with a length of rope."

"I see. You know, I'm very intrigued by his connection to the Ferris wheel case. But I'm an old man and my memory's not what it was. Can you give me some details about the Dominic Dean business? Just something to get the ball rolling."

"Well all right . . . a husband and wife went up on a Ferris wheel at a fairground in Golders Green. Whilst they were up there, a gunshot was heard, followed by the wife screaming. When the carriage came back down to earth again, the husband was found to have been shot at close range. The pistol was in his wife's hand. She said she picked it up from the floor of the carriage."

"And the wife denies any wrongdoing?"

"Right. But the burns on the husband's shirt indicate the barrel of the pistol was right up against his belly."

"And what about the gun itself?"

"Well, there's no question it was the pistol that was used in the shooting. It had two sets of fingerprints on it, the husband's and the wife's. That makes sense because it was the husband's gun."

Ibbs couldn't resist stepping in at this point. "A Nagant M1895," he said.

"Where did he get it?"

"I don't know," Ibbs answered. Which was true—nobody did. "But from the very beginning everyone has been treating the Dean murder as an open-and-shut case, and I don't believe it is."

Spector narrowed his eyes. "You think she's protecting someone?"

"Could be. I just can't fathom why a wife would do that—shoot her husband under circumstances where she would be the only conceivable suspect."

"Then whom do you think she is protecting?"

"No one. At least, I've not yet found anyone."

"Then that just leaves the husband," suggested Inspector Flint.

"Suicide, you mean? But why shoot yourself in the stomach? It's a hell of a painful way to go."

"Mm." Spector scratched his chin. "And Dominic Dean was . . . a bank manager, is that right?"

"Yes. In Golders Green. There was a violent robbery at his bank just a fortnight before his murder. I happen to think the crimes are connected."

At this, Spector arched his eyebrows. "Indeed? This is turning out to be quite a trail of breadcrumbs. Tell me about the bank robbery. I'm afraid that story passed me by."

Ibbs kept it brief: "A three-man raid, by all accounts. At least, three men were spotted climbing into a van immediately after the robbery."

"Three men?"

"Only three."

"Hm. Typically professional robbery gangs are at least four men strong."

"My theory is that the gang paid Dean off, to get inside information that would let them into the building and into the vault."

"But it went wrong." This was not posed as a question.

"Yes, it went wrong. There was a watchman on duty who got in the way. They beat him to death."

Spector tutted and shook his head. "Dear, dear."

"So the robbery gang became a murder gang. I believe Dominic Dean was overcome by guilt about the death of that watchman. So naturally he threatened to go to the police. And the gang had no choice but to have him killed."

"It's an interesting theory, Mr. Ibbs. But why would a man plagued by guilt—as Dean hypothetically was—let the rest of the gang in on his plan to go to the police? Surely he'd be aware of what they were capable of, how ruthless they were?"

"I've had accounts from Dean's colleagues of his increasing paranoia. It seems he wasn't in his right mind."

"What about his wife? Did she say anything of that sort to you?"

"Not in so many words. But I gather their relationship was rather troubled. She's being very careful with her phrasing. She knows the slightest slip could get her into trouble."

"Well, she sounds like an interesting lady. I'd like to see her at some point if I may."

"Another time," cut in Flint. "Right now I'm more concerned about the murder that just took place in front of seven hundred people."

"Let's dispel a misinterpretation, first of all," said Spector. "The audience did not see a murder committed, did they? They saw a corpse. That is not the same thing. Let's not forget that the illusionist's art lies in exploiting the 'modal gap,' the mind's innate perception of disparate entities as a single whole. A corpse equals a murder. That's what an untrained observer will tell you. But we know better, don't we, gentlemen?"

Flint just looked vexed. "Come on," he said, "I want to question Toomey. Alf the doorman said the two of them were playing cards when it all went down."

A brief chat with Max Toomey yielded a virtual mirror of Alf's account. After his turn onstage relatively early in the show for the Assistant's Revenge, he and Alf had played cards together in Alf's booth beside the stage door. They were still playing when the body was discovered, and all hell broke loose. Flint was content to cross the two men off his list.

"Well, Mr. Toomey, I think that's all your movements accounted for. For the moment at least."

"So can I go?"

"Yes, Mr. Toomey. But don't go far. We may need to speak to you again tomorrow."

"And what about me?" Alf chipped in.

"Yes, Alf. Get some sleep. I want you back here bright and early."

Alf and Toomey shared a telling look and left without another word.

"So where does that leave us?" Ibbs said.

"It leaves us with several promising leads," said Flint. "But now, Mr. Ibbs, it might be best if you left Spector and me to get on with our work."

Ibbs cast a forlorn glance at the old conjuror, who merely shrugged helplessly. Duly chastened, the young lawyer sloped off.

But no sooner had he left the dressing room than he stumbled on an interesting sight. It was Paolini, using the telephone in the corridor—evidently the one Draper had used to take his call during the preshow card game. He pressed himself discreetly against the wall, just out of sight.

"Get me Morgan. Andrew Morgan." Paolini was clutching the receiver to his ear, speaking in rasping, urgent tones. Ibbs flattened himself against the wall as best he could, ears pricked.

"Morgan," Paolini spat, "where the hell are you? I *know* you're back at the office. I was speaking rhetorically. I mean, why in hell's name aren't you *here* where I told you to be? I don't give a damn how many corpses there were up on that stage, it's no excuse for you to go scuttling off without seeing the coup de théâtre.

"No. I don't care. I want you back here *now*." That last word dripped with venom. "Our business is not yet concluded. Don't you understand? *I know who did it*." With that, Paolini slammed the receiver down and whirled round before Ibbs could slink away.

Ibbs had to think on his feet. "So sorry to disturb you. I know this has been quite a taxing evening for you."

Paolini snorted, but said nothing.

"I . . . I just wanted to tell you that I'm an admirer of your act. I really am. I've even been studying magic myself. Just a pale imitation of your own work, of course, but I enjoy it."

Paolini remained sphinxlike, clearly wondering how much Ibbs had heard.

"Well," Ibbs persisted, "I've been practising the Charlier cut in front of the mirror; you know, the one-handed . . ."

"I'm aware of the Charlier cut," said Paolini.

"Of course you are. Well, what it is, I just can't get the hang of it. I'm afraid my thumb's a fraction of an inch too short, I wonder if you could possibly . . . ?"

"You want me to show you?"

"Oh would you? That would be wonderful if you could, Professor . . ."

Paolini's eyes narrowed and a mean-spirited smile spread across his face. "No, I couldn't. Now leave me alone if you value your life."

Ibbs did so, gladly. Then he waited for an opportune moment and caught the attention of Flint and Spector. "Inspector Flint, could I speak with you about something?"

Flint tutted. "What is it, Ibbs?"

"I thought I'd better tell you—I just heard something that may be useful."

"Oh yes? And what's that?"

"It's Paolini. He was on the telephone just now with somebody named Morgan."

"Morgan, eh? And who's that?"

"I've no idea, but they had quite an argument. Looks like this Andrew Morgan was supposed to be here at the theatre tonight.

They had some sort of business or other. But that's not all. Paolini also claimed to know who killed Varga."

"He what!"

Spector stepped in. "I shouldn't get my hopes up if I were you, Flint. Paolini has a habit of overstating his abilities."

"All the same, I can hardly let go of a lead like that . . ."

"Personally," said Spector, "I am more interested in this Morgan fellow."

"Morgan," Flint repeated the name thoughtfully. "Not much to go on, but it might be useful, Mr. Ibbs. Good work."

"Are you going to question him about it?"

"All in good time. Wouldn't want to show our hand too early, would we?"

Taking this as a summary dismissal, Ibbs skulked away. Never before in his life had he been so confused, so bewildered, and so utterly at a loss.

Ibbs did not immediately perceive the presence at the other end of that dimly lit and curiously empty corridor. But the slow creak of a floorboard brought him back to reality, and drew his attention to a malign shape. It was a man, a dim silhouette in the murky light.

"Hello?" Ibbs called out, and was perturbed to hear his voice catch slightly in his throat. "Who's that?"

The fellow took a step forward. He was both tall and broad, wrapped in a heavy overcoat. He wore a bowler hat. His eyes were slightly bulbous, casting his face in the glow of mania. But when he spoke, his voice was soft. Almost childlike. "So it's you," he said.

The next instant he was barrelling toward Ibbs, almost seeming to skid on the carpeted floor, reaching out with clutching claws.

Ibbs was about to say something, but no sooner had a word formed on his lips than this fellow's hands were around his throat, throttling. He heard himself gasp; a desperate, scratching sound. A white flare blossomed before his eyes and the man's face faded in and out of focus. But there was no escaping the faint gleam of madness in those bulbous eyes.

CHAPTER SEVEN

THE EX-HUSBAND

A feminine voice punctured Ibbs's fading consciousness. "Ned! What in hell's name are you playing at?"

The giant snapped to attention, letting go his grip on the lawyer's swanlike. Ibbs dropped like a stone. It was most embarrassing. And the next instant Martha was standing over him, dusting him off and helping him to his feet, all while she continued to berate the monster who did this to him. "You're such a complete moron, Ned; I can't believe it—did you honestly think this was Toomey? Does he *look* like Toomey? This is poor Mr. Nibbs, he just came to see the show!"

Ibbs cleared his throat—which took some doing. "It's Ibbs actually," he said hoarsely.

Ned was immediately chastened. "I'm very sorry," he mumbled, "hope I haven't hurt you too badly." He held out a hand and Ibbs flinched, then shook it. "Ned Winchester's my name."

"How . . . how do you do?"

Martha tutted. "Oh come on, both of you. Come into my dressing room."

As they followed her down the corridor, Ibbs got a better look at his assailant. He was broad all right, almost filling the entire corridor. This gave him the appearance of having an unusually small head. His hair was thick—thicker than Ibbs's, anyway—and his nose was conspicuously broken and crooked. Other than that he was tolerably handsome, with half-lidded eyes which evoked either extreme dullness or pronounced perspicacity. The look on his face now was one of benign affability. He had removed his bowler hat and respectfully gripped it with both hands as though he were attending a church service.

When they were in her dressing room, Martha sat Ibbs down and calmed him with the promise of another cup of tea from the small stove. "Who *is* this fellow?" Ibbs said. "Your brother or something?"

Martha gave a short, harsh laugh, then looked at Winchester, who was smiling. "He certainly acts more like a brother. But no, Mr. Ibbs. Ned's my husband."

Had Ibbs been sipping tea at that moment, he would have spat it all over the floor. "Husband?"

"Ex-husband, I should say. But he acts like a brother. Don't you find that rather perverse?"

Ibbs did not find it especially perverse. He was, however, mildly scandalised by the news of the ex-husband; he grew up in rural Berkshire, so this was the first knowing encounter he had ever had with a divorcée. He glanced over at Winchester, who winked at him.

"Ned's got this foolish idea that he's my guardian angel," Martha explained. "He thinks he can crop up out of the woodwork and make everything all right for me. When I was young and stupid I thought he was a hero. Now I realise he's just a kindhearted idiot. Aren't we, sweet?"

"If you say so, darling." Winchester gave a modest smile.

Flint and Spector came rapping at the dressing-room door, no doubt drawn by the commotion. They had Sidney Draper with them.

"And who is *this*?" Flint demanded.

"Ned Winchester," said Martha without hesitation. "I'm sorry Inspector. I lied to you earlier. You see, I let Ned in through the fire door before the show. He was backstage the whole time."

Flint turned puce. "So . . . he was here when the murder took place?"

"Yes," said Martha, "I suppose he was."

"Just a mo'," said Winchester, "*what* murder?"

"Well, well," Flint continued, striding expansively into the dressing room. "Ned Winchester. Seems to me I do recognise your name after all. I gather you're well-known to my colleagues."

Winchester was shuffling his feet, a picture of contrition. "I made a few iffy decisions in the past, Mr. Flint. But that's all behind me. And I don't know nothing about a murder."

"Really? You sure? Because it looks to me like you're right in the middle of a very 'iffy decision' indeed. Why did you come here tonight?"

A pause. "To watch the show."

"From backstage?"

"All right, I didn't come to watch the show. I came to see Toomey. Catch him unawares, like."

"Toomey? Paolini's double? What did you want with him?"

"I wanted . . ." he slumped down in the other chair, the one beside the dressing table. "I wanted him to leave Martha alone. He'd been badgering her. Telling her he was in love with her. Isn't that right, Martha? She didn't want none of it. It was getting right up her nose. She told me about it, so I decided to come and set him straight."

Spector seized the reins. "Now correct me if I'm wrong, but you just mistook young Mr. Ibbs for Toomey, is that so?"

"Well, I don't know what Toomey looks like. I've never seen him outside of his Paolini gear."

"Very well. Then let's go back to the beginning. What time did you get to the theatre?"

"I'd say around half-past seven."

"And Martha let you in."

"Yes."

"Right," said Flint, seizing Winchester by the arm, "come with me. I have one or two questions for you." And he marched him out into the corridor, followed by a sly-looking Spector.

"Please don't hurt him," said Martha, "this is all my fault." She glanced at Ibbs, then at Draper, then bit her lip. "God, I need another cigarette." She sidled out, leaving Ibbs alone with a bemused-looking Sidney Draper. The old stage manager sighed and shook his head.

"She's a dark horse, that one. Plays her cards close to her chest, if you know what I mean." For the briefest moment Ibbs's imagination dwelled on Martha's chest and he felt a crimson flush come to his cheeks.

"Did you know she had a husband?" he asked, feigning casualness.

"A husband? I'm afraid I did. Poor brainless old Ned. I know him very well. You see, he's my nephew." When Draper smiled—as he did now—he showed off a row of perfectly even, white teeth. Much too impressive to be the real thing. "Never was too bright, that lad. Even in the early days, when I'd take him along the pier at Margate. I remember he walked slap-bang into the glass in the hall of mirrors once. Nearly had someone's eye out at the coconut shy. Not bad at hook-a-duck, mind you . . ."

Ibbs raised a finger to his lips and pressed an ear to the door just in time to hear three sets of footsteps retreating. He twisted the door handle as quietly as possible and slipped out into the corridor, leaving Draper alone. He followed the three men in the direction of the stage door, watching from a discreet distance as Flint settled Winchester in the now-vacant booth.

Flint paced up and down a little. Spector, however, was conspicuously still. Of course he knew Ibbs was there, but he evidently did not deem it expedient to acknowledge him.

After a few tense moments, Flint spoke. "So you got here before the show?" he demanded.

Ned Winchester hung his head. "Yes, sir."

"And you were here during?"

"Yes, sir."

"Where?"

"I stayed in Martha's dressing room for a bit. Till after curtain-up. Then Sid Draper came to fetch me when the coast was clear. He's my uncle. Then we played cards backstage."

"Aha. The plot thickens. So your uncle knew you were here too."

Winchester nodded. "I told him I was here for Toomey. Uncle Sid got all fraught and started trying to talk me out of doing anything stupid. I told him, I said: 'I'm just here to talk, that's all I want.' He gave me a whisky and we had a little chat."

"Did you see anybody else while you were backstage?"

Winchester nodded again. "A few. Ken Fabris, I saw him get in the crate. He was in that suit of armour getup. And then there was Will Cope, the lighting man . . ."

"The lighting man. No wonder he was looking nervous earlier," Flint observed, casting a wry eye in Spector's direction. "And what about Varga?"

"Who's Varga?"

"The dead man. The man this is all about."

"Never heard of him."

"No? Come with me."

Flint took Winchester back down the corridor the way they had come, then strode out onto the boards from stage-right, halting beside an insensate mass on the ground, which was covered by a grubby sheet. Flint knelt down and lifted a corner of the sheet, revealing the remains of Miklos Varga.

"Have you ever met this man before?"

Winchester's mouth dropped open. "Yes I have."

"You have? When?"

"About ten minutes before the start of the show . . ."

"Where was he? Backstage?"

"No. He was out in the street."

"Outside the stage door?"

"No. Outside the fire door I came in through. I propped the door open for a minute to smoke a quick cig while Martha and Uncle Sid were getting ready for curtain-up. You're not supposed to smoke backstage because of all the flammable bits and pieces. And just as I was about to close the door, this fellow comes charging up along the pavement, says can I let him in, he's in the show and he's running late. So I let him in and he scuttles off without so much as a thank-you."

"Scuttles off where?"

"Don't know. Didn't see."

Flint was writing all this down. "So *you* were the one who let him backstage."

Winchester nodded. "But he was alive when I saw him, I can tell you that. I thought he might be Toomey out of his disguise. But when he spoke I heard he had a foreign accent—Toomey's a Londoner. So I knew this chap wasn't him."

"What can you tell me about Titus Pilgrim?" Flint asked.

Winchester's whole body grew taut. "Now I don't go messing about with any of that lot anymore, Mr. Flint."

"That wasn't my question."

"I've only met him a couple of times, and that was over two years ago. Back in the bad old days, that was."

"What about Dominic Dean?"

"Who?"

"You never heard of him?"

Winchester shook his head.

For the first time, Joseph Spector seized the reins of the conversation. He had been looming throughout like a sort of cadaverous sibyl, silent but perpetually observant. He stepped out onto the stage and said: "What about Boyd Remiston?"

Winchester screwed up his face thoughtfully, then said: "No, I haven't. And who are you anyway?"

"That's Joseph Spector," said Flint, "and you'll treat him with respect."

Spector smiled disarmingly. "How do you do, Mr. Winchester? I understand you got into something of a scuffle with young Mr. Ibbs?"

Winchester glanced at Ibbs, who was now emerging from the wings. "Uh . . . yes, well, that was all a bit of a misunderstanding."

"I see. So do you come to the Pomegranate often?"

"Sometimes. To see my uncle. Or Martha. We have a laugh. Play a bit of cards."

"But you came this evening with the especial intention of beating Max Toomey to a pulp?"

Winchester laughed. "You might say that. I don't like lechers. That's what Toomey is. Where is he by the way?"

"Far away, I'm afraid. Inspector Flint sent him home."

"Pity. I don't like the way he treats Martha."

"You and Martha were married briefly, is that so?" In a matter of moments, Spector had wrested control of the situation away from Flint.

Winchester frowned. "What's it to you?"

"Colour me inquisitive. Now how long did the marriage last?"

Winchester exhaled. "Not long. A few months."

"And you're divorced now?"

"This is nobody's business but mine and Martha's. It's got nothing to do with all this."

"Well, for a divorced couple you still seem awfully protective of your former wife."

"She's . . . she needs someone to take care of her."

"I see." Spector changed tack. "The dead man—you say you'd never seen him before this evening?"

"No. Never laid eyes on him."

"And how do *you* think he came to be in that crate that was wheeled onstage?"

"Haven't the foggiest. And I mean that truly. I saw Uncle Sid strapping Fabris into the crate. I even helped him wheel it into position by the side of the stage. Then me and Uncle Sid sat down to play cards for a bit."

"So the crate was not out of your sight?"

"No. I even saw Martha reach out and drag it onto the stage just before the start of the trick."

"And what about the other crate? I understand Paolini keeps duplicates of all his props?"

"That was with the other props. Nobody touched it. Why would they need to?"

Spector steepled his fingers under his chin. "Now, Mr. Winchester, I'd like you to describe for me as accurately as you can the order of events concerning the crate illusion."

Winchester considered this question very carefully. "All right. Me and Uncle Sid were playing cards when he looks at his watch and says, 'Wait here, Ned, while I undo the rope lock for that blasted crate trick.' So I'm sitting at the table while he goes over to sort it out. But then he comes back looking sort of worried and says, 'Ned, there's something wrong. The ropes have got knotted up somehow. I can't get the backcloth to shift. Will you go up there and cut the rope attached to arbour number six? I have to go and roust Fabris.'"

"He sent you up to the overhead walkway?"

"Yes. Up the spiral staircase. I've seen my uncle do it a lot of times, so I know the ropes, so to speak."

"I see. So you went up to cut the rope holding the backcloth in place. How long did that take?"

"Longer than it should have," Winchester grumbled. "Whenever I've gone up there before, the lights have been on so I could read the numbers. But this time it was completely dark!" He said this as though it had come as a surprise. "So I struck a match to get a better look. That's when Cope came hobbling over, clanking on the metal walkway. I thought he was going to bring the whole thing down!"

"Cope, eh? What did he want?"

"He was hissing at me to put the match out. Said the ropes and everything were highly flammable. I mean, how was I supposed to know that? I knew I was up against it time-wise, so I just counted along the ropes and cut the sixth one. Seems to have done the trick, because the backcloth dropped, didn't it?"

Spector conceded that it had.

"Do you and Cope get on well? Are you friends?"

"Not friends, no. But he's all right. He's got a sick kid, you know. A boy. The wife died, so he's all the little lad's got left."

Spector nodded. "And what happened after that?"

Winchester hesitated. "I went back down."

"You went back down the spiral staircase?"

A pause. Then, somewhat coyly, "Yes."

Flint stepped in. "Why do I feel as though you're lying to me, Winchester? You're already in enough trouble as it is. I'd spit it out if I were you."

Winchester gave a petulant sigh. "All right. I didn't go straight down. I . . . I didn't like the way Cope spoke to me. Treating me like I'm an idiot. So I went over to give him a piece of my mind."

"You threatened him?"

"No, nothing like that!" But it was evident from the way Winchester's gaze was darting around the room, and the way he moistened his lips with a quick flick of the tongue, that it was *exactly* like that. "It's just that I don't like being talked down to. That, and I was bothered he might warn Toomey I was in the building."

So Cope's caginess and his willingness to lie to the police made sense. He was trying to avoid getting on Ned Winchester's bad side.

"Where was your uncle while you were messing about up in the fly loft?"

At this, Ned Winchester shrugged. "You'd better ask him."

"Don't worry," said Flint, "we will."

"Personally," Spector murmured absently, "I'm more interested in *why* your uncle sent you up in the first place. If he was trying to keep you hidden, why delegate a task which he knew would put you in contact with more of the backstage crew?"

Winchester shrugged. "Uncle Sid was a bit flustered. He gets that way sometimes. My uncle's not got the strength he once had. He shouldn't be climbing up and down steps. Anyway, as I went

I called out 'Don't you worry, uncle,' and next thing I heard him going 'Shhh!'" Winchester smiled. "No pleasing some people."

"So you saw Cope. We know you didn't see Toomey. He was fortunate enough to evade you. Did you see Alf, the doorman, at all?"

"No. I couldn't have done. If he was by the stage door, he would have been just out of my sight. Uncle Sid didn't want Alf knowing I was backstage. There's a bit of a rivalry between them."

"So you didn't see Alf and Alf didn't see you. All right. But you saw your uncle helping Fabris into the crate?"

"Yes."

"What time was that?"

"Nine fifteen on the nose. It's *always* nine fifteen for the suit of armour trick. That was when I was coming back down the steps."

"And what precisely did you see?"

"Like you said—I saw my uncle getting Fabris into the crate."

"What happened?"

"Well, Fabris was just making sure the armour was secured to the hook in the rear door, so there was no danger of a mishap and his coming loose."

"Did either man say anything?"

"Yes, Uncle Sid said something along the lines of 'You all right in there, Ken?' and he answered 'All quiet on the Western Front,' and gave a thumbs-up sign."

"What happened then?"

"Fabris started to lean out of the crate and said: 'That you, Ned?' We're chums. Drunk together a few times. But Uncle Sid told him something like, 'No time,' so he settled back into the crate. Just before the door closed, he called out: 'See you on the other side then, fellows!'"

"And you watched your uncle seal the crate."

"Yes. Then I helped him wheel it into position."

"And there didn't seem to be anything unusual about it? It didn't seem heavier, for example, than you were used to?"

Winchester shook his head. "I'm not here every night of course. But I've seen the show a few times, and been backstage a bit too. No, there was nothing that struck me as being out of the ordinary at all. But you'd better ask Uncle. Or Fabris."

"And the cabinet was not out of your sight until Martha dragged it onstage from the wings?"

"That's right. After that, my uncle and I played a round of whist while I waited."

"And what about the duplicate crate?"

"Yes, that was in sight too."

"Was it open? Closed?"

Winchester thought about this. "Closed. I think."

"But you can't be sure."

"Well, I didn't pay much attention to it. Anyway, not long after that we realised something had gone wrong onstage. My uncle told me to clear out before anyone saw me. But I was . . . what's the word?"

"Stupid?" Flint supplied.

"Curious. So I headed back up into the rafters and hid for a while. No one saw me this time, not even Cope. And I managed to get back down again before your constables could find me. I hid in a storage room opposite the dressing rooms for a bit, then by chance I bumped into Mr. Ibbs, thought he was Toomey and . . . the rest you know."

"I have a question," said Flint, "why would your uncle lie to us? He didn't mention you when we asked him who was backstage."

"He's protective, Mr. Flint. He knows I've struggled. He knows I've not always . . . done the right thing. I reckon he was scared you lot'd get the wrong end of the stick."

"Well, we'll know soon enough. Please give your address to Sergeant Hook. And don't go anywhere. We'll be back to take your statement in further detail."

Leaving him, they headed back into the wings with Ibbs trailing behind like an obedient puppy. As they headed back to Martha's dressing room, Flint was oddly chipper. That's when he seemed to notice Ibbs for the first time in a while.

"Hop it would you, Ibbs? I need a word with Draper in here."

Ibbs opened his mouth to protest, but thought twice about it. He watched them enter the room and slam the door behind them.

Then he ducked forward and pressed his eye to the keyhole. There was no one around to see. In the dressing room, Flint was towering over Draper while Spector stood to one side, looking thoughtful. "Why didn't you tell us your nephew was backstage with you?" Flint demanded.

If the Inspector had anticipated a confrontation, he was disappointed. Sidney Draper caved in immediately. "I wanted to try and keep him out of it. I know now I did the wrong thing."

"Your nephew's well-known to the police. He has quite a temper."

Again, Draper could hardly deny it. "He's been in trouble before. But he's a good lad. He *is*. All he wanted to do was come and say hello to his uncle. He's . . . not a bad lad, Inspector. You have to believe me. I've known him since he was a little tot. When I was a Punch and Judy man, his mother used to bring him down to the pier at Margate to watch my show. Then I'd buy him ice cream and what have you and we'd have a fine old time."

"That's all very well. But it's no excuse for lying to Scotland Yard in the midst of a murder investigation."

"I know. And I'm sorry. I am."

"So when did your nephew arrive?"

"Not sure."

"You didn't let him in?"

"No. I reckon that was Martha. She must have let him in through the fire door." This tallied with what Winchester had said.

"Ah yes. The door that doesn't open from the outside."

"That's the one. He wouldn't have wanted to use the stage door, because of Alf. Anyway, he came to see me not long after curtain-up. We had a chat for a bit. We played some cards. Then he helped me get ready for the crate illusion."

"So Fabris saw him too?"

Draper bit his lip. "I don't want to get anyone in trouble."

Flint sighed and headed for the door. Ibbs bolted out of the way. "Mr. Fabris," he bellowed along the corridor, "will you come in here please?"

Fabris appeared, blinking innocently. "Yes?"

"It's come to our attention that you lied to us."

"Really?" he seemed shocked. "About what?"

"Ned Winchester."

"Oh," said Fabris. "Him. Well, you didn't ask about him. And I'm not a mind reader. That's Paolini's purview."

"You lied by omission. So you *did* see Ned Winchester backstage before you got into the crate?"

"No, but I heard him just before Sid came to fetch me. I'm pretty hopeless with timekeeping unfortunately, so poor old Sid has quite a bit of legwork to do. But I definitely heard that dopey voice: 'Don't you worry, uncle!'" Fabris produced a cruelly accurate approximation of Winchester's speech pattern.

"Did you see the crates?"

"I did. They were both there. *My* crate was open and ready for me to climb in. The other was in the far corner, where it always is."

"And what did Sid Draper say to you?"

"He said 'All set, Ken?' Nice and polite like he always is. He's a gent. I told him yes, and so we set about getting me in the crate."

"Could you see Ned Winchester?"

"No. He was up in the rafters. I could hear him stomping about, but he was hidden by the lights."

"And was there anything *else* unusual which took place in the few minutes prior to your climbing into the crate?"

"Everything went *exactly* as normal. I stepped up onto the ledge, Sid Draper came to help make sure the hooks were in place. He said something along the lines of 'You all right in there, Kenny?' and I said, 'Yes,' or, I think, 'All quiet on the Western Front.' And I gave him the thumbs-up. That's when I heard Ned coming back down. I thought I'd say hello, but Sid told me there wasn't time.

He's always on the ball, and punctual to a fault. So he swung the crate shut and I was sealed inside."

"What happened then?"

"I can't say. You have to believe me when I tell you I can't see *anything* from inside that helmet. I'm relying entirely on Paolini and Martha to free me from the crate. So whoever it was that swapped the crates around, I was entirely at their mercy."

"I see. All right then. Thank you." Flint waved a hand, dismissing Fabris.

At that moment, the nervous lighting man, Will Cope, approached. Ibbs ducked out of sight around the corner as he tapped nervously on the door.

"Enter!" Flint bellowed.

"Inspector," Cope said, sheepishly peeking around the door, "I feel I should perhaps inform you . . ."

"We know already, Cope. You lied about seeing Ned Winchester. He came up into the rafters during the show, didn't he?"

Cope hung his head. "Yes, he did. At first I didn't recognise him—he was just a shape looming in the dark. Then he lit a match and I saw who it was. At first, I didn't know what he was doing there. I thought perhaps he was looking to make trouble of some kind. But he told me his uncle had sent him to cut one of the backcloth ropes. They had got tangled up somehow."

"Does that happen often?"

Cope nodded. "It's not unheard of. Sometimes one of the doors gets left open and a breeze starts the sandbags swinging. They bump into each other and the ropes get knotted. Perfectly natural."

"Doesn't anyone check them *before* the show starts?"

"Oh yes! Always. But it can happen during a show as well, you know, and a man can hardly be in two places at once."

"Wasn't it unusual for Sidney Draper to send his nephew to tackle a snarl-up like that, rather than taking care of it himself?" Spector asked.

"Now that you come to mention it, yes. Draper likes being in charge of things. But—though he's the last one to admit it—he's not the man he used to be. I reckon he's finding the job harder and harder. In fact, if you asked me it won't be long till he . . ."

Flint silenced Cope with a wave of his hand. "All right. Thank you, Mr. Cope."

Cope bowed obsequiously, then scuttled away.

Now that Flint and Spector had the dressing room to themselves, Ibbs took the opportunity to emerge from hiding and sidle up to them once more. His curiosity was insatiable. Flint continued to ignore him, and looked over at Spector, who was conspicuous in his quietude.

"So what do you reckon?"

"You know me, Flint. Though I may appear idle to the untrained eye, there's always something bubbling away between my ears. As it happens, I'm contemplating the immortality of the crab."

"What's that supposed to mean?"

Spector closed his eyes, deep in thought.

"All right, I'll ask you another," Flint persisted. "Who killed Varga? And how did they get him in the crate?"

"Let's consider it chronologically," said Spector. "Varga must have been killed *and* stashed in the crate between eight and nine. During that time, Toomey and Alf were playing cards by the stage door. Draper and Winchester were playing cards behind the stage. Cope was manning the lights. Fabris flitted between the two games and then went away to get into his suit of armour."

"That means he's the only one without a solid alibi," Flint observed.

"Does it?" Spector raised an eyebrow. "I suppose it does, in a way. I'm still intrigued by this Winchester fellow. All very curious. I can't quite fathom precisely why he came to the theatre in the first place. Initially, he claims he was here to see his uncle. Then he says he was here to see Martha—in addition to the fact that *she* let him into the building. Then he changes his mind and says he was here to see his uncle after all."

"When we all know the *real* reason he came was to give Toomey a ruddy good pasting," Flint concluded.

"Yes, and ended up getting the unfortunate Mr. Ibbs instead. Even *that* excuse sounds a little spurious to me. Especially the fact he doesn't know what Toomey looks like. Add to that the unfortunate fact that he is the one who admitted Varga to the backstage area, mistaking him for part of the show."

"Do you believe that?"

"I suppose I do," said Spector. "It has just the right amount of absurdity to be true. Besides, if he were the one who *killed* him, it would make little sense for Winchester to admit letting him into the building."

"True. But what did Varga do once he was in the theatre?"

Spector shrugged. "Dead end. If anybody other than Winchester saw him, they're keeping that fact to themselves."

"Do you think perhaps he may have deliberately hidden himself?"

"In the crate you mean? It's an idea, but it doesn't tally with the head wound and the strangulation."

"Not necessarily *in* the crate. Somewhere else backstage perhaps."

"Did you see the suit he was wearing? That bold, chequered pattern? I find it difficult to imagine a getup like that going unnoticed." Spector snapped his fingers. "Of course. He hid himself because he was afraid. Somebody was after him, so he sought refuge in the theatre."

"But how did he come to be here?"

"He must have followed Ibbs. It's the only way I can think of. Ibbs is the sole connection between Varga and the Pomegranate Theatre. Besides, Ibbs also claims he caught a glimpse of Varga outside the Old Bailey. Isn't that so, Ibbs?"

The lawyer jumped slightly. He had not expected to be addressed directly. In fact, he'd almost got used to being treated as though he weren't there. "Yes," he said. "That's where we saw Titus Pilgrim."

Spector considered this briefly. "Do you reckon Pilgrim is involved in all this?"

He seemed to be asking Ibbs, but Flint was the one who answered. "I don't see how. Guess where he is this evening? Coincidentally at the very moment Varga put in his posthumous appearance? At a police benefit event in Hampstead. Plenty of witnesses. Hundreds, in fact. He was careful to ensure he was nowhere near this place."

"That doesn't rule out his operatives, of course."

"Right. That was my thinking originally. But I don't see how a hired killer could have got backstage. We have Winchester's word that he let Varga through the fire door. That's the one door through which anybody could have entered the backstage area unseen. But if Winchester closed the door again when he finished his smoke, there's no way anyone else could have got in unseen."

Spector nodded. "That rules out a killer from outside. He *must* already have been backstage. It also seems to rule out Winchester. If *he* were the murderer, he could quite easily have claimed that he left the door open and unattended, to make it *seem* as though the killer came from outside. If he killed Varga, it would be counterintuitive to tell us the door was closed. It would be advantageous for him to make our suspect list as open-ended as possible."

"What about Draper?"

"He claims he'd never seen Varga before in his life up until the moment he came tumbling out of the crate. We know Draper was playing cards with Martha, Cope, and Fabris up until five minutes before show time. Apart from a brief telephone call, he was never out of their company."

Spector grinned. "I must say, whoever this killer is, I'm envious of his stagecraft. Very impressive! What we are presented with here is a trick within a trick. Fabris is strapped into the crate in readiness for the beginning of the illusion. The crate is wheeled onstage and the trick goes ahead as planned. However, when the time comes for the 'reveal,' it is not Fabris but the corpse of Varga which comes tumbling out in front of the audience. The crate swings shut and is shoved offstage while the corpse is examined. But it is never far away. When the crate itself is examined, we find Fabris still inside, wondering what on earth has gone wrong. Amazing!"

"I find it difficult to share your enthusiasm," said Flint. "What I want is a nice simple murder case. Maybe where the murderer is standing over the victim with a smoking gun in his hand."

Spector ignored him. "Initially, a few prospective solutions present themselves. For instance, Fabris escaped from the crate somehow and put the corpse in his place. But that's impossible. Both Draper and Winchester confirm that Fabris was inside the crate the whole time. They had their eyes on it up until the moment it was wheeled out onstage. Also, it would be impossible for Fabris to have extricated himself from the crate without considerable effort, as it's designed to only be opened from the outside.

"This causes us to direct our attention to Draper and Winchester. Though they are uncle and nephew, I find it difficult to imagine a conspiracy between the two. Winchester lacks the wit and Draper lacks the impetus. Couple that with the fact that neither fellow has any verifiable links with the late lamented Varga. And when we take the two gentlemen as lone operatives, it becomes more unlikely still. Draper sent Winchester off on an errand while he helped Fabris into the crate. But Winchester was back in time to see Draper closing the door, and to help him wheel the crate into position. Both testimonies exonerate the other. Then there's Cope the lighting man. We know for a fact that he was manning the lighting rig throughout the show. How do we know that? By virtue of the simple fact that not one lighting cue was missed. If he had left his spot for even a moment, it would have been painfully obvious to both the audience and the performers onstage. What a problem! I don't think I've ever had one quite like it."

"Well, I've pieced together a timeline," said Flint. "I've managed to get corroboration for pretty much all the activities listed. That is, at least one other person was witness. There are exceptions, but I'm fairly happy with the accuracy of the list."

"Bravo, Flint. Hand it over will you?"

Spector took the sheaf of paper from him and scrutinised it carefully.

7:30—Ned Winchester arrives and is admitted to the theatre by Martha via the fire door, unseen by Paolini, Fabris, Toomey, Alf. They retire to Martha's dressing room, and Martha fetches Sidney Draper.

7:30–7:50—Winchester, who has violent intentions toward Toomey, is gradually calmed by Martha and Sidney Draper. He, Winchester, departs for a cigarette, going out via the fire door through which he entered. Throughout this time, his presence backstage is kept a secret from the others. That's why, when he goes for a smoke, he does not use the stage door (where he might be observed by Alf) but instead uses the fire door, which must be propped open.

7:50—Varga arrives at the theatre from the street. Rather than making for the stage door, which is down an alleyway and visibly closed, he seizes his opportunity and heads for the fire door, which is propped open. He is let in by Ned Winchester. Inside the theatre, no one sees him.

7:51—Winchester finishes cigarette and returns to Martha's dressing room. Varga nowhere in sight.

8:00—Curtain-up.

8:15—The coast clear, Winchester comes out of Martha's dressing room to play cards with his uncle.

9:09 (approx.)—Door closed on crate.

9:10—Crate in position offstage right.

9:15—Martha pulls the crate onstage for the start of the knight trick. At this point Varga's body is in the crate.

Spector handed the sheet back. "Bravo, Flint. This is a useful reference. The important factor to consider is that there are gaps in just about everybody's accounts. Also, your timeline ends abruptly with the discovery of Varga's corpse. Really, you ought to take into account what happened immediately *afterward*."

"Meaning what?"

"When the crate was shoved out of the way so that Varga's body could be examined, it had rolled offstage slightly, and its door had swung shut. When I went to open it, I found Kenneth Fabris inside, in his suit of armour, wondering why his cue had been missed and generally nonplussed as to what was going on."

Obviously there had been some chicanery with the two crates, but it was all but impossible to determine how this trick-within-a-trick had been worked. Paolini himself could not say whether the crate he wheeled onstage was the original or the duplicate. Both Sidney Draper and Ned Winchester had seen Kenneth Fabris climb into the original crate—that was what they claimed. Fabris himself recounted being helped into the crate by Draper and had seen—no, not *seen*, not quite—but had *perceived* Ned Winchester coming down the steps to his right. The accounts of all three men tallied. And why should they lie? What manner of conspiracy might all three of them be party to?

"Come on," said Flint, "what do you say we go up and get a look at that lighting rig, and those numbered ropes? I want to see exactly what Cope and Winchester were up to during the show."

"I'm game," Ibbs said.

"Not you, Mr. Ibbs. I appreciate your enthusiasm, but you have to remember you're still a civilian. You have no standing here."

The young lawyer appealed to Spector. "But surely my involvement with the Dean case . . ."

To his surprise, Spector remained stony-faced. "I'm afraid Flint here is right. It's best for you to keep out of the way of the investigation, Mr. Ibbs. For your own good." Evidently the old conjuror was simply trying to mollify him, and they were afraid he would get under their feet. But what choice did he have?

Flint and Spector left Ibbs alone in the corridor. He made instinctively for Martha's dressing room, but was surprised to find it locked. He rapped on the door and she called out: "Wait! Wait a moment, I'm changing."

Suddenly feeling decidedly useless and depressed, Ibbs skulked farther along the corridor in the direction of Paolini's dressing room, and the fire door that led to the street. Just as he was passing by, the dressing room door opened.

"Ibbs." The sound of his name made him jump. "Ibbs, I need to speak with you."

"What is it, Professor?"

"In here. Quickly."

With a flourish of his cape, Paolini ushered him into his room. He followed, easing the door shut as quietly as possible. There was something troubling in the magician's manner—something hushed and secretive which had not been there before. The gregariousness was gone and in its place was an icy sheen of fear.

"Professor," Ibbs repeated, "what's all this about?"

"It's something I wanted to speak to you about in private. Something I didn't want the others to hear." He paused a moment, evidently summoning up as much drama as he could duly muster. "It's about Dominic Dean."

That was not a name Ibbs had anticipated hearing on the lips of the conjuror. The death of Varga at this theatre had until that moment seemed to be the most monstrous and unholy coincidence. But now Ibbs began to perceive it for what it really was—part of a pattern.

"You know something about Dominic Dean?"

"Yes. I know *everything*."

At that moment, Paolini froze, transfixed by the sight of something looming just behind Ibbs. "Good God . . ." he murmured.

The lawyer felt a stab of fear and slowly turned. But he never saw the person standing behind him. All he saw was an abyss, and he tumbled right into it.

CHAPTER EIGHT

A LOCKED ROOM

There was a pneumatic throb in Ibbs's skull, followed by a blossoming white light growing brighter and brighter until it seemed to envelop the world and everything in it. He blinked, and that's when he realised he was lying on the carpeted ground.

Slowly, the world came back into focus. The pain in his head intensified. He must have taken a fierce crack to the skull. When he placed his palms flat on the ground to try and heave himself upright, he found that his right hand was holding something. He tried to let go of it, but couldn't. It was stuck to him somehow.

As his eyes regained their ability to focus, he saw that it was a revolver. He jumped at the sight of it, which sent another jet of pain shooting through his brain. With his left hand he tried to prise it free but it wouldn't come; the revolver's handle stretched his skin almost to a tearing point. He squinted, trying to see exactly what had happened, but it was obvious that some sort of glue had been used to adhere the weapon to his hand. He sniffed the barrel. It smelt of . . . something, at least. Some sort of burning. Obviously it had been fired.

He glanced around, and that's when he saw the body at the other end of the room.

He didn't need to look too close to see that it was Paolini, lying in a pool of drying blood. There was a hole in his right temple, and another in his left. Entry and exit wounds. And a bullet hole in the left-hand wall.

Ibbs redoubled his efforts to remove the gun, but it wouldn't come. Whatever substance had been used, it was industrial-strength stuff.

"Professor! Hey, Paolini!" came a muffled voice from the corridor. Of *course* people were gathering. There had been a shooting.

There was little to do except to face the music. But as Ibbs lurched toward the door handle, he saw the key lodged in the lock. He frowned and looked back at the window. It was rusted shut, and barred. That's when he realised the full extent of his predicament. He made one last half-hearted attempt to remove the gun from his right hand, but of course it wouldn't budge. The killer must still be in the room! In a sudden frenzy of activity, Ibbs pulled open the drawers in the dressing table, and then turned his attention to the wardrobe. He wrenched open the doors. Nothing.

There was nothing else for it. He would simply have to face the music. He headed for the locked door, and with a quivering left hand reached out and twisted the key. The door swung open (outward into the corridor) and he was face to face with Flint, Sergeant Hook, and Joseph Spector.

"Gentlemen," he said, and his voice cracked.

"Well," said Flint, "let's just relieve you of *that*, shall we? Hook."

Hook stepped forward to take the revolver. When it wouldn't budge, he said: "It's stuck somehow, sir." Then he noticed Paolini crumpled in the far corner. He dashed over to feel the conjuror's pulse. "He's dead, sir."

Before Flint could comment, Spector stepped in. "Can't you see this fellow's hurt too? He's obviously taken a crack on the head. Here, Edmund, let me get you a flannel . . ." Spector took a small square cloth from the dressing table and headed for the sink. When he eventually coaxed a thin trickle of water from the tap, he ran the flannel underneath it till it was nice and cool and damp. Then he handed it to Ibbs, who rubbed it gratefully against the lump on the back of his head.

"Feeling better now?" said Flint with mock concern. "Good. What a merry dance you've led us on this evening, Mr. Ibbs. Cuff him please, Sergeant Hook."

"But I didn't do anything!" Ibbs yelped. "Really, I didn't!" He looked imploringly at Spector, who was hovering in the doorway with an enigmatic and difficult-to-read expression on his face.

"You must think I'm mad. Why should *I* kill him? And why in a locked room? With all those people outside?"

Flint was having none of it. "You might well be mad as far as I'm concerned, sir. I'm sure it's none of my business."

"I'm telling you, I was coshed. Somebody knocked me out, killed Paolini, and then left me here to take the flak."

"Clever blighter, eh sir? And was it the same person who shot that Dean fellow on top of the Ferris wheel?"

"Yes! That's exactly who it was. It's the same person, the same trick, I'm telling you."

The inspector was still unimpressed. "Mr. Ibbs, you must take me for a fool."

"No, no! I realise how it looks, I do! But I know I didn't kill him. And what sort of lunatic would stick the gun to his own hand?"

"Beats me, sir. All I know is it's the sort of lunatic that doesn't belong on the streets."

"Can't you see what's happened? I'm being framed! Just like Carla Dean was framed! Whoever killed Dominic Dean has used the same exact method to kill Paolini."

"And just what method is that, Mr. Ibbs?"

"I . . . I don't know. If I knew, believe me, I'd tell you. But it's all a trick. I swear to you—I did not kill that man."

This was rapidly turning into the worst night of Edmund Ibbs's life. It took an age to finally extricate the weapon from his hand. This was achieved with a cocktail of solvents and some vigorous scrubbing. It left his palm red and raw. Next, he was handcuffed by Sergeant Hook. When the sergeant seized Ibbs by the elbow, a fierce pain leapt up his arm all the way to the shoulder. Ibbs shrieked.

"Ah, there it is," said Flint. "I see it in amateurs all the time. Kickback a little more than you bargained for, eh?" The inspector turned to the others and explained: "The revolver is always a little more powerful than they expect it to be. I've known blunderers like Ibbs here to dislocate their shoulders with a single shot."

Then he instructed Ibbs to sit on the long wooden bench in the backstage corridor. From that vantage point the young lawyer watched the investigators come and go from the dressing room, and saw the corpse carried out beneath a murky shroud.

Occasionally somebody glanced in his direction. When they did, he would say: "It's not me. I swear it's not." But nobody listened.

"Mr. Ibbs, I'm arresting you for the murder of Professor Paolini."

"You're making a big mistake, Inspector . . ."

"Listen, Ibbs, I don't know what to make of all this. But we found you locked in a room with a corpse, with a smoking revolver in your hand. What would *you* do if you were in my shoes?"

"Please. I know how this looks, don't think that I don't, but you have to listen to me . . ."

"There'll be plenty of time for that."

Eventually he was escorted into a dimly lit side room at the far end of the corridor and seated at a wooden table. Opposite him sat George Flint. Every scintilla of clumsy affability was gone from the inspector's demeanour. He was ice cold.

In the corner of the room, seemingly absenting himself from proceedings, was Joseph Spector. He smoked a cigarillo quietly and gave occasional smiles of encouragement.

"I think you'd better tell us everything," said Flint.

"You know as much as I do," Ibbs told them. "I went to his dressing room because he asked me to, no other reason. He said he had something he wanted to show me. It seemed urgent. At least, his behaviour was rather erratic."

Flint pounced on the word. "In what way 'erratic'?"

"Excitable. Like a kiddie in a sweet shop. I thought it might be something relevant to the case."

"So you thought he'd perhaps stumbled across some useful fact that might aid the investigation?"

"It's possible."

"And why, Mr. Ibbs, would he share such a prize with *you*?"

"I can't answer that. I've no idea."

"Tell me what happened when you were in the dressing room."

"Like I say, he was agitated. He seemed to think there might be somebody spying on us. He checked the corridor, and locked the door behind him."

"But presumably the assailant was already in the room?"

"He must have been. Hidden somehow, I don't know. But the fact is, Paolini started to tell me something. Then all of a sudden he stopped and looked at someone standing behind me. I felt the presence at my shoulder. And he said 'My God, it's you!' I spun round to get a look at the fellow, but before I could latch onto his face he clocked me round the head. I must have dropped like a stone."

"So you never saw this mysterious third man?"

"I wish I had."

"I'll bet you do." Flint's tone was hard and unkind.

"The next instant it seemed to me that I was sitting up in the smoky little room, realising I had a gun in my hand and I couldn't get rid of it. I looked around for Paolini, and that's when I saw him lying facedown on the rug. He was dead."

"How do you know that?"

"Because he *looked* dead. I don't know. He had a bullet hole right through his head."

"And what about the door?"

Ibbs shut his eyes. He knew that he was damning himself. "It was still locked."

Flint turned in his seat to look at Spector. Spector scarcely seemed aware of what was going on around him. The old magician merely smoked his cigarillo and fixed his gaze on nothing in particular.

A shock of dread shot through Ibbs's heart as he imagined his poor mother and father, hearing the news that their only son was in jail for murder. And as for his colleagues . . . well, he would never live it down. He was finished; he knew he was.

Flint, methodical even in the face of chaos, followed Spector's advice and started canvassing alibis, though Ibbs could have told him it wouldn't help much. After all, Martha was locked up in her dressing room two doors away from Paolini's at the time of the shot. Fabris was in his own room across the corridor. Draper was off on his own somewhere, Ibbs wasn't sure where. And as for Ned Winchester, who could say?

The only one with a genuinely airtight alibi for the moment Paolini was shot was the lighting man, Will Cope. He had been up in the rafters with Flint and Spector, showing them the rig, and recounting his brief meeting with Winchester. Of course, when the shot was heard, Ibbs no longer gave a damn how Miklos Varga had been placed in a crate without anybody noticing. That was the least of his worries.

But all the others had what you might call "alibis by omission." Sergeant Hook was in the corridor outside Paolini's dressing room at the moment the shot was fired. If anybody had come running out of the room at that moment, he would have been the first to notice. This certainly did not help the case for Ibbs's defence.

The dressing room where Paolini died was the largest room in the entire backstage area at the Pomegranate. Of course, that was not saying much. There was a single door; that which opened onto the narrow corridor—outside which Sergeant Hook had been on unwitting sentry duty, and could confirm that nobody had gone in or out. There were two windows with bars on the outside. Even if the bars had not been there, the windows were caked shut with rust. Flint tried them both multiple times in order to convince himself of this fact. They would not budge. And even if the windows could have been opened, the lethal shot was made from close range. Too close, in other words, to have been fired from out in the alley.

Next door to the crime scene was another dressing room, this one considerably smaller and unoccupied. Unlike the crime scene, this one had a connecting door that led directly into Martha's dressing room. Not that it made much difference: the connecting door had a chunky metal lock mechanism that had clearly not been tampered with.

"I hope you don't mind," Spector said to Martha, eyeing the lock, "but it's best to check these things."

"It won't budge—try it for yourself." She rattled the handle and motioned for Spector to do the same. He did.

"Kept very firmly in place," he said to no one in particular. Then, without warning, he dropped to his knees and peered through the keyhole. "There's no key in the other side . . . but of course, there's no need for one. The door won't unlock even *with* a key."

"What?" said Flint. "I don't understand, how come? Looks to be a common or garden lock to me."

"Oh, far from it!" said Spector. "This is a Chubb lock."

"And what's *that* when it's at home?"

"A Chubb lock," Spector expounded, getting to his feet, "is a lock made to the specifications of the Temple Street maestros, Jeremiah and Charles Chubb. Known throughout the country as an 'unpickable' lock. It really is a masterpiece of design. Of course, this model is significantly older than those on all the other doors. Almost as if this door has been neglected for some reason."

"I can tell you all about it," said Sidney Draper. "You see, those Chubb locks or whatever you call them have got something in them that means if you try and jimmy the lock or pick it then it sort of jams up. The idea is that the owner can see whenever someone has been trying funny business with the lock. And it takes a special regulator key to get it open again. Well, the regulator key went missing a long time ago. Decades, I'd wager. And some bright spark tried to fiddle with the lock, so now it's gummed up good and proper."

"Why wasn't this lock replaced when the others were?" Spector asked.

"Mister Teasel doesn't like to spend money if he can help it. And after all, there's never been any need for a connecting door between dressing rooms."

"Quite so," said Spector. "But in my time I've come up against all sorts of locks, and I must say that this is one of the best. I believe that the Koh-i-Noor diamond is secured by a Chubb lock."

Lastly, at the end of the corridor adjacent to Martha's dressing room, was the little alcove where Alf traditionally sat, and finally the stage door, which led out into the alley. Though Hook did not have a direct view of the stage door when he was loitering in the corridor, he would most likely have heard if anyone had entered or exited this way. But even if they had, how might they have entered Paolini's dressing room through a window that was sealed and barred? It made no sense.

From the very beginning, the death of Professor Paolini seemed to be a problem with only one solution. The scene of the crime was essentially a sealed box. The windows—like the windows of every other room along this accursed corridor—had narrow windows embedded high in the wall. Windows of thick, frosted glass, through which no ordinary mortal could be expected to climb.

As for Ned Winchester, when the shot was fired he was nowhere in sight. He had briefly evaded Flint's net. Within two minutes, uniformed officers were scouring the building for the elusive giant. They found him in the alleyway outside the stage door, perched on a dustbin and smoking a cigarette.

"What's happened now?"

"Will you come with us please, Mr. Winchester?"

"Why? What's this? I'm getting tired of being messed about."

"Step inside, Mr. Winchester," said Flint, framed magnificently in the stage doorway.

Grudgingly, Winchester flicked his cigarette butt away and obliged.

With everyone gathered inside once more, Flint made an announcement. And what a showstopper it was. "Ladies and gentlemen, there has been a second murder this evening. Professor Paolini has been shot dead." There were generalised murmurs of consternation. "We will be questioning you all once again.

Please—and I cannot emphasise this enough—do not leave the theatre."

"Well who did it then?" said Winchester. "Shot him dead right under your nose?"

"It was Ibbs," said Sid Draper quietly. "I don't know why he did it."

Ibbs heard all of this through the wall, but he could not quite comprehend any of it. He sat looking down at his cuffed wrists, trying to work out what had happened. And that's when Joseph Spector ushered Ned Winchester into the room.

"Hope you don't mind my disturbing you, Mr. Ibbs?" said the old magician. "I thought it might be best to speak with Mr. Winchester in private."

Winchester looked the lawyer up and down. "Well, well," he said, "so Uncle Sid was right! I couldn't credit it."

"I didn't do it . . ." Ibbs protested, but Spector raised a hand for silence. He was all about the business once again.

"Why were you in the alley, Mr. Winchester?"

"Stepped out for a cigarette. Didn't think it would make much difference."

"And how long were you out there?"

"Does it matter? I couldn't have shot him from out there anyway. The windows are locked and barred."

A brief pause. Then Spector inquired softly, "How do you know that?"

But Winchester scarcely missed a beat. "This isn't my first time at the Pomegranate, you know."

Undeterred, Spector continued: "Did you hear the shot a few minutes ago?"

"I don't know if you noticed, but I was out in the night air. There's people and taxis and all sorts out there. You couldn't expect me to hear a revolver from there."

"Revolver?"

"Mm?"

"What makes you say revolver?"

"Why? Wasn't it a revolver?"

"It was. But I'm curious as to how you knew that."

"Your man Flint said so."

"No. He didn't."

"Then it was one of the constables."

There ensued another silence, and Ibbs studied Spector's unblinking, unsmiling face. Then all at once the spell was broken. "Perhaps you're correct," said Spector. "Care for a smoke?"

Caught off guard, Winchester answered: "All right."

No doubt he regretted it moments later, when the smoke was clogging his lungs, and he was hacking and spluttering like a dying man. Whatever was in those cigarillos, it was no ordinary tobacco. And yet Spector smoked them continuously. It was all very sinister. Like a portent of some very real and very dark magic.

Winchester headed back out into the corridor, and Spector swiftly followed without another word.

"Please!" Ibbs called out, rapping on the wall. "Let me out of here! It's all a mistake."

All at once the door swung open and Flint was filling the doorway. "Quiet, you. I won't tell you again."

"Let him out, Flint." It was Spector, still puffing on his cigarillo in quiet contemplation. It was amazing the way he directly contradicted Flint without incurring the policeman's estimable wrath. But Flint simply sighed.

"All right, Ibbs. Out you come."

And so Edmund Ibbs stepped back out into the corridor. All eyes were on him. Feeling distinctly uncomfortable, he asked: "Any chance you could loosen these cuffs . . . ?"

Flint shook his head. "No chance. You're out of the room. That's enough for now." Then he turned to Martha. "The weapon," he demanded, "where did it come from?"

If he had been trying to catch her out, he had failed. "It's the pistol we use for the bullet-catch trick," she explained.

"And where is it kept?"

"Locked up in a crate alongside some of the other props."

"Show me."

She led them along the corridor to the prop hold. Having little else to do, Ibbs trailed along behind. They were in the space directly behind the stage where the two crates were kept. In the corner was an iron staircase that spiralled up to the overhead walkway, which in turn led out across the stage. It was up there that Will Cope had been positioned throughout. And just beside the spiral staircase, on a wooden work surface, lay a small wooden chest with its lock broken and its lid hanging limply. "Somebody broke it open," she said.

Flint took the box from her. "There's another pistol in here," he said.

"Yes. That's just a prop. We . . . let me explain. In the bullet-catch trick, the real, loaded revolver is passed around members of the audience so they can be assured it's genuine. Then before it gets back onstage, we switch it for the prop. This one then shoots blanks. Wouldn't hurt a fly."

Flint nodded, taking it all in. "So, the hypothesis is this: Ibbs found out the revolver was in that box. When the time was right, he broke it open and stole the revolver. He had plenty of opportunity, of course."

Sergeant Hook, who had been a kind of éminence grise throughout the investigation so far, suddenly interposed: "How did he know he had the right weapon? I mean, how could he be sure he hadn't picked up the prop?"

"Listen," said Martha, "I don't think for a *moment* that Edmund Ibbs here killed Paolini. But whoever did, they must have got the revolver from that box. And to answer your question, Sergeant Hook, the revolver compartments are carefully labelled. As you can imagine, we have to be very careful to ensure there are no mix-ups with the weapons." She said a few more things, but Ibbs had stopped listening. He was just quietly flattered that she had remembered his name.

By the time his attention wandered back to the conversation at hand, Spector was speaking again. "I have another question, if you'd be so kind. Tell me this: Do you know if Paolini ever had dealings with a man named Dominic Dean?"

Martha phrased her response carefully. "I didn't take much interest in his social life. We moved in different circles, you might say."

"What about Carla Dean?"

Martha shook her head.

"And what about Titus Pilgrim?"

"What about him?"

"You've heard of him, then?"

"I reckon everybody's heard of him. You think he had it in for Paolini?"

"I wouldn't go that far. All I want to know is whether Paolini ever mentioned the name Titus Pilgrim to you."

She narrowed her eyes. "Possibly. Maybe he read about him in the newspaper. He had a fascination for all the crimes and murders he read about in the dailies. A morbid fascination."

"You say he never had any dealings with Dean, but did he ever *mention* the name to you?"

"Why yes, he did. Just this week, in fact. That's the chap whose wife murdered him on the Ferris wheel, am I right?"

Spector smiled. "More or less."

"Then yes, Paolini was talking about it. He was interested in the case. But then, I think *everybody's* interested in the case aren't they?"

"Do you remember what he said to you?"

"He said they were looking at it all wrong."

"Who?"

Kenneth Fabris stepped in. "Everybody. Police, I assume. Maybe the press. I heard him going on about it. He was a difficult man to get on with, Spector. He had a habit of assuming superiority over a chap. Take myself for instance. There was a definite tendency in him to lord it over me, to perpetuate the idea that I owed him my living. But if you think about it, surely *he* owed *me* his living? After all, I did a lot of the dirty work, going in the suit of armour and what have you."

Spector nodded slowly. "And now those days are over."

"Oh, don't think any of us will be destitute now that Paolini's out of the picture. I've got my share of irons in the fire. In many ways I'll be a lot better off. I won't have to listen to his insufferable braggadocio anymore, for one thing."

"That's awfully candid of you, Mr. Fabris."

Fabris grinned. "And do you know why? Because I have nothing to hide."

Edmund Ibbs cleared his throat. Immediately, the attention of the group focused on him. "Excuse me," he said, "but I believe I have the solution."

There was a brief, stunned silence. Then Joseph Spector said: "The solution to what?"

"To the Ferris wheel conundrum. I know how Dominic Dean was killed."

Flint and Hook traded ironic glances, but Spector seemed sincere when he said: "Please go on."

"All right." He paused for dramatic effect, making the most of an unpleasant situation. "It's important to take into account Dominic Dean's state of mind on the night he died. We've been told he was paranoid and that he'd become increasingly erratic."

"Duly noted."

"This makes his choice of the fair rather more understandable. He needed to get out of the house, but he didn't want to risk putting himself in danger. And so he chose a venue which was out of doors and filled with people. Hence, the fair.

"Carla Dean was adamant that her husband was unarmed when he was at the fair. She knew this because he placed his jacket over her shoulders, and she would have been able to see the outline of a revolver through his linen suit. This establishes that he was not armed *at that point*. But it does not mean that he wasn't armed earlier in the evening, and that he concealed the revolver before removing his jacket to lend to his wife."

"Interesting, Mr. Ibbs. I admire the logic so far."

"Then, when you think about it, there is only one place he could have concealed the pistol. Carla was equally adamant that she herself was unarmed when she left the house that evening. But how was she to know if her husband slipped the revolver into her bag? Perhaps when the time came to lend her his jacket, he knew the revolver would be visible and so he swiftly removed it and placed it inside the bag in a single motion which Carla did not notice."

"Excellent!" said Spector. "Oh yes, very good."

"So when they got onto the Ferris wheel, Carla was carrying the revolver in her bag. She just didn't know it."

"All right. You've done well so far. So what happened next?"

"They were seated in the car, both looking out over the side and down at the fair below. What if Dean saw something in that crowd which his wife did not? What if he saw the face of Boyd Remiston, waiting for him to come down? He knew what Pilgrim had planned for him. He knew he was trapped. So, while Carla was peeking over the side, he removed the revolver from her handbag once more and fired it into the air. Carla was facing the other way, so she didn't see. The noise was enough to scatter the crowd, and send Remiston ducking for cover. But he had to explain it away somehow. So he immediately clutched his stomach to make it look as though he had been shot. His plan was to be whisked away to safety in an ambulance with his wife at his side."

"So what happened then? The crowd that had scattered at the sound of the shot crept back. And a doctor was called for—by the time he got to Dean the bullet wound was there. So what do we infer? Remiston must have taken the opportunity to sidle up to Dean in the confusion and press the barrel of a pistol right into his gut and pull the trigger. Either the gun was silenced or the sound was masked by the general consternation plus the muffling effect of Dean's clothing. Then the assassin ducked away as quickly as he appeared. There it is. The explanation. The only explanation."

"Bravo!" said Spector, applauding heartily. "It's a triumph, I couldn't have done better myself."

Ibbs flushed with pride. At that moment, he began to think he might be able to find a way out of this little mess after all.

"A tour de force, absolutely," Spector continued, "and in a court of law I'm certain it would convince a jury that not only did Carla Dean *not* murder her husband, but that she never would have *considered* such a recourse. She was the innocent in the whole affair, naive and exploited by ruthless killers."

"Thank you. I think it's rather good myself."

"It is. There's no denying it. But I'm afraid it's wrong."

"What?"

"I mean, there's no way it could have happened like that."

"Why not?"

Spector exhaled softly. "Let's just say that the Ferris wheel component of the case is the *least* of our concerns at the moment. Currently, I'm more interested in the crate illusion and this fresh locked-room dilemma. Tell me, when you were in Paolini's dressing room, did you get the chance to consult the books on his shelf?"

"No. But I'm aware he had a copy of *The Master of Manipulation* if that's what you're referring to . . ."

"It isn't. There was a well-thumbed book amongst them—I recognised it as I myself own the same edition: *The Case-Book of Sherlock Holmes* by Arthur Conan Doyle. There was a bookmark in place when I flipped the book open; it marked the beginning of 'The Problem of Thor Bridge.' Do you know the Holmes stories, Mr. Ibbs?"

"To a degree."

"Then I'm sure you remember 'The Problem of Thor Bridge.' It's a famous one."

"I do, yes."

Spector smiled wistfully. "I wonder what it was about the story that appealed to Paolini?"

"All right," said Flint, taking charge once again. "I think I've heard enough. Ibbs, may I congratulate you on the merry little dance you've led us on this evening? And the clever sleight of hand in turning one murder into three? I can honestly tell you I never saw it coming. But now it's time for the grim farce to end."

"Inspector," said Ibbs, drawing himself up to look imperious, "you're a damn fool if you think I did this."

"Well, I'll admit the circumstances are somewhat bizarre. And it does defy logic somewhat. But then, your other murders defy logic too."

"Now wait a moment . . . are you honestly trying to tell me you think I killed Dominic Dean and Varga now as well?"

"Well," the inspector favoured him with a patronising smile, "you said it, not me."

"This is a joke. Can't you see I've been set up?"

Suddenly Flint was serious. "There's nothing comical about three deaths, Mr. Ibbs. And whether or not you've been set up is something we'll need to determine. But let me tell you this . . ." he leaned forward threateningly. "I don't like having the wool pulled over my eyes. And whether or not you pulled the trigger on Paolini, I know you're in this up to your neck. Understand?"

"But I *didn't* do it! I swear! There has to be another explanation! I *know* there is!"

"So what's your hypothesis? Come on, you'd better tell me."

"Well, that somebody crept into the room . . ."

"Clobbered you and shot Paolini? Then somehow managed to leave the room, locking the door and windows from the inside? All in the space of about a second? Listen, if there's one thing in this life which I have come to understand in great depth, it's locked rooms. The ways they can be worked, and the mentality it takes to work one. Because you see, really the only locked room is the one up here." He tapped his temple. "I've been over that dressing room, and I can tell you that there is no way another person could have got in or out of there."

"But . . ."

"Please. Let me finish. First, we looked at the window. Sealed on the inside. Understand?

"So that leaves us with the door itself. Now it's hard wood, mahogany, and double-layered. There's a thin hollow between the two frames, but of course it's not wide enough for a human to hide in. It's not wide enough for a slip of *paper* to hide in. The door was bolted. That was how you described it yourself, I think? After all, *you* were the one who unlocked it. Now there is literally speaking *no conceivable way* that a murderer could have got out of the room."

"In that case," Ibbs recommenced slowly, "he must still have been in there when the door was unlocked."

Flint sighed. "I was afraid you'd say something like that. Because if I were in your shoes, it's the kind of thing I would say. But again, there's just no way. Where could a killer have hidden that was not searched almost immediately? The wardrobe. The dressing table. The laundry hamper. We checked them all."

Ibbs slumped down on the bench along the back wall and put his head in his hands. "Then I don't know. I just don't know." He tried to puzzle the whole thing out. There *was* a third man in the dressing room; Paolini had addressed the fellow directly. Ibbs had then turned round to get a look at his face but . . . nothing. Blackness. How long had he been unconscious? Not long. Between five and ten minutes, but it was hard to tell because he wasn't sure exactly when Paolini invited him in. So, the killer knocked him out and then shot Paolini. A single shot through the left temple, which exited through the right and pierced the dressing room wall. Next, he took the weapon, wiped it clean of his fingerprints and applied an adhesive to it which he then used to attach it to Ibbs's hand. Then he left the dressing room unseen, somehow rigging the door so that it was locked on the inside.

"The glue is a common enough brand," Flint said. "LePage, I believe. The sort that comes in a tube, and dries fast."

"There are a few tubes around the place," Sidney said. "We use it for repairs and such like. I've got some myself, I was fixing a few props earlier today."

Spector hummed thoughtfully. "That doesn't tell us much, I'm afraid. But it *does* pose the ineffably fascinating question: Why?"

Ibbs was struck by a thought. He sat upright and rubbed his bleary eyes. "Mr. Spector, do you think this might have something to do with *The Master of Manipulation*?"

Spector frowned. "What makes you say that?"

"Well, it strikes me that the book was almost a targeted attack on Paolini. After all, most of the illusions it exposes are ones he featured in his act."

Spector pursed his lips. "You may be right."

"At first I thought Paolini himself wrote the book. You know, a sort of devil may care farewell to the world of show business. But I gather that wasn't the case, and he was genuinely upset by it. So somebody else wrote the book. Somebody with a vendetta. What's the best way to destroy a magician? Expose his secrets."

"I admire your enthusiasm. But you're wrong, I'm afraid. The best way to destroy a magician is to put a bullet in him."

"All the same, there's something in it, don't you think?"

"Possibly. What do you reckon, Flint?"

Flint shook his head sadly. "I reckon it'll be a good few hours yet before I can get some sleep."

"Paolini had a copy on his shelf," said Spector. "It may be worth taking a look at it."

They headed back to the crime scene. As they stepped back into the dressing room, Sergeant Hook took hold of Ibbs's arm. He wasn't giving an inch.

Spector seized the book from the shelf and flipped it open. "There's a clue in here, I'm sure of it," he said. "Though it may not be the clue Ibbs is anticipating. It's published by Tweedy." He checked his pocket watch. "It's a little late, but perhaps a telephone call will yield some fresh information."

"Please," Ibbs ventured, "is there any chance of you letting me out of these cuffs?"

Flint weighed up the situation, and finally said: "All right, Hook. Uncuff him."

Once the handcuffs had been removed, Ibbs rubbed his wrists gratefully. Was this a vindication? Was Flint now feeling dubious about making the arrest in the first place?

It was close to midnight, but Inspector Flint had no qualms about calling the eponymous Tweedy at home. He used the telephone out in the corridor, the one Paolini had used to call the mysterious "Morgan," whoever he might be. Flint had to sweet-talk the operator into making the connection to Tweedy's private residence. There then followed a couple of minutes of silence, waiting for Tweedy himself to pick up.

With everyone's attention elsewhere, Edmund Ibbs took the opportunity to do some detective work of his own. He headed for the hatch by the stage door, where Alf and Max Toomey had sat throughout the show. There, he leaned over the desk and picked up the receiver of a second telephone extension he had noticed earlier. Holding it to his ear, he realised the publisher had answered the phone himself.

"Scotland Yard?" Tweedy inquired. "Is something the matter?"

"Nothing of direct concern to yourself, sir, though we are looking into a matter that you might hopefully assist us with."

"I see. Make it quick, will you? My wife and I are hosting an *intime soiree*."

"Sorry to hear that, sir. Well, I'll keep it brief. Your publishing house recently issued a book called *The Master of Manipulation*."

"That's correct."

"The author listed in the book is one . . . um . . ." he referred to the book itself, "'Doctor Anne L. . . .'"

"Surazal. Yes. I'm quite aware," Tweedy said, "that there is nobody named Anne L. Surazal. The name is a pseudonym, common practice in the publishing game as I'm sure you know."

"I am looking to identify the author of *The Master of Manipulation*. It's imperative to the resolution of a murder investigation."

This stumped Tweedy for a moment. "Well," he eventually said, "I'll do what I can to help, but I'm afraid I don't have much to offer."

"Any information will be of value, Mr. Tweedy."

"All I can tell you, Inspector—Flint, was it?—is that the contract was negotiated through a firm of solicitors. I never met with the author directly."

"And who was the solicitor?"

"Pepperdine, Struthers, and Mull," said Tweedy.

"They represented the author's concern?"

"Precisely. In fact we deal with them quite often. If you're trying to trace the author, they'll be able to offer some guidance. I warn you though, they're a canny bunch."

Now *there* was a name Ibbs knew. Though he had never come up against them in a professional context, their reputation certainly preceded them.

"All right. Thank you for your time, Mr. Tweedy."

Next, Flint was onto the solicitors' office. Luckily, they kept extraordinarily late hours, and he was able to get hold of Struthers without too much hassle. Ibbs listened to the whole thing—no doubt Spector had noticed his absence from the group, but he evidently did not consider it a noteworthy infraction.

"Mr. Struthers, I'm very sorry to bother you, but I've been referred to you by Tweedy's publishing house. I'm trying to find out about an author named Anne L. Surazal. We have reason to believe the name is a pseudonym, but I understand you've been representing the author's concern."

Struthers had a most condescending way about him. When Flint had finished speaking, the old lawyer simply said—at great length—"Indeed?"

"That's why I'm calling," Flint persisted. "I need to know who this 'Surazal' really is."

"Well, as I'm sure you are aware, it would be a violation of trust to disclose any information—no matter how general—concerning a client without their expressed permission. So even if I were in a position to disclose the identity of Anne L. Surazal . . ."

"Wait a moment. You mean you don't *know* who it is?"

"We were engaged purely via correspondence."

"Do you have the letters to hand?"

"They will have been filed with all other papers concerning Doctor Surazal. And before you ask, my good man, it will not be possible for you to consult them."

"What about," Spector whispered, "Lazarus Lennard?"

Flint repeated the question over the telephone.

"Mr. Lennard was also a client of ours," Struthers acknowledged.

"Was?"

"I can tell you nothing more about him except that he is deceased."

"When did he die?"

"Really, this is . . ."

"Let me remind you," said Flint, "that this is a murder case."

"Very well. Lazarus Lennard died over ten years ago. A tragic, untimely demise. He was rather young."

Ibbs didn't hear any more of the conversation, because at that point a uniformed constable came haring down the corridor from the wings. He was out of breath, and looked as though he had been dispatched with a very important message. "Sorry to bother you, sir," he panted, "but there's a gentleman just arrived in the foyer."

Ibbs hung up the receiver and returned to the group before anyone else noticed he had gone.

"Just arrived? Who is he?"

"Says his name is Andrew Morgan."

Morgan! thought Ibbs. *The fellow Paolini called earlier!*

"Well?" said Flint. "What are you waiting for? Bring him down here at once! I want to see if *he* can shed some light on this mess . . ."

When Andrew Morgan appeared, he was distinctly unimpressive; even a little shabby-looking. It didn't help that he was yawning uproariously. Introductions were made, but Morgan didn't seem to be paying much attention. He just nodded and grunted. Soon, he said: "I was looking for Paolini. He around?"

Flint and Spector glanced at each other. "In a manner of speaking," said Flint. "I understand you were supposed to meet with him this evening, but that you broke the appointment?"

Morgan sighed. "This whole evening has been a wretched wild-goose chase. He told me he'd have a story for me. An 'exclusive.' Said he'd spill the beans tonight, if I'd come to the show. So I did. And . . . well, you know what happened. But I'm afraid *that* little story broke before I'd even left the theatre. It was hardly the exclusive I'd been promised. Bloody Paolini! All that hype and it turns out to be a ham-fisted publicity stunt. I have much better things I could have been doing with my evening."

"If you're referring to the body on the stage, it was no publicity stunt, Mr. Morgan."

"What do you mean?"

"It was very real and very dead."

Morgan was incredulous. "I think you're pulling my leg aren't you? Anyway, he's dragged me all the way back here now. It turns out I missed the 'scoop.' Where is he? If he's got something to say to me he may as well say it and I'll be on my way."

"I'm afraid he won't be saying anything. He's dead."

Morgan shuffled his feet a little. He was getting uncomfortable. "Now look here, I don't like this. I come all the way across London for some half-baked stage gimmick, and now you're telling me the magician's dead?"

"They don't come any deader, Mr. Morgan. He was shot in the head a short while ago."

"Are you serious?"

"Very."

"And the body on the stage . . ."

"Was real."

"Well . . . Well I never. Old Paolini, dead." From his inside pocket Morgan produced a notebook. "Then . . . perhaps this wasn't a wasted journey after all."

"Why did Paolini call you back here?"

"Paolini was damnably close-mouthed when it came to anything that might prove to be a story."

"You'd worked with him before, then?"

"Yes, he and I had something of a professional relationship. I gave him some free publicity for his shows and he would occasionally provide me with a stunt or two to fire up flagging sales."

"Such as?"

"Well, he recently got into the world of séances and mediumship. He had the idea he was going to be the next Houdini, debunking all these old frauds and generally causing a stir."

"And were you involved at all?"

"Yes. I accompanied him on a couple of trips. He was full of his usual bluster, and wrenched away tablecloths and pulled on hidden strings and generally made a nuisance of himself to these old women who try to make money out of such things."

"You sound rather unimpressed."

"Well, the truth of it was that there just wasn't much of a story. Of course we got some mileage out of exposing the mediums, but for all Paolini's bluster he just wasn't able to come up with a creditable personality, something for the readers to latch on to. He was too pompous, with that ridiculous moustache and that top hat which he insisted on wearing every single time."

"So," said Flint, "you don't think there's anything in the idea that a disgruntled medium might have been responsible for his death?"

"Well, that's not for me to say. But from my experience, they seemed to be more doddery old dears than fearsome assassins. That's why the whole thing had the air of swinging a sledgehammer to crack a walnut. It was as if Paolini was afraid of tackling anyone truly important, and instead he just went about making himself look almost as foolish as those tired old mediums."

"Very well," said Flint, changing tack. "Then what can you tell me about his last story? The one which was so important it required your presence at the theatre tonight?"

"I've no clue, I'm afraid. That's another reason why working with him was so difficult. He wouldn't simply *tell* me what the job was. He had to make a guessing game of it. But he *did* happen to mention that it was something to do with the *Chronicle*."

"That newspaper specifically?"

"Yes. And that's what made me think it might be something to do with that Ferris wheel business. You know, Carla Dean."

" 'Can *you* solve the Ferris wheel murder case?'" Ibbs quoted.

"What?" Flint was impatient.

"They were running a competition," Morgan continued. "If you can come up with a viable solution for how the killer got to Dominic Dean up on the Ferris wheel, then you can win two thousand pounds."

"And you think that's what Paolini had done? Come up with a solution? Did he let slip anything when he spoke to you on the telephone?"

"No. He just outright *demanded* that I come back to the theatre. He first called me up a few days ago and he told me to come to the show tonight, and afterward he'd have a story for me. So I came," but I beat a hasty retreat when all that cabinet nonsense was going on. I headed for the office to get it typed up at the night desk. You see, I assumed *that* was the story after all. A morbid little gimmick with an apparently dead body. Who am I to quibble? It seemed like decent copy. But then the telephone rang—it was Paolini. He wanted to know why I'd skulked out without hearing his story. Told me to come right back for the main event. The *real* main event."

"So you did."

"So I did. I'm an obedient little puppy dog, aren't I? I thought if the corpse was just a curtain-raiser then what the hell was the star turn? And now I get here and it turns out I've missed him by minutes. Don't I just have the worst luck?"

"Diabolical," said Flint without expression. "So you really think he had cracked the Dean case?"

"I tell you, I've no idea. But Paolini clearly thought he was going to make a big splash—bigger even than the body in the cabinet."

"And maybe he would have," said Flint, "only somebody beat him to it."

"Of course, it makes sense that he wouldn't spill the beans over the phone. After all, he wouldn't want anyone nicking his idea and beating him to the two thousand pounds. So now he takes his secret to the grave . . ." Morgan chewed on his pen nib, then began to scribble in his little notebook. "You're on the case, is that right? What can you tell me about the murder?"

"Nothing whatsoever," Flint said. "A statement for the press will be prepared, and you'll be privy to it along with every other reporter first thing in the morning."

"So there's nothing you can tell me? Not even the smallest detail?"

"Nothing. Constable, would you see Mr. Morgan out please?"

Morgan was still protesting as he was (somewhat roughly) escorted down the corridor and out the way he had come.

Spector, who had watched this little exchange curiously, had now lit himself another cigarillo and was exhaling more unholy smoke. He had evidently been struck by a thought. "Tell me about this 'Boyd Remiston' fellow, Flint. I've heard his name mentioned, but he seems a decidedly intangible presence in this story."

"The name *has* cropped up a few times in this case, but I reckon it's an alias."

"What about the description?"

"Oh, you mean the fellow the eyewitnesses at the fair described? I don't put much stock in eyewitness testimony. Some of them said he was tall, others short. Some that he wore black, others brown. It's a mess. Nothing that might produce a usable profile for the fellow. All they seem to agree on is the fact that he had a limp. If it's any interest to you, Remiston also turned up at Dean's bank by all accounts. At least, that's according to one of the cashiers who dealt with him."

"Do you think he might be one of Pilgrim's men?"

"All Pilgrim's known associates have alibis for the night Dominic Dean died. Almost too-conspicuous alibis."

"Staged, you mean?"

"Staged, quite possibly. But genuine all the same. I've not been able to pick a hole in a single one of them."

"And what about Pilgrim himself?"

"Very embarrassing, this. Just like tonight, Pilgrim was at some sort of Police Association event. His alibis are not only unbreakable, but they make Scotland Yard look like a bunch of buffoons. I don't know *how* he came to be there, but there he indisputably was."

Spector sighed. "I feel as though we've hit another brick wall, my friend. Because the fact remains, even if by some miracle we *do* manage to track down this Mr. Remiston, we still have no way whatsoever of tying him to the Dominic Dean shooting, let alone the killings of Varga and Paolini."

Flint joined in with a riotously loud theatrical sigh. "That brings us round full circle. To the only person who can *possibly* have pulled the trigger. Carla Dean."

"Here's another question: did Carla Dean have gunpowder on her hands at all?"

"None at all."

"All right. Then in virtually every aspect, this case neatly parallels Paolini's murder, doesn't it?"

Flint nodded. "It is getting rather close for comfort." He thought for a few silent moments, then changed tack. "Answer me this, Spector. You knew Paolini yonks ago, correct?"

Spector nodded. "He first appeared on the scene some fifteen years ago. Long after I had retired, of course, but he was always one to show his face at dinners and the like. The London Occult Practice Collective, for example, of which I am a founding member. He wasn't called Paolini then, though. In those days he went by Paul Zaibus."

"Did he ever seem like the sort of fellow to be involved with a cove like Titus Pilgrim?"

"He was certainly young and ambitious when I knew him. Back then he would most definitely have fallen for Titus Pilgrim's insalubrious charms. He was a fellow willing to do whatever it took to be the best at his chosen profession. Note my use of the word 'profession,' not 'vocation.' For some of us, it's a calling in life. But for Paolini I couldn't escape the notion that it was all a means to an end. He loved the high life. Show business. Entertaining royalty. Travelling the world. But a true magician performs and practises endlessly. He flips coins and riffle shuffles when no one is watching. He recites his patter to himself in the mirror. He yearns to read more, discover more, *know* more. Paolini did not have that extra something in him. And so he aged before his time. This life," he gestured expansively, referring to the world around them, the theatre, "this life wore him down."

"A man in his position," Flint commenced, "could have got desperate. Maybe he had money troubles. Maybe he borrowed from Titus Pilgrim and couldn't pay him back. In those circumstances, he might easily have been convinced to do something foolish."

So the next inevitable question arose: Where was Paolini the night Dominic Dean was murdered?

The answer was an obvious one: he was at the theatre. Onstage in front of a packed house. "And there's no way he could have slipped out at all, without anybody noticing?" Flint pressed.

Sidney Draper was adamant. "None at all. I was back here all night every night during show time. This is my domain. Whatever I say goes around here. Ha!" He gave a snort of derisive laughter. "Can you imagine? The star of the show sneaks out midperformance and nobody notices! What a joke. No, I'm afraid you're most certainly barking up the wrong tree this time, Mr. Flint."

Flint could not help but agree.

His nebulous investigation having so far yielded precisely nothing, Flint came back over to Ibbs, brandishing the handcuffs again. "I'm afraid I've got no choice, Mr. Ibbs. Till we can sort this whole mess out . . ." And he clipped them back into place around the lawyer's wrists.

"I don't understand," Ibbs protested. "You *know* I didn't kill Paolini . . ."

"Yes, well . . ." Flint huffed, evidently embarrassed, "I found you standing over the dead body, with a smoking gun in your hand. If I *didn't* place you under arrest, I'd never hear the end of it."

Ibbs couldn't fault the inspector's logic. In his shoes, Ibbs would likely have done the same thing. "So what happens next?"

"I'm afraid it's a night in the cells for you. We can look at things afresh in the morning."

Taking this as his cue, Sergeant Hook grasped Edmund Ibbs by the elbow and led him away. This time, they headed for the stage door, out into the alley where Winchester had stepped for his illicit cigarette, and toward a Black Maria waiting ominously at the other end of the alley. Ibbs had never seen the inside of one before.

As he approached the police vehicle, he could not resist one last glance back over his shoulder. He saw that the assembled company—Martha, Sid Draper, Ned Winchester, and the rest—had spilled out into the alley to watch him go.

Among them, he thought, was the one responsible for all this. Paolini's killer.

PART THREE

HE FADED INTO AIR

I am the very slave of circumstance

—Lord Byron, *Sardanapalus*,
Act IV, Scene I

The illusionist must play many roles.

—*The Master of Manipulation*,
"The Role of the Magician"

CHAPTER NINE

DR. ANNE L. SURAZAL

As the police van carried him through the cold London night, Edmund Ibbs could scarcely raise his head. He was trapped in his own mind, staring down at his cuffed wrists and running again and again through the night's events in sequence. He barely noticed when the van coasted to a halt.

He was marched through more corridors, paraded past the disinterested eyes of various desk sergeants, then deposited in a square grey cell somewhere in the bowels of the earth. Just before the cell door slammed he mustered sufficient presence of mind to turn to the uniformed jailers and say: "It's a mistake."

"Course it is, chum."

Slam.

He wasn't alone for long though. After what seemed like an hour, Joseph Spector put in an appearance, accompanied by Martha.

The guard—who knew Spector by sight—saluted and leapt from his seat to unlock the cell door.

"Thank you, Henry," said Spector, "and remember—not a word to the guv'nor, eh?"

"Right you are, Mr. Spector. Ibbs! Visitor for you."

By then Ibbs was on his feet, heart racing. "Mr. Spector! You've got to believe me when I tell you I didn't kill Paolini. I would never . . ."

Spector held up his hand for silence. It was a practised gesture he used to use on the music hall stage. And it worked. "I don't know you well, Mr. Ibbs, but my—let's call it 'experience'—tells me there's more to this than meets the eye. Don't think too harshly of Flint, though. The poor fellow's just doing his job."

"You believe me, then?"

"My dear fellow, of course I believe you. Even the most elementary logic dictates that a killer does not adhere the weapon to his own hand, seal himself in the room with his victim, and then knock himself unconscious. But there are two details that do not look so good. One is that a single shot was fired. That is evidenced by the revolver itself, which is missing a single bullet, not to mention the sound of a gunshot that we heard in the corridor."

"It's a conspiracy," Ibbs said. "It's all to do with *The Master of Manipulation*. You see, the *name* on *Master of Manipulation* is Doctor Anne L. Surazal, which is 'Lazarus Lennard' spelled backward. Now all we need to do is to find Lazarus Lennard and we'll have our first clue as to who would want Paolini dead. . . ."

"Calm yourself, Edmund. We've found him."

That stopped Ibbs in his tracks. "You have?"

Spector nodded. Then he turned to Martha. "Haven't we?"

She looked decidedly embarrassed. "Uh, yes," she sighed. "I wrote *The Master of Manipulation*."

Ibbs was aghast. "You . . . you what?"

162

Spector closed his eyes and intoned: "He cried with a loud voice, 'Lazarus, come forth!' And he that was dead came forth, bound hand and foot with graveclothes: and his face was bound about with a napkin. Jesus saith unto them, 'Loose him, and let him go.'"

He grinned at Ibbs. "Lazarus—that is, the biblical Lazarus—had two sisters. Mary of Bethany, who anointed the Lord with ointment, and . . . Martha."

Martha drew in a deep breath, then sighed heavily. "Lazarus was the eldest," she said. "Mary came next, but she got all knotted up with the cord and died in the womb. Then there was me."

Spector was nodding. "Children of pious parents. And they themselves died soon after, didn't they? Leaving you and Lazarus orphaned. Really the only thing you had in this cruel world was each other, isn't that so? Lazarus had a certain knack when it came to magic tricks. And his sister was his loyal assistant." His pale eyes levelled on Martha, who was hanging her head, as though succumbing to the suffocating weight of her loss. "Fiercely loyal. They performed together. Did quite well on the music-hall scene. But then tragedy struck. Lazarus Lennard died. And his poor sister was bereft. She had lost her other half. But she was also a pragmatist. She needed to eat. So eventually she fell in with a second-rate conjuror going by the name of Paul Zaibus. Soon he recruited her as his full-time assistant. Now, why would he do a thing like that? As you yourself said earlier tonight, Martha, assistants are ten a penny. Well, this particular assistant had something else to offer. A book of tricks. Her late brother's tricks. And Paul Zaibus performed those tricks. They made him famous. He changed his name to Professor Paolini, and he toured the world with his marvellous act. But through it all he never failed to remind Martha that *he* was the star. That without him, she was nobody. So, after fifteen long years, she decided to take her brother's tricks back. She wrote a book. And let it be published. She exposed every single illusion. Just because she could. It was her revenge. Have I missed anything, Martha?"

"You've got almost everything right, Mr. Spector," Martha said evenly, "except for one important thing. My brother came up with the tricks, certainly. But not *all* the tricks. Many of them were mine and mine alone." She spoke with a quiet pride that was laced with the sadness of opportunities missed, and potential unfulfilled. But at last a part of the problem made sense. Paolini—or Zaibus, or whatever his name was—had conned her into giving up her tricks fifteen years ago. She was relegated to the role of assistant while Paolini astounded audiences with his genius. But her resentment had festered into hatred. So she came up with a perfect method of reclaiming what was hers. *She* had written the book, but *Paolini* was the real master of manipulation.

"In many ways the greatest trick was yours," Spector said benignly. "The trick to making Paolini's career vanish in the blink of an eye."

"He treated me like a slave. That's all I was to him. But he wouldn't have *had* a career if not for me."

"No. I think you may be right."

With this revelation still fresh in their minds, there was too much to discuss in such a short space of time, and Spector cut short their tête-à-tête. "We must go now, Martha and I. But stay strong, Ibbs. We'll have you out of here soon enough. In the meantime, I have some more work to do."

Martha gave Ibbs a thin smile. "Good night, Edmund."

Still stupefied by the revelation, Ibbs answered blankly: "Good night, Martha."

She was a portrait of decorum. But Edmund could not help but notice the sly glance she threw in his direction as she was escorted away from the cell. Did she wink at him? Perhaps it was just a trick of the fading light. Or his overactive, hopeful imagination.

He sat there alone, on the bench that was as cold and hard as a tombstone, and wondered what he was going to do. Eventually, he decided to do nothing. Let the wheels of justice move at their own stately pace. (Those same wheels which were inevitably going to lead the innocent Carla Dean to the gallows. Ibbs rubbed his forehead and tried to banish this unwelcome thought from his mind.)

He was not, and never would be, a man of action. That was what made the whole thing so absurd. He was the cerebral type; that was what his doting mother had always said. He thought of her receiving the news that her only son was a stone-cold killer. He blinked away a few tears then lay back, wide awake, to look at the ceiling.

※

For Joseph Spector, the night was still young. He had other visits to make. He said good night to Martha before making the trek across London from one prison cell—in the depths of Scotland Yard—to another. Holloway.

Using Flint's credentials he was able to talk his way into a brief late-night visit with their latest celebrity prisoner. The woman of the moment.

"Mrs. Dean. Forgive me for waking you in the middle of the night."

She greeted him affably. "Sleep is not much good to me anyway. I have dreams, you see."

Spector inclined his head. "We've never met before, but of course I know you by reputation. My name is Joseph Spector, and I'm working with Scotland Yard. But I'm not a policeman, so you needn't worry about that. The reason that I've come here is to ask you a few very pressing questions."

"Ask away. I'm so used to answering questions."

"These may not be the kind you are used to. Firstly, have you ever heard of a magician named Professor Paolini?"

Her expression betrayed acute surprise. He really had caught her off guard this time. "Professor . . . ?"

"Paolini."

"Paolini. No. I'm afraid the name means nothing to me, Mr. Spector. Why do you ask?"

"I must beg your indulgence—I don't have much time for explanations just yet. But all will be revealed, as they say. Next question: have you ever been to the Pomegranate Theatre in the Strand?"

That same perplexed look. "Well, yes, I believe I have. But not for many years."

"Had your husband?"

"Not to my knowledge."

Spector produced a sheaf of paper from his inside pocket, which he delicately unfolded and placed on the small table in front of

Carla. "I'd like you to look at these names, please, and tell me if you recognise any of them."

As instructed, she studied them closely. "Remiston? An unusual name."

"You recognise it?"

"Yes. I rather think I heard Dominic mention it once or twice."

"In what context?"

"Oh, not to me. I heard him mention it on the telephone. He was always on the telephone in his study at home, sometimes long into the night. Discussing business, he said. Anyway, I heard the name Remiston."

"And what about the other names?"

"Well, Edmund Ibbs came to see me today. I believe he's acting on behalf of my defence."

"Quite so. And the others?"

"Hugh Ransome . . . Doctor Ransome! Why, he was there that dreadful night they killed Dominic. Let me see . . . Sidney Draper. No. Kenneth Fabris. No. Ned Winchester. No. Martha Lennard . . . No. Varga . . . yes, that's the gentleman from the Ferris wheel."

She slid the paper back toward him.

"So the only names on that list which you recognise are Remiston, Ibbs, Ransome, and Varga?"

"Correct."

"Very good. Thank you. There's just one last name I'd like to put to you, if I may."

"Please."

"Titus Pilgrim."

He watched her reaction very carefully. She did not flinch; evidently she had heard the name before. "Pilgrim. Yes. Again, that's a name Dominic used from time to time. Quite possibly on the telephone."

"Can you think of anybody else he spoke with or about on the telephone?"

"I'm afraid I took little interest in his business affairs. I know now that I should have paid more attention, but he always seemed so secretive about things, I just couldn't muster the energy."

"All right. Thank you very much. Another question: Who killed your husband, Mrs. Dean?"

This blindsided her. She stumbled over her answer. "Well, I have no idea."

"You must have an idea. You were there, after all. Unless . . . I don't suppose you were unconscious at all during your time on the Ferris wheel?"

"Certainly not!"

"Then you were awake at the precise moment your husband was shot. The bullet came from the revolver that was found in *your* hand, Mrs. Dean."

"You think I don't know that?" she snapped.

"Sometimes the solution to a problem presents itself when we reframe said problem in an abstract sense. *You* did not shoot your husband. Very well, in the context of our abstract assessment, we accept that. But who *did*?"

"You think it's one of the people on that list? Then why did you include Mr. Ibbs? Surely he's got nothing to do with any of it. He's entirely bona fide."

"Oh, quite bona fide, I imagine. But one can't be too careful. Very well, thank you for your time, Mrs. Dean. Get some rest. Things may not seem quite so bleak come the morning."

That night, Miss Maudie Cash, cashier at what had once been Dominic Dean's bank in Golders Green, went to bed early. She slept for several hours but woke at about one o'clock, her lips parched and her mouth dry. She did not know it—no one had ever had the occasion to tell her—but it was because she snored so stertorously, with her mouth wide open and her nostrils flaring. Every night her routine was the same. She eased herself out of bed and into a warm dressing gown. Then she trudged down the stairs to the kitchen. She did this in the dark, ever mindful of the cost of candles. She fumbled for a clean glass and filled it at the sink. It was only when she had taken a lengthy, welcome sip of water that she realised she was not alone in the house.

"Who's there?" she bellowed. "I know there's somebody there."

A shadow moved.

Miss Cash opened her mouth to scream. But before she could emit so much as a squeak, the room was filled with light.

"Apologies," said the old man in black, "but I prefer not to work in the dark."

"Who . . . ?"

"You'll forgive the intrusion, Miss Cash. But I hope you'll understand that it is a necessary evil. My name is Joseph Spector. I'm with Scotland Yard."

"You're a policeman?"

Spector smiled. "I need you to tell me everything you can about Boyd Remiston."

⁂

It had been a difficult labour. One of the most troublesome Hugh Ransome had ever come across. But now the little fellow was out and shrieking up a storm. His poor mother sedated at long last. Having done all that he could do, Ransome returned to his surgery. His Spartan living quarters were upstairs; he would be glad to see them.

When he switched on the electric overhead light, his heart all but gave out at what he saw. It was an old man all dressed in black, with a silver-topped cane. The man himself was not threatening, but his presence was. He had a Mephisthophelean smile.

"Doctor Ransome, I presume?"

"Who the hell are you? How did you get in here?"

"If only there were time enough to answer your questions satisfactorily. As things stand, I'm up against it somewhat. So I'll keep it brief: Why did you lie to Scotland Yard, Doctor? And to Mr. Edmund Ibbs when he called on you earlier today?"

"How dare you! I don't care to be accused of lying by a complete stranger."

"I'll bet you don't. Nonetheless, the fact remains: You lied about what you saw at the fair. About who was there that night. And when the Dean case goes to court, you'll be called into the witness box to perjure yourself before God and man. Can you do it? *Will* you do it?"

Ransome had begun to sweat. His eyes darted round, but there was no escape.

"You tended to Dominic Dean as he died, didn't you? You did your best to save him. You ought to be commended for that. But what about what you *saw*? Would you care to tell me about that? Tell me *precisely* what you saw. And Doctor Ransome," the old man's face hardened. "Don't lie to me."

—⁂—

"Oi! Ibbs!"

Ibbs sat upright, his head swimming. God knows how—or for how long—but he had slept. In the interim Henry the guard must have gone off duty. The constable who now stood framed in the barred cell doorway was a stranger. "Someone to see you."

Ibbs cleared his throat. "Who?"

"Your fiancée. Count yourself lucky I'm an old romantic."

"But I . . ."

Before he could say a word, Martha appeared beside the constable. Out of her stage clothes she cut a different figure entirely. She was dressed demurely, and a hint of makeup accentuated the aquiline curves of her features. But this was no more the real Martha than the magician's sequined assistant. It was just another performance.

"Darling," she said.

Ibbs swallowed.

"Darling, I had to come and see you. The constable has very kindly allowed me to see you for five minutes. I tried to tell him this whole thing is all a dreadful misunderstanding but, well, he has his job to do, I suppose."

The constable inclined his head.

"Thank you for coming," Ibbs stammered.

"What else could I do, my sweet? Come a little closer, let me get a look at you."

Ibbs shuffled toward the door.

"Oh darling, what have they done to you? You look a positive fright."

The constable cleared his throat.

"Well, I think this gentleman is trying to tell me that our brief reconnoitre is almost over. But don't you fret—we'll have you out of here sooner than you might think. But please—just one little kiss for the road?" She leaned forward, pressing her face between the bars.

"Stand away from the cell door please," said the constable.

"Please—that policewoman gave me an extensive search and found nothing that might possibly constitute contraband. Not even a hatpin. All I ask is a single kiss from my beloved."

The constable blushed slightly, shuffling his feet. "One kiss," he said.

Ibbs leaned in and he and Martha kissed through the bars. It lasted perhaps less than three seconds, but it was enough. Ibbs felt something thin and cold sliding involuntarily between his lips. Taking a step back, Martha winked at him. It was unmistakable this time. "Good night, my darling."

Ibbs stowed the small object under his tongue. "Good night," he said.

And with that, Martha breezed away.

The constable was shaking his head. "You know what, Ibbs? Murder or no murder, you're a lucky chap."

Ibbs smiled stupidly and returned to the bench. When he was sure the constable was back at his desk, he spat out the object Martha had passed to him and examined it on his palm. It was a key.

Ibbs waited. He paced his cell. Occasionally he peeped out between the bars at the constable on guard duty. The fellow was reading a newspaper. Yesterday's. Ibbs could only imagine what the morning headlines would bring.

Soon the constable grew tired of his paper and folded it at his side. Ibbs watched the fellow's eyes flutter and ease slowly shut. Within minutes he was asleep. But this was no ordinary snooze. He seemed a little too leaden, his breathing too slow. He did not snore, though languid breaths escaped him in hisses. Experimentally, Ibbs rattled the bars. The fellow did not stir. Next he hoarsely called out: "Hey! You!" Nothing from the constable. Ibbs spotted the empty teacup on the table and wondered just what Martha had dosed it with.

Eventually—when he dared—Ibbs slid the key into the cell keyhole. It fit perfectly. He gave it a firm twist and felt the lock give. All he could hear was his heart thundering in his ears. All he could feel was the blood pumping at his temples as he stepped out of the cell.

He had the presence of mind—and sufficient fascination with locked-room mysteries—to lock the cell door behind him.

He cautiously retraced his steps through the building, which was now almost uncannily empty. A clock in the corridor told him it was twenty-five minutes past two. The only sounds that followed him through the building were the clock's tick and the echo of his own footsteps. He stepped out into the night air a free man.

He waited until he was well clear of the building before he broke into a run. When he finally ran out of breath and stood panting on a corner, a midnight-blue Austin 5 rolled up beside him.

"Psst!" the driver hissed. It was Martha. "Get in," she instructed, "and for God's sake keep your head down."

Ibbs did as he was told without complaint. She fired up the engine and eased the auto away from the kerb. Nice and leisurely, so as not to attract attention. Soon they were on the open road, roaring across London. Ibbs's heart felt as though it might peter out at any moment—he was picturing the empty cell he had left behind him, and the carnage that would ensue when his escape was discovered. But what choice did he have? Martha knew something. He trusted her.

"Where are we going?" he hissed, his head still between his knees.

"I think you can sit up safely now," she said. He did, and a bone in his back cracked painfully. He moaned. "Poor Mr. Ibbs," said Martha, "you are rather out of shape aren't you?"

"Never mind that, just tell me where we're going."

"Putney," she said.

"Putney? What for?"

"For one very good reason. You'll see."

And she returned her gaze to the road, her thin white hands snared tightly round the wheel. Ibbs studied her moonlit profile. In moments like this—times of pregnant silence—she had a

melancholy, contemplative air about her. Ibbs wanted to say something, but he couldn't find the words.

Putney was not an area he knew at all. Truth be told, he had
always avoided it. The stories he had heard were not flattering. But
by darkness there was little he could make out of the place itself.
Narrow residential streets, the wheels thundering over cobbles. The
houses were just nebulous shadows beyond the glass.

Martha was concentrating hard—no doubt looking for an
address.

"Please," said Ibbs, "tell me where we're heading."

"Jubilee Court," she answered.

They found it eventually. A dank little cul-de-sac. No sooner
had they rounded the bend than Ibbs saw their destination. Tucked
away in the far corner, a squat little house that did not seem to fit
somehow with the rest of the street, as though it had been dropped
in, fully formed, from above. Unlike all these other houses, which
were in darkness, every room of this particular residence looked to
be lit, giving the building the appearance of a hollowed-out skull
with blazing eyes.

"Is this—?" Ibbs began.

"Mm-hm," said Martha, coasting the car to a halt.

CHAPTER TEN

MIDNIGHT VISITOR

Ibbs's legs were shaking as he and Martha approached the house, climbing the three stone steps to the mahogany door. The knocker, he noticed, was also skull-shaped. It was Martha who did the honours.

The door was opened by a young housemaid. She looked a little nonplussed at the sight of the pair, but did not say a word and merely stood to one side to let them enter. They headed through a narrow hallway to a parlour-cum-study at the rear of the house. The room was dimly lit and stank of incense and Spector's strange tobacco. Candles at each corner gave the place a dreamy look; the sort of room where weird and occult rites might be enacted.

Sitting in an armchair by the fire was Joseph Spector. For the briefest instant a look of surprise flitted across his saturnine face. Then his habitual composure returned.

"Well," he said, "Martha, nice of you to drop by. And I see you've brought a guest. Clotilde, will you bring us some tea?" The housemaid bobbed and left the room. "You'd better sit down," Spector continued.

"I never meant for this to happen," Ibbs told him.

"I had to get him out, Mr. Spector," Martha explained. "You must understand that."

"Oh, I understand. I also understand I'm currently harbouring a wanted criminal. Correct?"

"It's all a mistake," Martha persisted. "Ibbs here would never have killed Paolini."

"I must say, you have a lot of faith in this young man. I hope he is worthy of it. Because all I know at the moment is that a prisoner is now at large and in my study, and that my good friend Inspector Flint will no doubt be on his way here as soon as he finds out. Have you any reason why I shouldn't hand you over to him straight away?"

"Please hear me out," Ibbs continued. "If you just hear my version of events you'll see how ludicrous the whole thing is."

"Well, I don't deny that it already seems fairly ludicrous. But please, tell me. And try to keep it concise. I believe our time may be running short."

"Very well. First, I have no motive. None. I'd never met Paolini before tonight. Second, even if I *did* have a motive, why should I choose to commit murder in such ridiculous circumstances?"

"That's not a good argument, as you well know, son. Murderers are by their very nature irrational most of the time. Killing is fundamentally an irrational act."

"All right. How about this, why in the name of hell would I adhere the revolver to my hand? And what about *this*?" he parted his thinning hair to show the wound on his head. "Somebody cracked me on the head, they knocked me unconscious."

"Paolini might have done that while fighting for his life."

"For God's sake! What do I have to do to convince you I didn't shoot him?"

Spector studied the young man for a long moment, then his face creased into a smile. "Forgive me. I have to play devil's advocate sometimes. It helps to put myself in the shoes of the most objectionable and immoveable critic. Then I know how my good friend Flint will look at things. There *is* another theory, but I must warn you, Mr. Ibbs, that you're not going to like it."

"Tell me."

"The theory Flint will pursue is that you murdered Paolini in such absurdly incriminating circumstances precisely *because* they were so incriminating. A kind of double bluff. In other words, you know his previous experience with locked-room mysteries and so-called impossible crimes. So you framed yourself for a murder that you had really committed all along."

"That's utterly bizarre."

"But not altogether unheard of. And Flint will be able to congratulate himself for being so clever, all the while searching for the right method by which you may have killed Varga too. He tends to work backward, you see, once he latches onto an idea. It's not so much a matter of making the solution fit the facts, but of making the facts fit the solution."

"But that's utterly foolish," chipped in Martha.

"Is it? It's worked before. All I can say is Flint's lucky he has me around. Otherwise mistakes like this one might be a more common occurrence."

"But it would take some sort of criminal genius to come up with a scheme like that. I'm just an ordinary fellow."

Spector, still smiling, did not comment. He turned to Martha. "You did a very brave thing in freeing this young man. I only hope you've done the *right* thing."

At that moment, Clotilde arrived with the tea. "I'll be mother, shall I?" said Spector.

"You see why I brought you here now?" Martha said to Ibbs. "Mr. Spector is the best in the business when it comes to things like this. If anyone's going to work out the truth behind what's gone on, it'll be him."

"I hope so," said Spector, pouring the tea. "Because I'm going to have to do a considerable amount of smoothing-over with Flint and Scotland Yard. I'm sure you are well aware that the British justice system is ultimately impervious to logic. It will take rather more than common sense to establish your innocence." Spector sat silently for a moment, drumming his fingers on the arms of his chair. "Do you see that painting over there?"

Ibbs followed his gaze to the wall at the far end of the room. "Yes."

"Well, it contains the key to the whole problem. As well as a rather nifty précis of the entire magic business."

Ibbs scowled at the image, an engraving depicting a cup-and-ball magician performing for a crowd of onlookers. But the onlookers did not seem particularly interested in the show; rather, their collective gaze was fixed on a man amongst their number, evidently a wealthy fellow, who seemed enraptured by the legerdemain.

"It is 'The Conjuror' by Hieronymus Bosch," Spector explained. "It also happens to be a master class in the art of misdirection. See how the wealthy man is entranced by the cup-and-ball trick.

See how he leans in close to observe the magician's hands, to see if he can spot the sleight-of-hand. But look behind him, and you see a sneaky thief is relieving him of his coin purse."

"I don't understand," Ibbs said—a neat summation of the entire evening thus far.

"It aids us in framing the problem, so to speak. The portrait shows a deception within a deception. The trick—what we would *consider* to be the trick, at least—is really a misdirection. The *real* conjuror is the pickpocket filching the foolish rich man's purse. And yet there is also a third level of deception. You see, this painting is actually one of five duplicate paintings. No one—not even the finest art experts in the world—knows which is the original, or the extent of Bosch's involvement in each. So of course the value is impossible to estimate. A real-life cup-and-ball trick, you might say. So the painting depicts a trick, and yet it is also a trick itself."

"And you think that applies here somehow?"

Spector nodded. "There's an 'odd one out' somewhere in all this. All we need to do is find it. Dear old Flint is under the impression that it's you, that *you* are the only factor linking the Golders Green robbery and the Dean case and this mess at the Pomegranate, but he's wrong of course. Really we should focus our attention on poor unfortunate Miklos Varga. Just why did he have to die? When you spoke to him at the fair this morning, did he mention Paolini? Or anything that might have implied he was planning to come to the show?"

"No. Not at all."

"And yet you're convinced he was following you during the day."

"I thought I caught sight of him outside the Old Bailey, that's all."

"Then it's safe to assume he was keeping tabs on your movements."

"So you reckon *that's* why he turned up at the Pomegranate? He was following *me*?"

"It would make sense in a way. Maybe he wasn't sure he could trust you. So he decided to follow you, to try and make up his mind. Maybe there was something he did not tell you at the fair, something important. Something he forgot, or was afraid to disclose. Maybe it was something he didn't want to put in writing or entrust to someone else. And just maybe it was something that would have helped to crack the Ferris wheel case."

"And that's what got him killed," Ibbs said conclusively. "I see . . . In that case, I have an idea what it might be."

"Oh yes? What?"

"It's so simple. It explains everything. I can't believe I didn't think of it before. He saw Boyd Remiston shoot Dominic Dean. He must have done! It's the only way it could have happened. Remiston *must* have been the killer. Dominic Dean cried out because he saw Boyd Remiston waiting for him on the ground. This attracted a crowd, but it wasn't until the Ferris wheel car reached the ground that Remiston actually pulled the trigger, then threw the weapon into the car, where Carla Dean foolishly picked it up."

Spector steepled his fingers. "The shot was heard while the Deans were still in the air."

"That was an illusion! Or a mistake, or something. The witnesses *thought* they heard a shot, but they can't have done! So they must have convinced themselves of it after the fact."

Spector, devil's advocate once more, said: "The fair must have been very noisy. I imagine there were all kinds of clatters and bangs that might have been mistaken for gunfire."

"Then I'm right, aren't I? Boyd Remiston shot Dominic Dean in full view of a crowd of people."

That's when Martha asked the obvious question: "Then how come nobody saw it?"

Spector was smiling. We had reached the crux of the problem.

"Let me think . . ." Ibbs murmured, rubbing his temples as though that might help to soothe his frantic brain. "Yes! I've got it. Miklos Varga told police that he saw Boyd Remiston walking *away* from the crime scene. But if Remiston shot Dominic Dean, Varga was either lying or mistaken. If he was lying, it was because someone bribed him. Personally, I think that's the likeliest explanation. It establishes *why* he was reluctant to tell me the whole story when I visited him this morning. But it also provides a solution as to why he was following me. He was having a crisis of conscience. He wore a crucifix—I presume he was a religious man. I think he accepted a bribe in a moment of weakness. A payoff to lie to the police about what he saw that night. But maybe my visit caused him to reconsider. That's why he followed me across London. He'd changed his mind; he wanted to tell me the truth."

The smile had not left Spector's face. "You think he perceived in you a certain . . . integrity? And it caused this crisis of conscience, and led him to follow you when you left the Golders Green fair."

"That's what I believe, yes."

"Well . . ." At last the conjuror took centre stage. He removed a cigarillo from a silver case and lit it. "First of all, let's be completely accurate. Miklos Varga did not tell police he saw Boyd Remiston walking away from the Ferris wheel. He told them he saw a sinister, limping man. We have all leapt to the conclusion that it was Boyd Remiston, based on Remiston's subsequent appearance at the bank. But, for the sake of argument, let's pursue your theory. Miklos Varga saw Remiston shoot Dominic Dean, and was then either bribed or intimidated into lying about it. That means the others are lying too. Doctor Ransome. All of them."

"Only Doctor Ransome and Varga explicitly described the limping man walking away from the Ferris wheel. Nobody else mentioned him at all. Here's a thought: perhaps Remiston shot Dean with a silenced pistol, and then a second, unsilenced shot was fired to draw the crowd. That way, Remiston could indeed have been walking away at the moment Dean was apparently killed."

"But every witness testimony includes the detail that they heard the shot while the Deans were still in the air."

"Then they were wrong!" Ibbs snapped. He was getting frustrated. They were going round in circles, so to speak.

Spector exhaled a plume of pungent smoke. "Your idea is sound in principle. If we assume that Titus Pilgrim was the mastermind behind the whole thing, it's well within his capabilities to bribe or intimidate a handful of witnesses into providing false testimonies. And naturally Pilgrim himself would ensure that he had an impenetrable alibi for the moment the shot was fired. Boyd Remiston—a false name, naturally—will likely never be found. In some ways it's a perfect crime. But there's one piece of the puzzle that doesn't quite fit."

"What do you mean?"

"Carla. I can imagine Varga and Ransome lying. But why her? *She* couldn't be bribed. Especially when it's her life and liberty which is now at stake. Even Titus Pilgrim's threats wouldn't be enough to silence a condemned woman."

Ibbs frowned. "What a fool I am. I'd forgotten Carla completely."

"You mustn't be so hard on yourself. I do think your idea has merit. Parts of it, anyway. And it provides a rationale for Miklos Varga's unlikely behaviour. I can imagine him acquiescing to the intimidation of Pilgrim and his cohort, only to relent when faced with the real prospect of perjuring himself before his God. In those circumstances, he might well have followed you, waiting for the right moment to accost you in private and tell you the truth."

Now, Ibbs smacked his forehead. "But how could I forget about Carla? It doesn't make sense. If Boyd Remiston shot Dean, Carla would have seen the whole thing. No, no. It makes no sense at all."

"It has the bare bones of a solution," Spector said consolingly. "But I think we may perhaps be looking at things from the wrong angle. And the fact remains that Titus Pilgrim's metaphorical fingerprints are all over this murky charade."

And that was when there came a knock at the door. It was an immense, petrifying sound. Ibbs looked at Martha and found that she was staring back at him intensely.

"Well, well," said Spector, "an unexpected guest. I wonder who it might be? Clotilde, take Mr. Ibbs upstairs, would you? And Martha, please remain here."

Without a word, Ibbs followed the maid out into the hallway and up the stairs. She installed him in a small bedroom to the rear of the house. It was nondescript—the sort of room you might find in any ordinary seaside boardinghouse. Clotilde pulled shut the curtains and lit a candle beside the bed. Then she turned expectantly toward him.

Unsure what was expected of him, Ibbs just said: "Thank you."

She gave a little curtsey and made for the door, pulling it shut behind her. His heart pounding, Ibbs slumped down on the bed with his head in my hands. He was vaguely conscious of movement and creaking floorboards downstairs, so he got up from the bed and pressed an ear to the thin wooden door. But of course, he knew there was only one person the midnight visitor was likely to be.

CHAPTER ELEVEN

OVER THE FENCE

"Flint, my dear man. Come in out of the cold."

"I assume you know why I'm here," said Inspector Flint.

"Yes, I'm afraid I do," answered Spector, standing aside to let the top-coated policeman into his house.

"Well I don't know *how*. How is it that you know everything I'm going to say to you before I say it? And where's Clotilde? Not often I see you answer your own door."

"Clotilde is busy. She'll be down presently. Come into my salon, we can talk more comfortably in there."

"So you heard about that damn fool Ibbs?"

"Yes. I'm still not quite sure how it happened."

"Well if *you* don't know, what hope is there for the rest of us? The fact is, one minute he was in his cell and the next minute he vanished. The whole thing's very embarrassing. It makes everybody look bad. But can you honestly say to me now that you believe he's innocent?"

There followed a brief pause, then Spector spoke in hushed tones: "Honestly, yes. I think he's a fool—misguided and easily led—but I don't believe he's a murderer."

Flint humphed. "Well, I reckon Martha's in on the act. I've sent Hook round to her place now and I'm waiting to hear what he says."

"I see. You think they're in collusion?"

"Perhaps."

"But to what end?"

"A quid pro quo, maybe. It's happened before. Maybe she helped him kill Dominic Dean and he helped her kill Paolini. It would make sense, in a way."

Spector was sceptical. "Would it? I don't think you've explained to me what motive Ibbs had for murdering Dean."

"Maybe he's in love with Carla. Maybe they have some kind of long-standing affair that hasn't yet come to light. After all, we have no choice but to take Carla Dean at her word on the subject of her marriage."

"Interesting thought."

"Come on now, Spector. Don't be so vague. I want to hear your ideas."

"Well, all right," said Spector, clearing his throat and drawing himself up so that he seemed to grow in height. "I'd be very interested to know where Titus Pilgrim fits into this."

"Yes!" Flint exclaimed. "And so would I! He's at the back of all this, I'll wager. Maybe Martha and Ibbs are both in his employ. Maybe *he's* the one having an affair with Carla . . ."

"Please, Flint. Give it a rest. This is a first-class case of pareidolia. You're trying to pick out patterns where there aren't any, like those fools who look for faces in clouds."

"Well, all right," said Flint. "Your turn."

Flint stopped in the salon doorway, paralysed at the sight of Martha. "Oh. Evening, Miss. I, um, I wasn't aware that you were . . ."

"Not to worry, Inspector," said Martha. "Good evening to you."

"Something to drink?" Spector offered. "Warm the cockles?"

Still a little nonplussed by Martha's presence, Flint declined.

"So, what is it that brings you here, Inspector?"

"Do you have to ask? We've had a new development, and an ugly one at that. Honestly I couldn't bring myself to believe that Ibbs had it in for Paolini. I agree with you that the whole thing was too contrived. But the young lad has confessed."

"Confessed?" Martha sat forward in her seat.

"Well, more or less. Not in words, but in deeds. He escaped from the cell we had him in. He's out on the loose somewhere in London. What's that but an admission of guilt?"

Spector lit a cigarillo. "I see. So what you mean is that he has *not* confessed at all, but merely vanished. A different thing altogether."

"But why should an innocent man run?"

"I can think of a lot of reasons. Firstly, he's afraid. Secondly, he wishes to prove his innocence."

"And just how is he going to do that?"

Spector shrugged. "I'm merely speculating. But I can see how this poses a problem for Scotland Yard."

"Well, what do you suggest?"

"To begin with, I suggest you forego your habitual formalities and have a drop of whisky. It'll cheer you up immensely, and take the edge off a cold, thankless evening's work."

Clearly Flint was desperate to accept. He threw a forlorn look in Martha's direction.

"Oh, don't mind me, Inspector. Remember, *I* have a vested interest in this business too. Paolini was my employer, after all. And as for Mr. Ibbs . . . well, you could say I took a shine to him."

"Begging your pardon, Miss, I'd love a dram."

Spector, grinning, poured out a glass and handed it to Flint. After a long, languorous sip, Flint gave a grateful sigh. "All right," he said. "All right."

"Better now?" Spector inquired. "So, where would you like to begin?"

"Good question. I haven't a clue. Varga and the dual cabinets, maybe. That aspect of the case is really getting on my nerves. What makes the whole thing so impossible is the unshakeable testimony of everybody backstage. The cabinets were in plain sight of at least two people at all times. There's just no way a body could have been sneaked into either of them."

"Incorrect," said Spector. "The fact is a body *was* infiltrated into one of the cabinets. Ipso facto, it's not impossible. We must alter our perception of the whole event. We have to look for a gap somewhere. Even the tiniest blind spot."

"And do you know where that might be?"

"No. But I will. Have faith in me, Flint. I can spot an inconsistency like no man on earth. What about the mysterious man that Varga and Doctor Ransome saw the night Dominic Dean was killed? Boyd Remiston, the fabled limping man? Have you had any luck tracing him?"

"What do you think? Of course not. Just like everything else in this case, it's a dead end. But even if we found him, he was on the ground when the murder took place some fifty feet in the air. There's no way we can link him to it."

Martha cleared her throat softly. "With all due respect, I think there are plenty of ways a man on the ground could commit a murder in the air."

Spector and Flint looked at her expectantly.

"Well," she continued, "before I fell in with Paolini, my brother and I were with the circus for a couple years. My brother was a magician, and I was on the flying trapeze. So there's one possible angle: an agile killer could have got up onto the Ferris wheel with comparative ease and speed."

Flint gave a derisive snort. "Forgive me, Miss, but I think even *we* could have tracked down a killer trapeze artist."

Martha frowned at him. "You're overestimating the eyewitnesses. Think of the lights and music on the ground. A killer in black could easily have scaled the Ferris wheel completely camouflaged against the night sky."

"Without even Mrs. Dean spotting him?"

"All right, since you're determined to be difficult. Another act when I was in the circus was the trick shooting. We had a fellow who could angle bullets around corners, knock a row of bottles from a fence, and what have you."

Flint thought about this. "So you're saying a man on the ground could have fired a pistol upward, but achieve the effect of a bullet fired horizontally?"

"I'm no expert. But the fellow I knew could certainly have attempted a feat like that."

Flint rubbed his chin and finished his whisky.

"Another?" said Spector.

Flint nodded and the old conjuror refilled his glass. "But I don't see how that can be the case here. Particularly with the sworn testimony from a weapons expert that the bullet was fired at close range. In other words, within two feet of Dominic Dean."

Martha considered. "I still think there's a way it could have been done."

"Hmm. Well, we may have to agree to disagree. But one indisputable fact is that Varga saw something he shouldn't have. Maybe something that didn't make sense at first, which is why he was following Ibbs. He wanted to speak to him again, to confide in him. But it couldn't wait. He needed to get it off his chest as soon as possible. He followed Ibbs into the theatre, but unfortunately his pursuer caught up with him."

Spector, who had been unusually quiet during this exchange, put in: "And what about Paolini?"

"Right. So far, Ibbs is the sole factor which links all three deaths. He was investigating the first, and was present at the last two."

"But that still doesn't provide him with a motive for killing Paolini. In fact, from what I can tell, young Ibbs was a staunch admirer of Paolini's. And, I have to say, he doesn't seem the type to be capable of violence."

"They rarely do," said Flint. He was on his feet now, admiring the various macabre artefacts which cluttered the room.

"Never took you for a Bible-basher, Spector," said Flint, spotting a big black book on the desk.

"Hm? Oh, I see what you mean. Well, I wanted to refresh my memory of a particular verse . . ." He gave Martha a sideways glance. "And I should perhaps point out that's no ordinary Bible. It's what's known colloquially as the 'Wicked Bible.' Exceedingly rare and exceedingly blasphemous."

Flint, who had reached out to touch the book's cover, withdrew his hand as though from a hot stove.

Spector laughed. "Nothing to trouble yourself about. It was simply intended to be a harmless reprint of the King James Bible, save for one typographical error which caused havoc. The word 'not' was thoughtlessly omitted from one of the commandments. Specifically, the one about adultery. Needless to say, seventeenth century society did not take to being exhorted 'Thou shalt commit adultery.' The scandal was immense. Most copies of this edition were seized and destroyed. That makes mine something of a treasure." Spector was clearly in a contemplative mood. He continued: "Funny, isn't it, how the omission of a single word completely reverses meaning? Makes one wonder what other minuscule shifts in focus can fundamentally change our perception of an idea."

"You're thinking about the locked dressing room, aren't you?"

"Yes. Specifically, I'm thinking about the sink."

"Well, that's one way for a killer to get out, I suppose. Down the plug hole. Good God!" Flint was startled by a mummified creature in a glass case—a demonic, reptilian figure with scowling features and scaled flesh. In the dim light, it had almost seemed to appear from nowhere, lurching out at him.

"Don't tell me you've never encountered a Jenny Haniver before?" Spector chuckled.

"What on earth *is* it?"

"Don't be alarmed. It's quite harmless. No doubt you're familiar with the so-called 'sea monk' that was discovered off the coast of Denmark in 1546?"

"Strangely enough, no."

"Well, some reckon *that* was a Jenny Haniver. A moderately sophisticated humbug, that's all. What they do, these fraudulent artisans, is they obtain some species of cartilaginous fish and manipulate it by hand before treating it chemically so that it eventually resembles some manner of mythological beast. A basilisk, or some such. This fellow is a particularly fine example of the breed. One of the oldest extant too; conservative estimates date him to around 1600."

"He's repulsive."

"Indeed. And several hundred years ago, he would have been the stuff of nightmares. There's a lesson in that, don't you think? One man's inhuman monster is another man's dead fish. Doesn't that put things in perspective?"

Flint, still in an ornery mood, answered: "No. It doesn't. Now I want you to be honest with me, Spector. What do you *really* make of it all?"

"Candidly, this is a case where it's very difficult to discern the wood for the trees. First of all, if we operate under the assumption that the same individual killed Paolini as killed Dominic Dean, then what possible motive could there be for both murders? As far as I can tell, there's nothing at all that links the two men. That also leaves us with a quandary concerning just *how* the murders were effectuated. But if we satisfy ourselves with the conclusion that it was in fact young Mr. Ibbs who murdered Paolini, we must ask why in heaven's name he locked himself in the room, adhered the weapon to his hand and clubbed himself into unconsciousness."

Flint threw Spector a sideways glance. "I think you're pulling my leg, aren't you? I'll have to take him in, you know. No matter how unlikely it seems, I can't rule him out purely on the basis that it would be an utterly idiotic way to go about a murder. After all, he might be a madman. Oh, I know he doesn't look it. But looks can be deceiving."

"There," said Spector, snapping his fingers and producing a Jack of Clubs, "we agree."

"I've been looking into Ned Winchester."

"And?"

"Begging your pardon, Martha, he seems like a harmless knucklehead to me. He's had his brushes with the law, but it's mainly barroom brawls and similar petty offences. I don't think he's capable of anything as sophisticated as this."

"Well *there* you and I agree," said Spector. "However, men like Ned Winchester may be taken advantage of. They may be exploited by a diabolical mastermind, and induced to play a part unwittingly."

"You think that's what happened here?"

"I don't know yet. But his presence backstage at the Pomegranate is interesting, to say the least."

"Then there's Fabris. Not much to be said about him."

"No? Why not?"

"Well, I don't see how he could have done it. And let's not forget, he was strapped into the crate at the time."

"Only when the body was discovered. I should have thought it quite possible for him to have committed the murder beforehand."

"Not timewise. Timewise, he couldn't have pulled it off."

"No. But then again, none of them could, could they? When Varga was killed, Alf was manning the stage door and Sid Draper had Winchester, Cope, Martha, and Fabris in his sights. Then he put Fabris in the crate—something both Fabris himself and Ned Winchester can attest to. If we focus purely on establishing a timeline, I'm afraid we're doomed to fail. A clever killer has worked hard to skew our perception of the events backstage. Then of course there's Paolini's murder. Again, it's a matter of perception. And please, let's not pursue the foolish notion that Ibbs could have done the deed. After all, the police doctor could attest that he had suffered a nasty blow to the head which would likely have rendered him unconscious. Also, there's the question of why he would commit murder in a locked room where only he could possibly be the culprit. And the less said on the matter of motive, the better. Simply put, there was none."

"This is starting to sound like the Dean case all over again," Flint observed.

"You're right. That could mean one of two things. Either it is the same murderer using the same modus operandi, or else it is a different killer who is attempting to mislead us by establishing an aesthetic link between two unconnected murders."

"And which do you think it is?"

"I don't know. But once I do, I think we shall be well on the way to putting this messy business to bed once and for all. But I still have several questions. For instance, what can we infer from Varga's unanticipated appearance at the Paolini show last night? Two things: either there was something he did not tell Ibbs which he wished to impart as a matter of urgency—some forgotten and seemingly trivial detail. Or else he was there to warn Ibbs."

"Warn him of what?"

"A threat."

"But that implies Varga himself was somehow involved with the conspiracy surrounding Dean's death."

"Maybe he was. We may never know. But the important factor is, whatever he was planning to do at the Pomegranate, he was killed before he could accomplish it. And what about the robbery at Dean's bank? Is there anything else you can tell me about that? Something which didn't make it into the papers?"

"Well, in spite of alibis, I'm convinced it was Titus Pilgrim."

"Why?"

"Just the circumstances of the case, the way it was handled. It fits in very nicely with Pilgrim's other works of art."

"And what about the dead night watchman?"

"Yes, that was a mistake. And Pilgrim doesn't look kindly on mistakes. I have to admit, the security guard doesn't really fit. It's out of character."

"Am I right in thinking that poor Morrison was not even meant to be on duty that night, but that it was a last-minute change to the schedule?"

"The bank doesn't normally *have* a night watchman. But that night Dominic Dean made the decision to pay Morrison a little overtime."

"And it cost him his life."

"Right. Perhaps it cost *both* of them their lives."

"Well that poses another logical problem," said Spector. "We're operating under the assumption that Dominic Dean was in on the robbery. That he was somehow in the employ of Titus Pilgrim. Then *why* would he put in place additional security measures on that night of all nights? When he knew something very bad was going to happen?"

"You're right," Flint sighed. "It doesn't make sense, does it?"

"Do any of our other suspects have links to Titus Pilgrim?"

"Yes and no. You may not be aware, but Pilgrim owns a stake in the Pomegranate Theatre. It's likely just another means for him to clean up his dirty money."

Spector closed his eyes ruminatively. "It makes sense. After all, I'm aware that he has attended some of Benjamin Teasel's showbusiness soirees. Pilgrim haunts this case like a phantom. First, the Golders Green robbery. Then the Dean murder. Then, by association, the Varga murder."

"What about Paolini?"

"That's the question I've been trying to answer for myself. *What about Paolini?*"

"And on top of all that, I still need to find Ibbs."

"Oh Flint, don't you think you have more pressing concerns?"

"No I don't! That lad knows something he's not telling."

Martha opened her mouth to say something, but Spector beat her to the punch. "Take my word for it, Flint—he doesn't."

"How can you say that?"

"Oh for goodness' sake. I had hoped I wouldn't have to spell it out. Because the first place he came after he broke out of his cell was *here*. He was desperate, and he wanted me to look into this mess to try and clear his name."

"He was here?" Flint spoke quietly, but his cheeks deepened to a bold claret.

"Flint, there's no need to fly off the handle. Edmund Ibbs had nothing to do with Paolini's murder."

"He . . . was here?" Flint repeated. He almost quivered with rage.

"Flint! Be sensible."

"Sensible?" Flint barked. "He knocked out one of my constables. He made the whole of Scotland Yard look like imbeciles."

"Your men will only look like imbeciles if they continue to persecute an innocent man."

"Where is he? Spector, I'm being polite about this. I could just as easily throw *you* in a cell."

Now Spector laughed. In many ways it was the worst thing he could have done. The only *worse* thing would have been telling the truth. And that was what he did next: "Edmund Ibbs is upstairs. He's been up there the entire duration of our conversation. He's been getting a much-needed rest after all the horrors of the last twenty-four hours."

Flint was on his feet and trampling up the stairs. "Where?" he demanded. "Which room? I want to see him."

"Top of the stairs," Spector called up, "second door on the right."

The creak of a door frame. A few seconds' silence. Then Flint came storming back down again. "He's not there now."

"Slipped the net again, eh?" Spector did not seem unduly troubled. "I imagine he was listening to our conversation. Perhaps he didn't like what he heard."

Flint approached Spector. His voice was low and dangerous. "All I can say, Spector, is that you'd better find this killer for us. And if it turns out to be Ibbs, I won't be held accountable for the consequences."

⸺⸱⸺

Spector was right; Ibbs had snuck out of his hiding place upstairs and crept back down the narrow staircase to listen at the salon door. He heard everything. But that wasn't the reason he made a break for it. In fact, it was because he had solved the problem. Part of it, at least. Listening to Flint and Spector, something clicked in his brain and the Dean murder made sense at long last. He knew how, why, and most importantly *who*. Spector was right when he told Ibbs the answer had been knocking around in his brain all along. It was an apparently idle, harmless comment that contained the key to the whole thing. And now that he knew why Dominic Dean had to die, he was well on my way to understanding everything else too. Varga. Paolini. Even Lazarus Lennard.

But he had to get out of that house. He didn't dare risk the front door; Flint had apparently come alone, but Ibbs could well imagine one or two of his cronies lurking around outside. So he headed through to the back of the house. The place was in darkness, but he tried a door handle and slipped into a chilly parlour. A candle burned at the other end of the room, and Clotilde was sitting motionless in a high-backed chair, watching him. He raised a finger to his lips and headed for the back door, which led out into a narrow yard. Clotilde's eyes followed him incuriously as he stepped out into the night air once again.

At the bottom of the garden was a rickety wooden fence, which he quickly clambered over. He found himself in a cobbled alleyway, ill-lit by a dingy lamp at one end. And that's when he saw them.

Two men, silhouetted at the far end of the alley. They were not in uniform; they appeared to be wearing overcoats and bowler hats. Not standard police issue. Evidently they had been waiting there for Ibbs. He headed down the alley in the opposite direction, his footsteps clattering carelessly. He needed to get away.

At the other end of the alley, his escape was cut off by a brick wall. He reached up and tried to scale it, but it was just too high. He glanced over his shoulder. The men were approaching. He could not see their faces. He didn't need to; he could tell they meant to do him harm. One reached into his coat and emerged with something long and black. Initially, Ibbs thought it was a revolver. But in fact it was a cosh.

He backed up against the wall, flattening himself against its cold surface. Then they were on him.

"Have a drink, Flint. You're a good man and a good friend. I know I'm not always the easiest chap to get along with. I imagine I try your patience terribly. But please do me this one favour: trust me."

Snaring a conciliatory arm around Flint's shoulders, Spector led him back to his chair by the fire. He poured out a hefty dram of whisky, which Flint downed gratefully.

"I need a good night's sleep," said Flint.

"You're more than welcome to stay here. Especially since it appears Ibbs has shunned my hospitality."

Flint gave a little smile. "No. I'd better be going. After all, there's a fugitive on the loose. He can't have got far."

Flint left Jubilee Court with a bounce in his step that had not been there when he arrived. Whisky, Spector reflected, was a wonderful thing.

As the old conjuror returned to his salon, Martha came out to meet him. The smile left her face when she saw his troubled expression. "What is it? It's all right, isn't it? Ibbs has got away."

Spector slumped in front of his desk and rubbed his forehead. "Oh God," he said, "I hope I haven't made a terrible mistake."

"What do you mean? What mistake?"

"Letting him go."

"But he's innocent, isn't he?"

Next second, Clotilde appeared in the study doorway, beckoning. Spector and Martha followed her through to the kitchen at the rear of the house. There they found the back door ajar. Spector stepped out into the cool night air. He struck a match and examined the ground.

"He went over the fence," Spector said, "just as I thought he would. But then . . ."

The old magician traipsed down to the bottom of the garden with Martha in tow. He opened a wooden gate in the fence and stepped out into the alley. His gaze was fixed on the ground at his feet. "Footprints," he said. "Fresh ones."

Martha, who could not make out the prints in the darkness, asked: "Which way do they go?"

"Both ways. To the right, toward the dead end. And then back again, toward the road."

"Then he did get away?"

"You misunderstand me, Martha. There are two sets of footprints heading toward the road; neither of them Ibbs's. He's gone all right, but he didn't go willingly. I'd say he was carried."

"But . . . I don't understand . . ." Martha protested.

"We're dealing with professionals. I doubt poor Mr. Ibbs has any idea what he's let himself in for."

"Do you mean Titus Pilgrim?"

"That's exactly what I mean."

Spector led the way back into the study, where he began pacing in front of the fireplace. More than once, he moved toward the telephone on his desk, but he could never quite summon the energy to make a call. "No," he said repeatedly. "I can't."

"Can't what?"

"I can't call Flint after all that hullabaloo. He has his own leads to follow. No, I'm afraid, Martha, that you and I must retrieve Mr. Ibbs without official involvement."

"Well how are we going to do that? We don't even know where they've taken him."

For the first time, Spector's voice grew slightly clipped. "It's a pity," he said, "that you couldn't have left him where he was. He might have been safe there, you know."

"I'm sorry," Martha said. "I was only trying to help."

At once, Spector's attitude softened. "I know. And it very nearly paid off. You see, Mr. Ibbs has behaved very stupidly in some respects. But in other respects, he has been very clever indeed."

"What do you mean? What are you talking about, Mr. Spector?"

"I mean that he now knows who really killed Dominic Dean. I hope that knowledge will not cost him his life."

CHAPTER TWELVE

FINAL JOURNEY

I bbs was on the move. He didn't know where he was heading, or who was with him, but he knew he was moving. It brought to his bleary mind a recollection of childhood, when he had fished from a small wooden boat. When there was sun, and water, and air.

Now there was only blackness.

His head throbbed to the pulsing rhythm of an engine. He was in some sort of vehicle, but could see nothing. His hands were bound in front of him. There was something covering his eyes, obstructing his view . . .

Suddenly, a sack was whipped away from his head and he found himself face to face with a man he had never seen before.

He blinked several times, trying desperately to imprint the fellow's features on his brain. He needed to remember.

Then it dawned on him that this man must be showing his face for a reason. Evidently Ibbs would soon be out of action permanently. Otherwise, he would be an insurmountable risk.

"Where am I?" he said. Or tried to say; his throat was dry and he barely managed a croak.

"You'll see." The fellow's voice had a killer's rasp to it. His face was gaunt and hollow-cheeked, with bulbous blue eyes. His head was shaven, but he wore a grey beard. In his forties, perhaps?

It was a cramped little Ford delivery van—a Model A. Its olive-green frame was just the sort of inconspicuous hulk that crept around quiet streets crammed with groceries and essentials. Ibbs saw them every day. They were unnoticeable, untraceable.

The van came to a juddering halt. The rear doors were thrown open and a man, evidently the driver, was silhouetted in dingy lamplight. He was a corpulent figure, and unlike his comrade boasted a mane of long black hair, over which he wore a soft felt cap. "How goes it, Branning?" he said.

The thin-faced fellow, glancing sideways at Ibbs, smiled. "You see, Mr. Ibbs sir, that we need not worry about you hearing our names. It's true that my name is Branning. This fellow is Keegan. And ours are the last two faces you shall ever see. Now: on your feet."

Branning shoved Ibbs out of the van into the chilly night air. He dropped face-first into the dirt, which sent a flare of pain coursing through his injured shoulder. With a groan he rolled onto his back and propped himself up on his elbows to look around. The nearby streetlamp illuminated a colourfully painted sign. When he spotted it, he gave a morbid chuckle.

"What the hell are you laughing at?" said Branning. He gave Ibbs a hard kick in the side, and Ibbs moaned as a couple of his ribs snapped. He tasted blood in the back of his throat, but he resumed chuckling as the pain flared through him.

"This place. I had a feeling we'd end up here somehow. You're Pilgrim's men, aren't you?"

The rides and attractions were ghostly and dark, like great shadowed tombstones. Looming in the distance, like some monstrous behemoth, was the Ferris wheel.

"Oh Mr. Ibbs. It's almost a shame to kill you without telling you the whole story. But we follow orders. Don't we, Branning?"

"We do, Mr. Keegan." He produced a revolver from inside his coat and trained the muzzle on Ibbs. "This way. I promise we'll make it quick."

"Not so fast," said another voice. A hulking figure stepped from the shadows. "Nice to see you again, Mr. Ibbs," said Titus Pilgrim, "but you don't seem all that pleased to see me. That's a shame. I have some questions for you, and I'm hoping you can answer them toot sweet."

"Let me go," Ibbs told him, getting to his knees. "It'll be better for all of us. I won't say a word, you know."

"Oh, I wish I could believe you. But it's just not on the cards. At least, not till you answer these questions. And then . . . well, we'll see. Firstly, I want to know when you worked it out?"

"Worked what out?"

"Don't play the fool. I know you wouldn't have done a runner from Spector's place if you hadn't cracked the Dean business."

"I worked it out about two minutes before I left Spector's house. But the funny thing is, the answer has been rattling around in my brain all day. Since this morning, anyway."

"Blabbed, did she?"

"Not at all. Mrs. Dean was very discreet when I paid a visit to her in her cell. But in spite of that, she let something slip. Most likely she did it without even realising."

Titus Pilgrim tutted. "Careless of her. Especially after all the trouble I went to."

For a few minutes, at least, Ibbs was able to play the great detective. He got to his feet with a moan, and looked Titus Pilgrim in the eye. Time enough, he thought, for a rescue mission. "You know, I found it hard to tell whether Carla Dean was the *most* likely suspect or the *least* likely suspect. Then I realised that was exactly the point. She was the most likely suspect all along, but you *contrived* to turn her into the least likely suspect. Isn't that so?"

Pilgrim removed a cigar from the inside pocket of his overcoat and bit the end off. He spat it venomously into the dirt. He did not answer the question, so Ibbs continued: "She killed him. I've looked at the problem from every angle, and she's the only one who could have done it."

Grudgingly, Pilgrim said: "Then you're not the fool I took you to be. Yes; of course Carla Dean shot her husband. They were up on a Ferris wheel, for God's sake!" And now he laughed, pluming pungent smoke.

"And that's exactly how you planned it. Isn't that so? I thought Dominic Dean was your inside man when it came to planning the bank heist. But it was his wife all along."

"Just for my own edification," Pilgrim said, gazing off into the distance, "what was it that she said to you? How did she give herself away?"

"It was the weapon. The Nagant M1895—a Russian Bolshevik pistol. I still have no idea where it came from—that's not important. What *is* important is that it holds seven bullets. After he died, it transpired that Dominic Dean always kept the chamber empty, in case of accidental discharge. Carla Dean knew that, though she claimed to know nothing about the weapon itself. She had never held it, or even looked at it. And yet she made a throwaway mention to 'emptying six bullets into another man' when she spoke with me today.*

"The natural assumption would be that the weapon was just like an ordinary revolver, which carries six bullets. In that case, Dean would have loaded it with only five. In the context of our conversation, it would have made sense for her to allude to firing *five* bullets. But she didn't, she said six. She knew that even with the chamber empty, the weapon held six bullets."

"She may have misspoken," said Pilgrim. "Or you may have misinterpreted the nature of her statement."

"Yes. You're right. Which is why my argument would never hold up in a court of law. But it's enough to convince me that she lied when she said she had never handled the murder weapon before. And if she lied about that, what else was she lying about?"

Ibbs gave a long rattling breath, and continued: "From the very beginning there was a question that bothered me. Namely, if Dominic Dean was the 'inside man,' why did he allow the watchman, Arthur Morrison, to be present the night of the robbery? It made no sense for a conspirator to place an obstacle in the way of his own scheme—and sign that poor old man's death warrant into the bargain. So I reframed the problem: what if Dominic Dean *wasn't* in on the robbery after all? But *somebody* must have been. And if not him, then who? And why did he subsequently have to die?

---

* See page 21.

"Looking at things from that angle, it's not such a complex problem after all. There are a number of suspects in the bank—Felix Draven, Miss Cash, et cetera—but who could have had access to Dominic Dean's personal papers? Who could have had access to the kind of confidential information that even his employees did not know? Who could have surreptitiously elicited the information from him by other means without arousing suspicion? Really, there was only one suspect. *Carla Dean.*

"I don't know whether you and she were having an affair. Maybe Carla is just an exploiter, out for whatever she can get. Either way, she's an accomplished deceiver. She managed to elicit information from her husband which she passed on to you and your gang. They in turn used this information to plan the robbery. But you and Carla bargained without one thing—Dominic's paranoia. He knew his wife rather better than she anticipated, and he sensed there was something afoot. That's why he asked Morrison to take a look around on the night in question. And we all know what happened next.

"Of course, Dominic was horrified to have his suspicions confirmed. That brought about the sudden changes his colleagues observed in his behaviour. His wife had betrayed him, and it had led to the unnecessary death of poor Arthur Morrison.

"So it became a game of cat and mouse between husband and wife. He knew she'd betrayed him, and she knew that he knew. But Carla Dean is a ruthless woman. She wasn't prepared to take a chance. So she worked out one of the cleverest tricks I've ever seen.

"It was really quite a brilliant double-bluff. A murder for which she could never, ever be convicted. She would shoot her husband dead in circumstances where she and she alone *must* be the murderer. She knew she would be arrested. But she also knew that the prosecution would never be able to convince a jury of her guilt. She did the dirty work, and relied on you, Mr. Pilgrim, to sow seeds of doubt among the witnesses. To bribe two men—Miklos Varga included—to spread stories of a phantom assailant, a mysterious limping man who did not exist. The second man was Doctor Ransome. They were paid to spread misinformation about 'Boyd Remiston,' the man who never was. The name is an anagram for 'Mister Nobody.' And this Mister Nobody served his purpose. Two words: reasonable doubt. You didn't need to prove she was innocent. All you needed to do was create *doubt*. If you threw in enough diversionary measures, there would be no way a jury could convict her *beyond reasonable doubt*. Even if they knew in their heart of hearts that she was guilty, the very possibility of a different killer would be enough to prevent conviction.

"The innate psychological bias among jurors means they will always believe those who claim they saw someone versus those who claim they did *not* see someone. You can't prove a negative. That's why only the disreputable Doctor Ransome and the ill-fated Miklos Varga were bribed. Their twin testimonies concerning the appearance of Boyd Remiston would far outweigh the testimonies of all the other witnesses who claimed there was no such man. Indeed, the vehemence of those fraudulent accounts might even have generated a few false memories among the other witnesses.

"But that wasn't all. This next part was a stroke of genius. Somebody—perhaps it was one of you, gentlemen?—went to the bank in the guise of this 'Boyd Remiston' and made himself known to Miss Cash, as well as a few other employees. I initially thought Miss Cash might be in on the trick herself, but she was duped just like the rest of us. This apparent reappearance of the killer after the fact added verisimilitude to the illusion. That was its sole purpose. It helped to convince people that Boyd Remiston was real.

"And in turn, it would have confounded the prosecution. Made the press ask awkward questions which couldn't be answered, because there *was* no answer. Carla shot her husband dead. She's the only one who could have done it. But her guilt seemed so blindingly obvious that I couldn't bring myself to accept it. There was also the fact she had no gunpowder on her hands, which is just the sort of detail a competent defence team could use to get her off. Though in fact, there are any number of reasons for her not to have gunpowder on her. For instance, she might have worn a glove which she then discreetly disposed of later. But by shifting the emphasis to an apparently contradictory detail like that, it would be possible to create doubt about her guilt.

"It also shifted the focus to Dominic Dean himself. I admit that I believed he must have been involved with the Golders Green robbery somehow. But he wasn't. He was just an unfortunate man who met an unfortunate end."

Pilgrim laughed heartily. "Wonderful work! Very neat. I think even Joseph Spector himself would be proud. I like that turn of phrase: 'an unfortunate man who met an unfortunate end.' Rather like you, eh Ibbs? And so we move from one likely suspect to another. Tell me this: why did you kill Paolini?"

Whatever Ibbs had expected, it was not this. He blinked a few times, then eventually stammered out: "I didn't!"

"So you keep saying. But you've just demonstrated how the most likely suspect in the Dean case proved to be the killer after all."

Ibbs hadn't considered that. Throughout the night, he had been trying to suss out a murder method that could have applied in *both* the Dean and Paolini cases. But whereas the shooting of Dominic Dean had been much simpler than it appeared, the shooting of Paolini was inestimably more complex. He still had no clue how it had been done. All he knew was that he wasn't the trigger man. Feeling like a broken Victrola, he said again: "I didn't kill him."

"I was afraid you'd say that." Pilgrim took a step toward him. He towered over Ibbs now. "I really hoped you wouldn't. Because now I know you're lying to me, and I don't like being lied to. It offends my sensibilities. It makes me want to hurt the person responsible. Understand?"

"Please . . . Mr. Pilgrim," Ibbs changed tack. "I swear to you on my life that I had nothing to do with what happened to Paolini."

"Don't swear on your life. Your life is quite literally in the balance, Mr. Ibbs. The only reason I'm showing you my face, you see, is that I know you'll be dead before daybreak. Before we bid you a fond adieu, we need to get a few things straightened out."

"You're a damn fool if you kill me," Ibbs said. It was a voice even he did not recognise.

"Wrong. Killing you will solve a number of problems. You will be killed in such a way that your death resembles suicide. The fact that you escaped from your jail cell will seem to indicate your guilt in the various criminal matters you have become embroiled with. And your suicide will confirm it. We'll be able to draw a line under it."

Ibbs said nothing. He had to concede that the plan made a kind of sense.

"But like I say," Pilgrim continued, "before you die, we need answers to some questions."

"I'm not saying another word."

"Let's be reasonable. You have it within your power to determine the manner of your death. How many people are given that opportunity? Will it be slow and painful, or quick and merciful? The choice is yours. I have men who can make it look like suicide either way. All I need from you are a few simple answers. But I'm a fair man. I'll trade an answer for an answer. So, first of all, what did Varga say to you at the theatre tonight?"

"Nothing. We didn't speak. The first I saw of him was when he tumbled out of that box."

Pilgrim smiled. "What a mess that was. But a handy distraction, I suppose." Then his expression hardened. "What did he say to you?"

"Nothing. I swear to you. Nothing."

"I'd like to take you at your word, Mr. Ibbs. But I'm afraid I'm a businessman, and we businessmen are a cautious breed. He spoke to you before the show, didn't he? He said something about the Ferris wheel?"

"I swear to you, he didn't!"

"My men know their trade, Mr. Ibbs. But all the same, things have been a bit close for comfort of late. Case in point: your good self. You have generally seen and heard too much for me to allow you to go on breathing. Fortunately, your death will put an end to the whole thing. The story will be told thus: you killed Dominic

Dean and framed his wife using methods unknown. You procured a role as her defender so that you might sabotage her case from the inside. You killed Varga because he witnessed your presence the night Dean died; he needed to be silenced. How did you do it? Who knows? Just another secret you will take to the grave. Eventually, overcome with guilt or mania, you returned to the scene of your original crime. There, you took your own life and so ended a crime spree like no other."

"You've forgotten something."

"Have I?"

"Paolini. Why did I kill Paolini?"

Pilgrim chuckled. "That brings us back to the matter at hand. Why *did* you kill Paolini?"

"I didn't!"

"Come along, Ibbs. You're amongst friends here."

"I tell you I didn't kill him!"

"Very well. A tight-lipped one aren't you? All right Branning, Keegan. Get it over with."

"You going to watch, boss?"

"Thank you, no. You've seen one dead man on a Ferris wheel, you've seen them all."

"Wait!" Ibbs was getting desperate. "All right. I killed Paolini. I don't know why I did it. It was a moment of madness. Now please: an answer for an answer. How did you kill Varga? Please, I need to know."

Pilgrim smiled. "I didn't. But I will concede to you that his death was to my advantage, just as yours will be. And Dominic Dean . . . well, the less said about that debacle the better. You're a very unsatisfactory man, Mr. Ibbs. I ask you several honest questions and you give me nothing at all. But then, you *are* a lawyer. And I suppose one less lawyer in the world is a good thing for everyone. Shakespeare, wasn't it, who said to kill all the lawyers? Well, I suppose one is a start."

He gave Branning and Keegan the nod and they led Ibbs slowly, funereally, toward the Ferris wheel. Sandwiched between them, he felt as if the very life was being squeezed out of him.

"Nothing to be afraid of," said Branning as they shoved him into the carriage.

"Gentlemen, you're making a mistake."

"We're not, honest. The mistake would be not doing what Mr. Pilgrim says."

Ibbs closed his eyes. Up there, the air was cold. He thought about Dominic Dean's final journey. How the bank manager had stepped onto that Ferris wheel in good faith. How he had a wife at his side. In many ways, Dean was lucky. He had not seen death coming. He had not felt its icy grip at his throat.

PART FOUR

THE WHEEL SPINS

Magic, like life, is a sequence of deceptions
culminating in a revelation. Unlike life, however,
the revelation is seldom disappointing.
—*The Master of Manipulation,*
"On Psychology and Other Casual Deceptions"

Against ill chances men are ever merry.
—**William Shakespeare,**
Henry IV, Part Two

CHAPTER THIRTEEN

ALL THE FUN OF THE FAIR

S pector had been examining the footprints in the alley for five solid minutes. Now he stood in sullen silence, smoking a cigarillo. Martha watched him and tried to gauge what was going on in his mind. Eventually, she could not bear it any longer. "Mr. Spector, what shall we do?"

He froze, as though startled. He had evidently forgotten she was there. But when he spoke, his voice was low and measured.

"Martha, there's only one reason Pilgrim's men would have kidnapped Edmund under cover of darkness. I think you and I both know what that reason is."

"They're going to kill him, aren't they?"

"Yes, it's highly likely. That's why time is of the utmost importance to us. We need to act with alacrity and precision. Pilgrim has considerable resources at his disposal. If he doesn't want Ibbs found, it's likely Scotland Yard would never find him. But he's made a grave error. He has underestimated you, and he's underestimated me. So we're going to beat him at his own game. We don't have much to go on. But I think we have enough. What do we know about Pilgrim? On the surface, not much. He is a professional éminence grise. But consider this: one of his primary fronts is the Red Star Shipping Company, based in Canary Wharf. That's a matter of public record. I think it's safe to say the kidnappers are dock workers. At least, that's what these footprints indicate."

"How?"

Spector smiled. "I'm glad you asked. The tread on these footprints is not that of a conventional work boot. Years ago—*many* years ago, before I was 'Joseph Spector'—I worked the docks myself, so I know whereof I speak. This groove here belongs to the steel toecap, you see, which helps to narrow the field. We are looking for a job with a lot of heavy lifting. Steel-capped boots are more expensive than the common or garden work boot, so our kidnappers would be unlikely to have them unless they were essential for work. And the bulky, tractor-like tread is best suited to either a farmworker or a stevedore—where the risks of slippery terrain are more pronounced. More so, for instance, than construction or factory work. Since there are no farms nearby, we must focus on the docks."

"All right, I suppose that makes sense. But where do you think they're taking him then? Canary Wharf?"

"Certainly not! Remember, the plan is to distance themselves from Ibbs and this whole string of impossible murders. They are crafting a neat conclusion to the narrative: one from which Titus Pilgrim is entirely absent. You see, they're going to pin it all on Ibbs. All of it. I'm talking about Varga, Paolini . . . and Dominic Dean."

"But how? I can see how it might work with Varga and Paolini—Ibbs was on the scene at least. But Dominic Dean? He has nothing to do with any of that business, surely?"

"You're absolutely right. It would appear to be a flaw in Pilgrim's plan. There is one conceivable method they could use to bring the story full circle. And that is to return to its beginning."

Spector was no longer looking at Martha. He was looking past her, into some nether realm of dark thoughts and ideas. Where the magic tricks come from.

"I know where they have him."

"You do?"

"Come on. I want you to have a drink of whisky before we go. It'll help you concentrate. I need you awake and alert for the drive."

They roared across London through desolate streets. Martha's foot was a little heavy on the accelerator and Spector found himself thumping from side to side in his seat as she swung the wheel.

When they rumbled into Golders Green, Spector took out his pocket watch. It was just after three o'clock. Pitch-black sky, chilly night air. They rounded a corner and the fairground came into view. Black shapes silhouetted against the moon. A dreadful, deathly stillness coupled with pervasive, melancholic silence. Martha coasted the car to a halt just outside the entrance gate. She switched off the engine and listened.

"It's awfully quiet," she said.

"Yes. Go to a telephone box, will you, Martha? I saw one at the corner. Call Inspector Flint."

"I don't think there's anybody here."

"That's just what they want us to think. It's altogether too quiet. A fairground on a Friday night should be thronged with merrymakers even into the early hours of the morning. I think it's safe to say Mr. Pilgrim has appropriated the place to set the stage for his own murky little drama."

"What are you going to do, Mr. Spector?"

"Go to the telephone box, Martha."

She did. Hunching her shoulders against the chill, she tiptoed back along the street toward the box. She glanced back over her shoulder, but Spector was already out of sight. There was only one direction in which he could have headed: into the heart of the fair.

She grabbed the telephone receiver and spoke hoarsely: "Scotland Yard."

Eventually, the operator put Martha through to Inspector Flint's office. It was Hook who picked up the phone.

"Yes?"

"This is Martha. I need to speak with Inspector Flint. It's very urgent."

"He's not here. What's happened?"

"Well where is he? We've found Edmund and he's in a lot of danger. Mr. Spector's gone in on his own."

"Give me the address."

As it happened, Flint was round the corner at the old Dean place going through some papers, still desperately trying to establish a link with Titus Pilgrim. Hook was able to get through to him on the telephone and he came running. In the meantime, Hook and several constables piled into a fleet of cars and headed for the fair.

Silently, the passenger car coasted upward, carrying Ibbs and his two murderers through the darkness. Titus Pilgrim remained on the ground, watching in contemplative silence.

When the car reached the summit—where the chill was at its most biting and the night sky at its blackest—the wheel abruptly halted. Ibbs closed his eyes.

At that moment, every single light in the Golders Green fair burst into blazing life. A sea of burning bulbs stretched out below them like a bejewelled sea. There was music too. That shrill, whistling fairground music. Like a great amorphous beast, the whole fair was awake.

Branning and Keegan looked at each other. This was not part of the plan.

"Up! On your feet!" The muzzle of the revolver dug into Ibbs's side. He stood up without a word, and the henchman made a spectacle of shoving the barrel into the back of his neck.

"*No!*" Pilgrim roared from down below. Ibbs heard the word and wondered if he might have a chance after all. That was when he glimpsed over the side and saw Pilgrim at the lever. Facing him was another thin figure, all dressed in black.

CHAPTER FOURTEEN

"I KNOW"

"You've made a rod for your own back, Mr. Pilgrim," said Joseph Spector. "Your men are just too eager. Truthfully, I doubt they comprehend all the nuances of your plan. If that fellow up there puts a bullet in the back of young Ibbs's head, you'll be in very big trouble indeed."

Pilgrim squared up to the old man. He produced a snub-nosed revolver from the folds of his coat.

"Needless to say, Scotland Yard will be with us momentarily," Spector pointed out. As if to punctuate this statement, the sound of approaching sirens commingled with the fairground music.

Pilgrim studied the old man gravely. "I'll remember your face, Mr. Spector."

Spector didn't blink. "And I'll remember yours."

With that, Titus Pilgrim silently withdrew. Spector stood and watched him go.

"Mr. Spector, are you all right?" Martha was back with him now, panting slightly from the sprint.

"Quite. It's Mr. Ibbs I'm concerned about."

"Where is he?"

Spector pointed upward.

Without as much as a moment's thought, Martha was away and running once again. She took a leap at the Ferris wheel and grabbed hold of the underside of the lowest carriage. It swiftly carried her skyward, and Spector could only watch as she swung herself up with feline celerity. No—not feline. She was more like a spider as she scrambled up, leaping from one carriage to another.

"Be careful for God's sake!" Spector yelled.

Ibbs tried to peer over the edge, but the lights were so blinding there was little he could distinguish.

"Come on," said Keegan. "Don't muck about."

"Hey," said Ibbs.

"Mm?" said Branning, turning. The next sound he made was a hoarse wheeze as Ibbs booted him in the gut.

Keegan brandished the revolver with a gloved hand—he squeezed the trigger a couple of times without troubling to aim. The thunderous shots whipcracked around the fairground. Ibbs went deaf in one ear. Fortunately, the bullets were wild. Keegan was too off-balance to focus fully, otherwise he would have been a dead man.

Martha made an audacious move—clearly her trapeze experience was coming back into play. She swung her legs high and vaulted onto the underside of Ibbs's carriage. This gave her leeway to swing her feet upward and kick Keegan square in the chest. The impact toppled him.

A third deafening shot accompanied his fall. Then it was merely the dreadful pipe organ—the last sound Keegan would ever hear. He hit the ground with a thump. Morbid curiosity compelled

Joseph Spector to head over and take a look. Yes, the fellow was indeed dead. But just to be on the safe side, Spector kicked the revolver away from him. It landed a few feet away—like its owner, cold and inert.

It was a curious trio that descended from the Ferris wheel. Martha and Ibbs were laughing giddily, no doubt still reeling from the mad delight of survival. And beside them an unconscious Brannigan sat slumped. When he woke, it would be in the rear of a Black Maria.

"Edmund. Martha. I think it's about time we brought this whole mess to a conclusion, don't you?"

"Thank you," said Ibbs. "Thank you both. I can't thank you enough. They were going to kill me. They really were."

"I don't doubt it," said Spector, lighting a cigarillo.

Ibbs took a few steps and dropped to his knees. "Goodness," he said. "Goodness me."

Martha patted his shoulder. "You're all right, Edmund. It's over and done with."

"Yes, I suppose it is."

She helped him to his feet as a pair of police cars shrieked into view, one behind the other. The first car was still moving when Flint leapt from it.

"Ibbs!" he roared.

"Be calm, Flint," said Spector. "It's over now."

"Ibbs, you're under arrest . . ."

"*There's* the man you should be arresting," said Martha, pointing to the unconscious Branning, who was still slumped in the Ferris wheel carriage.

"And who's this?" said Flint, prodding Keegan's corpse with the tip of his shoe.

"Whoever he may be," said Spector, "I think he's ready to come quietly." Spector perched on the edge of the nearby merry-go-round, which had just ceased to spin.

Flint wagged a finger at Ibbs. "You've got some explaining to do, you know."

"I'm just glad the whole wretched business is over," the young lawyer sighed.

A thin crease appeared between Spector's brows. "How do you mean?"

"I'm glad to finally know at long last who's responsible for this mess."

Spector ruminatively rolled the cigarillo between his spindly fingers. "Ah, Titus Pilgrim you mean. Well, though it pains me to admit it, Pilgrim is only responsible for the murders in an abstract sense."

"How do you mean?"

"He didn't actually *commit* murder. And neither did those two goons of his. The only provable death they are responsible for is Arthur Morrison's. That's all Flint will get them for, if anything."

"What do you mean?"

"This business is so much more complex than any of us could have imagined. Come here, sit by me. Care for a cigarillo? Or some absinthe? I have a flask here, I find it helps to clear my head."

"But it *makes sense*," Ibbs protested. "I mean, I think I understand. Pilgrim and Carla Dean were having an affair. She helped to plan the heist. But Dominic Dean became suspicious, so he arranged for Arthur Morrison to keep an eye on the place over-night. When the robbery took place, and Morrison was killed, Dominic Dean's worst suspicions were confirmed. So Carla shot him on the Ferris wheel."

"A perfect summation," Spector said, "of the *first part* of the problem, young Edmund. Flint, come over here. And Martha. I have your answers for you. It's all fallen into place at last."

"What do you mean?" Flint was incredulous.

"I mean I can tell you everything now. The whole sordid thing from beginning to end. I know who murdered Miklos Varga, and how they got him into the crate at the Pomegranate Theatre. And I know who killed Professor Paolini."

"Well for God's sake, tell us!"

Spector smiled.

CHAPTER FIFTEEN

THE THREE
GAUNTLETS

I bbs watched the sun come up over the Thames. It would be a bright day—unseasonably bright. Grudgingly, Flint had agreed not to arrest him after all. But it took considerable persuasion from Joseph Spector, culminating in a promise to stand him at least three pints in The Black Pig.

Keegan's corpse was carted away, and the other fellow, Branning, was revivified with a bucket of icy water. Once he was compos mentis, he freely admitted that he and his partner were the ones behind the Golders Green robbery, though he refused to name the third man. But when it became clear to him that Titus Pilgrim's empire was crumbling, and that the "Napoleon of Crime" had lost his lustre, Branning no longer seemed averse to trading a testimony or two for prison privileges. He gave up several low-level members of Pilgrim's organisation, who would in turn give up a few more. The house of cards had begun to tumble.

Flint seemed confident that they would have Pilgrim himself behind bars before the end of the year. While Edmund

Ibbs received medical attention (attended by a worried-looking Martha), Flint sidled up to Joseph Spector. "We'll get him, you know."

"I wouldn't be so sure," said Spector. "Pilgrim's a wily bird."

"Ah, but you forget, Spector: so am I."

Spector, Flint, Martha, and Edmund Ibbs made a bedraggled, careworn quartet when they arrived at Flint's office in Scotland Yard. The place was cramped and heaped with papers. It seemed to be a reflection of its owner, who was grizzled and ill-kempt, but who looked no less like someone who could get the job done. Flint was a model host, offering tea to all.

Ibbs was feeling elated; the weight of impending assassination lifted from his shoulders, not to mention the morphine coursing through him for his various aches and pains. His cracked ribs had been bandaged, and his wounded shoulder had been fitted with a sling. But as he gazed out the window at the amber morning sun, he knew there were still plenty of questions to be answered.

"You did very well, Mr. Ibbs, in seeing through Carla Dean," said Joseph Spector. "She was certainly a good liar, with a profound insight into human psychology. I have no doubt that *she* was the one who devised all the little complexities of the plan to murder her husband. In Titus Pilgrim, she found a man with the power to turn her ideas into a reality."

"It took me long enough," said Ibbs modestly.

"What's so infuriating," Spector observed, "is that I came up with the answer myself without even realising it, although I wrongly ascribed it to you.* It was an 'impossible murder' that wasn't impossible at all. Nobody is above suspicion in cases like these, but it's also important to remember that nobody is *below* suspicion either. Both Pilgrim and Carla Dean were counting on our *dis*counting her as a suspect purely *because* she was the most likely culprit. An interesting psychological technique which almost worked. Because it seemed impossible, didn't it? Why would a woman of her obvious culture and intelligence commit a murder *in that way?*"

"All right," said Flint, growing impatient. "Now, let's get this business over with once and for all, shall we, Spector? If Pilgrim's not the one responsible for the murders at the Pomegranate, then I need to know who is. Tell me everything."

Spector placed an unlit cigarillo in his mouth. "A matter of logic," he said. "Of untangling the skein. But if you really want to know, it was the three gauntlets which set me off on the right track."

---

* *See page 178.*

INTERLUDE

WHEREIN THE READER'S ATTENTION IS RESPECTFULLY REQUESTED

Once upon a time, this would be the point in the narrative where a challenge is issued to the reader. "All the data are in front of you," I would say, "that you will need to unravel this 'tangled skein' for yourself."

These days such practises are antiquated and rather passé. But who am I to stand in the way of a reader's fun? It's true that all the evidence is there, and in plain sight too. If there are any would-be sleuths amongst you, now is the time to make yourselves known. There is no prize, material or otherwise, save the quiet glory of having triumphed at what a wise man once termed "the grandest game in the world."

CHAPTER SIXTEEN

THE DEVIL'S OWN LUCK

The man who murdered Miklos Varga had passed a sleepless night. This was perhaps understandable; he'd been conscious of a paranoiac sense of entrapment ever since he snapped the poor fellow's neck several hours ago. He had been drinking long into the night and he awoke bleary-eyed, with a sharp stabbing pain behind his temples. His day began badly, and was soon to get worse.

He dressed and headed cumbersomely down the stairs. The little boardinghouse was sparsely furnished; he was able to pack his entire life into a suitcase. A good thing, he reflected, for a man who was soon to be on the run. But he would be all right. He knew he would. After all, he had a bargaining chip, didn't he?

He poked his head out of the house and into the brisk morning air: the coast was clear. Ducking back inside and easing shut the door, his heart all but stopped.

Standing in the corridor behind him was a horde of uniformed police officers. They had entered the house in silence—a dawn raid—and at their head, like a triumphant general fresh from the fight, stood Inspector George Flint.

"Sidney Draper?" he said. "I am arresting you for the murder of Miklos Varga. I'd recommend you come quietly. It's the best thing all round."

Sidney Draper seemed relieved that at last—after the longest night of his life—it was finally over. He went quietly.

At the police station, he was polite but subdued. He answered all questions put to him. He freely named names.

"It was Titus Pilgrim that made me do it," he told Flint. "If not for him, I'd never have done anything like that. I'm a good fellow, really. Honestly I am."

Being in Titus Pilgrim's pocket was no joke, but Draper had honestly thought he could get away with it. His "bargaining chip" was found in his pocket, where it had been throughout the previous evening at the Pomegranate. He had stolen it from Miklos Varga when he killed him.

It was a crisp, white lady's glove. And it was peppered with gunpowder.

"He almost seems relieved," Flint observed when he and Spector had reconvened in his office. Ibbs and Martha were there too; they would not have missed the denouement for the world.

"He *is* relieved," said Joseph Spector. "He's not a cold-blooded killer. Just a sad, desperate man. But he thought that glove was his ticket to freedom. After all, it was the one piece of physical evidence which proves Carla Dean killed her husband. He evidently had some sort of plan to blackmail Titus Pilgrim into helping him start a new life."

"That glove . . ." Flint said thoughtfully. "Presumably, Varga picked it up from the floor of the Ferris wheel car."

"That seems like a reasonable inference," Spector agreed. "Or perhaps she dropped it over the side. Either way, Carla evidently used it to prevent the gunpowder residue from getting on her hand when she killed her husband. Varga found it, and immediately understood its significance. He was no fool. Now, I suppose you would like me to tell you how the whole mess fits together?" Cue frantic nodding from Ibbs and Martha, along with a weary sigh from Flint. "All right. Well, let's take it from the top. I mean, from the *very* top. I'm referring to the Golders Green robbery which started this whole messy business in motion. Rather like the old woman who swallowed a fly, a simple enough bank robbery led to a sequence of murders. First, Dominic Dean—killed by his wife to keep him from revealing her part in the plan. And then Miklos Varga. Ultimately, Varga was condemned by his own conscience. You see, he accepted the payoff from Pilgrim. I imagine he was intimidated into doing so. That's why he fed Ibbs the line about the limping man.

"But from the moment the story left his lips, Varga regretted what he had done. He was a man of devout faith, as young Ibbs observed. The remorse was crippling. That's why, no sooner had Ibbs left the fairground yesterday morning than Varga was tailing him, waiting for an opportunity to tell the truth—and to hand over the incriminating glove. And Ibbs led him through a merry dance through London. He visited Scotland Yard. He visited the Old Bailey. That was where he encountered Titus Pilgrim and traded a few barbed words. But more importantly, it is where Pilgrim caught a glimpse of Varga in his fatefully colourful garb. Why, Pilgrim wondered, was the fairground man so desperate to see *Ibbs*, of all people?

"That was when he decided Varga had outlived his usefulness. He was a weak link, more useful dead than alive. And his death would serve two purposes: one, it would prevent him from going public with the fact that he had been paid off. And two, it would further enhance the idea of a conspiracy to protect the phantom killer, Boyd Remiston. Varga was killed not because he saw the real murderer at the fairground that night, as we all assumed—he was killed because he knew there *was no other murderer.*"

Flint was rubbing his forehead.

"Varga followed Ibbs to the Pomegranate. But he knew by then that Pilgrim's men were on his tail. His survival instinct led him to duck through the fire door. As we know, Ned Winchester let him into the backstage area. Pilgrim called off his goons rather than risk a splashy scene in a crowded theatre.

"But unbeknownst to Varga—or indeed anybody at the Pomegranate Theatre—there was a man working there who owed Titus Pilgrim a lot of money, and was willing to do anything to settle his debt."

"That was Sidney Draper," said Flint.

"Right."

"How did you work it out?"

"Well, the solution came twofold. I'll get to it in a moment. But when it became clear that Varga was ensconced in the theatre, all Pilgrim had to do was telephone Draper and inform him that he was willing to write off the debt in exchange for a single favour. You'll recall that we even hypothesised at one point that *Paolini* might have found himself in such a situation.* And you remember that the only time Sidney Draper's whereabouts were unaccounted for before the show was when he went to take a telephone call.** You can imagine his shock when it turned out to be Titus Pilgrim on the other end of the line, asking for a favour. And the 'favour' was to kill Varga. Needless to say, Draper was only too willing to oblige.

"You see, he is a gambler. That much was obvious after only five minutes' conversation with him. An examination of his personal finances will no doubt show escalating debts and increasingly insalubrious company. That gave me my first inkling that if anybody was in league with Titus Pilgrim, it was likely to be him. Think back to the chats we had with Draper. He punctuated almost every sentence with a gambling metaphor."***

"And how did you work out he was the one who killed Varga?" asked Flint.

"Simply a matter of probabilities. The old chestnuts: means, motive, and opportunity. While the means and motive remained a mystery to me, only Mr. Draper had the opportunity to commit the crime.

---

*   *See page 156.*
**   *See page 80.*
*** *See pages 86, 89, 101, etc.*

"And were I Sherlock Holmes, I would no doubt look at the man and perceive his loose-fitting clothing and the pale line around his ring finger indicating the sudden absence of a wedding ring and I would deduce that he was either freshly divorced or freshly widowed. But don't forget, I have spent much of my life in the music halls and I have seen areas of the world which Holmes could not have dreamt of. I noticed, for instance, the shadowed lump on each of Draper's thumbs.* To see it on one thumb is not perhaps so telling. But to see it on *both*? It shows that the man's thumbs have been broken. And for a man to be eating poorly and to have recently parted ways with his jewellery, that indicates that he is a gambler whose losses are mounting up. But for this man to *also* have had both thumbs broken at some point or other in his life, that indicates that he is not merely a poor gambler but an execrable one, one who is on the point of financial collapse. One who, in other words, will do anything for money."

"All right," said Flint, "stop beating around the bush. Tell us how he did it."

"Well, there is one fact to be got out of the way before anything else. *Sidney Draper killed Miklos Varga.* It does not particularly matter *when* he did it, but I imagine it was around ten past eight, when the show was in full swing and Ned Winchester was stowed in Martha's dressing room. Remember that he did not come out to play cards straight away—he waited a few minutes until he was sure the coast was clear.** Sidney Draper had a description of his

---

*   *See page 85.*
** *See page 102.*

target, and let's not forget quite how distinctive Varga's clothing was. There could be no mistake.

"Draper knew there was only one place where Varga was likely to be hiding, and that was in the storage room. So he went looking, and would you believe it, he struck lucky. Any conversation he had with Varga was necessarily brief. Perhaps he said, 'What are you doing here?' and Varga replied, 'I'm hiding—there are men after me.' Draper knew what he had to do. All it took was a brief distraction to draw Varga's attention away, and Draper grabbed him and strangled the life out of him, then retrieved the glove from the corpse. But that left him with a fresh dilemma: what to *do* with said corpse? The backstage area at the Pomegranate is horribly cramped and cluttered. There aren't too many places where a corpse might be stashed. Think about it. Where could the body have been, if it was nowhere to be found backstage and it was not up in the rafters?"

"Is this a riddle?" said Flint, placing unpleasant emphasis on the last word. "Please, I don't have the time or the patience."

"All right," Spector said, concealing a grin, "I'll give you the answer. If it's not on the ground and it's not in the rafters, there's only one place it can be. That's in the air.'

"In the *air*?" Flint repeated, making a face.

"Right. 'Sandbag man' is what Draper called himself. Some of those sandbags used as backcloth counterweights can weigh as much as a hundred and fifty pounds. In other words, more or less the equivalent of a grown man. Well, Draper was able to capitalise on that. Paolini, Martha, and Toomey were onstage for the Assistant's Revenge trick, Alf was by the stage door, Cope was in the fly loft, and Fabris was in his dressing room. Ned Winchester was still in hiding. So Draper strung Varga up and made sure the body was lost in the folds of the numerous backcloths. If Cope had happened to glimpse him hoisting the corpse into position—it was hanging by its feet—Draper could always try to convince him he had actually seen *Toomey*, who also happened to be hanging by his feet at that moment for the Assistant's Revenge trick. Picture it: two bodies, both hanging by their feet, both separated by a thin backcloth. But once poor Varga was hanging motionless up there in the darkness, there was no reason for Cope to see him. In many ways, it was a very elegant solution: there was no danger of anyone spotting him from either down below *or* up above. And the weight of the body served the same function as a sandbag. Then, Draper went to fetch Ned Winchester, and talked him into playing cards for a while. He needed someone to give him an alibi, you see. It was a neat little plan, which would have enabled him to remove the body after the show, when the backstage area was clear."

"Then why didn't he? Why all the nonsense with the crates?"

"Excellent question, and one which bothered me all the way through this murky affair. Surely there could be no advantage in having Varga's body unveiled before a crowd of a thousand people? That's what led me to realise that the corpse went into the crate as a matter of necessity. It was put there because *there was nowhere else for it to go.*

"Draper himself told us that he untied counterweight number six to lower the backcloth for the crate illusion, but that the ropes became knotted, so he sent Ned Winchester up to cut the rope with a knife.* At the time, I wondered why he would do a thing like that—a man as independent and in control as Sidney Draper, sending his 'dopey' nephew up to do an important job. But it occurred to me that perhaps there was a very simple reason he sent Ned up to the fly loft instead of going himself: because he *couldn't*. He was used to carrying sandbags. But he wasn't used to carrying sandbags *and* throttling a grown man to death. Think about the way Draper moved; the hunched gait and cautious step throughout the evening.** He had killed Miklos Varga scarcely an hour before, and he'd also gravely injured *himself* in the process. I'd wager a snapped tendon of some kind, making even the slightest movement agony. But he couldn't let on that he was in terrible physical pain, so he did his best to hide it. And he more or less succeeded, though he was forced to do one or two things which were distinctly out of character. One of these was sending Ned Winchester up to the fly loft. Either he had to miss the backcloth cue and thus draw unnecessary attention to the sandbags and the fly loft, or else he had to send Ned and take the risk. So he took the risk. But do you remember what Ned told us? He couldn't see the painted numbers, so he *counted the ropes* and cut the sixth one.*** He had no way of knowing there was an *extra* rope; the one with Miklos Varga's corpse hanging from it. And when he cut that rope—which was unfortunately placed between ropes five and six—Sidney Draper's plan came quite literally crashing down about his ears. The body dropped.

---

*   *See page 107.*
**   *See pages 61 and 78.*
*** *See page 107.*

"If things had gone according to plan, Varga's body would have remained hanging throughout the show, unnoticed. Then, once the theatre was empty, Draper could have removed it and dumped it somewhere; most likely in the Thames. That way, no one would ever have made the connection between Miklos Varga and the Pomegranate Theatre. Draper's debt would be cleared; he could start a new life. The slate would be wiped clean. Unfortunately for him, it didn't work out that way.

"Draper had to think fast. So, in spite of the terrible pain, he heaved the unfortunate Varga into one of the crates, then went to fetch Fabris. Like a lot of plans devised 'off the cuff,' this one left a great deal to be desired. But all the same, it fulfilled its purpose. Unwittingly, it also echoed the audacity of the plan cooked up by Pilgrim and Carla Dean. Draper is an inveterate gambler, so he gambled.

"He had two choices—place the corpse in a crate that he knew would be opened onstage within a matter of minutes (let's call that one Crate A)—or one which was destined to remain unopened (for the sake of argument, Crate B). Conventional logic dictates that he would place it in Crate B, the spare. But if we consider this closer, we see that it is not in fact the most desirable option. For one thing, he would need to remove the body by himself at a later date—this was naturally fraught with danger, particularly as the snapped tendon in his back made even the slightest movement cumbersome. And there was always the risk that somebody might open the crate in the meantime. If *that* were to happen, there would be no doubt at all as to who put the body there. Whereas if he allowed the corpse to be unveiled by Paolini in front of a full house, then the suspicion would be diffused among a larger number of people. And so it proved.

"I don't believe for a moment that Sidney Draper's train of thought in those few moments was anywhere near as categorical as mine was just then. But either way, he decided to gamble. He helped Fabris into Crate B, otherwise known as the duplicate crate. But he angled it in such a way that when Fabris was in position on the small ledge inside the rear door, he was facing *away* from the spiral steps leading up to the fly loft. Then Draper spoke aloud as though his nephew were coming down, when in fact Ned Winchester was still upstairs making a nuisance of himself to the lighting man, Cope. When Kenneth Fabris started to lean out to greet the lad, Draper stopped him and told him that there wasn't time. Hence Fabris's cry: 'I'll see you on the other side!'

"Then Draper sealed up Crate B and swiftly swapped it with Crate A. This little charade had taken perhaps three or four minutes in total. By this time, Ned Winchester really *was* making his descent from the fly loft. So Draper angled this crate in exactly the same position, and he reenacted the exact same conversation which had just taken place. That was his trick. Both witnesses—Ned and Fabris—saw *different enactments* of the same sequence of events, with a different crate each time. The same words were spoken, the same movements made—the thumbs-up, specifically. But when Ned saw the same thing as he was coming down the steps, he saw a performance by Draper which was purely for his benefit. He saw Draper securing *Varga's corpse* in the crate. He heard Draper mimicking Fabris's voice to provide the exact same dialogue which had taken place minutes earlier. And, perhaps the most macabre aspect of all, he saw Draper manipulating the corpse so that it appeared to move, and give him a thumbs-up. That's why there were *three* gauntlets rather than two inside the crate with Varga. Draper affixed one to Varga's right arm when he was positioning him in the crate. He knew that was the only part of the body that would be visible to Ned as he descended the steps. He waited until his nephew came back down, then he pretended to warn Fabris that there was no time. In fact he was talking to Varga's corpse, shielded from Ned's view. He managed to convince Ned that it was *Fabris* he was speaking to thanks to some deft but admittedly macabre manipulation—the hand Ned saw was in fact Varga's. Let's not forget, Draper was a Punch and Judy man in his day,* so puppetry was a particular skill of his. As was creative use of his vocal cords. As Mr. Punch and his ill-fated wife Judy, Draper was quite used to carrying out both sides of a conversation. So he warned "Fabris" that there was no time, and then—in a perfect approximation of Fabris's voice—he repeated the exact same words which Fabris himself had said only minutes before. It was enough to convince Ned Winchester that the man in the crate was alive and well. And by replicating the dialogue exactly, Draper was able to guarantee that both Winchester's and Fabris's accounts would tally. The only difference was the timing. But of course, as Fabris himself told us, he was a slave to Draper when it came to timing.** When Draper told him they were running short on time, he was quite willing to take the fellow at his word."

---

*   *See page 112.*
**   *See page 113.*

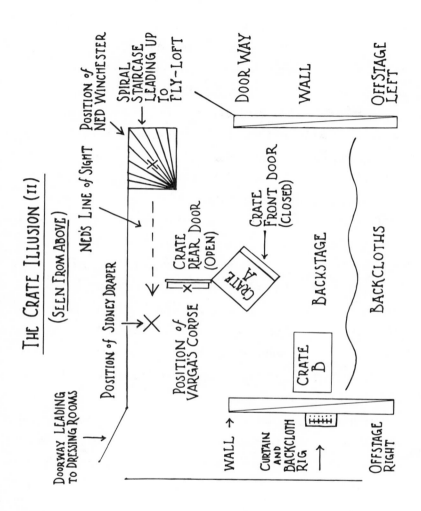

The Crate Illusion (II)
(Seen from Above)

Ned's Line of Sight

Position of Ned Winchester

Spiral Staircase Leading Up to Fly-Loft

Door Way

Wall

Offstage Left

Position of Sidney Draper

Crate Rear Door (Open)

Crate Front Door (Closed)

Backstage

Backcloths

Doorway Leading to Dressing Rooms

Position of Varga's Corpse

Crate A

Crate B

Wall

Curtain and Backcloth Rig

Offstage Right

"So Winchester was convinced that he was wheeling *Fabris* over to the side of the stage when in fact it was Varga's corpse. Very nasty," was Flint's verdict. "Very nasty indeed."

"Absolutely. And needless to say Fabris was in the dark both literally and figuratively. In that suit of armour he would never have heard Draper's little masquerade. He had no way of checking the time. He was helpless until Paolini opened the door of the crate to free him. But by then, Draper had already swapped the crates back again while we were all so busy examining the corpse on the stage.* It gave the appearance that the crate in which we found Fabris was the same one which had been wheeled out onstage. When of course that would have been impossible.

"And that brings us to the killing of Paolini."

"Why did he do it?" asked Martha.

"How did he do it?" asked Ibbs. They had spoken in perfect synchronicity.

"Martha, your question is the easiest to answer. He did it because he thought he had been found out. Remember, Ibbs, when you overheard Paolini speaking to Andrew Morgan on the phone? What did he say, again? Something about '*I know who did it*'? Of course, with the benefit of hindsight we can infer that he was talking about the Dean case, which he incorrectly believed that he had solved. But if a man who had just committed murder, a man suffering from both guilt and paranoia, happened to overhear that conversation, what other conclusion might he draw? He thought Paolini had found him out and was looking to capitalise on it before going to the police. So he decided to silence him."

"Just a moment," said Ibbs, raising his hand like a schoolchild, "it was just Paolini and me in the corridor. How could Draper have heard the conversation?"

---

* *See page 59.*

"When you heard Paolini talking on the telephone, Flint and I were in the midst of questioning Toomey and Alf in Toomey's dressing room. That means Alf's alcove by the stage door was vacant. I believe Draper stashed himself there, peeked around the corner and spotted Paolini using the telephone. Then he crept over and picked up the second extension. As you yourself did, Mr. Ibbs, when Flint here was trying to trace Lazarus Lennard.* He heard what Paolini said to Morgan, but he did not understand it. He saw it as a threat, when in fact it was anything but. Indeed, if Paolini had lived to expound his inaccurate theory, it would have added more confusion to what was already a decidedly tangled case. But Draper wasn't to know that. So he made another split-second decision, and another unfortunate gamble.

"He headed round to the backstage area where the pistols were kept and helped himself to one of them—the one with live ammunition. Then, he simply bided his time until the moment was right. And he slipped into Paolini's star dressing room and hid himself away, to lie in wait."

"Where?" Ibbs wanted to know.

"Why, in the wardrobe, of course."

"But the wardrobe was searched."

"Yes, but not until *after* he had managed to extricate himself. It was all a question of timing. He crouched in there (remember he was a Punch and Judy man, who was used to tucking himself into tight spaces) and waited until Paolini returned to the dressing room. Before Draper had the opportunity to finish Paolini off,

---

*   *See page 146.*

though, the Professor poked his head out into the corridor and called you over. He told you he had something he wished to discuss with you—most likely it was his theory about Dominic Dean. But Draper, overhearing this, stepped out of the wardrobe, clobbered you, Mr. Ibbs, and then executed Paolini with a single shot to the head. He knew the gunshot would draw a lot of attention, but he seized the opportunity to turn this murder into a locked-room mystery. He attached the weapon to Mr. Ibbs's hand . . ."

"Why did he do that?" Surprisingly, it was not Ibbs but Martha who had asked the question.

Spector shrugged. "More obfuscation. More confusion. But it had to have been *him* because, if you recall, he mentioned that he'd been undertaking some repairs to the props. He was also the one who stated how easy it would have been for a killer to find the glue backstage.* He must have had the glue in his pocket, so he decided to use it. He knew that if the police were clamouring around you, Mr. Ibbs, they would be less likely to look in the wardrobe straight away. And that's exactly what happened. It was a canny piece of misdirection. He retreated into the wardrobe once more, then slipped out while Flint, Hook, and myself were distracted by the sight of you with the gun in your hand."

There followed a moment's silence, and then Inspector Flint exhaled slowly, the way a man might sigh after enjoying a hearty

---

*   *See page 144.*

meal. "I can't decide whether he had the devil's own luck, or whether he was the most hapless killer I've ever encountered."

Spector gave a shrug. "Both, perhaps. Everything he did was a gamble. And each choice he made paid off in the short-term, but inevitably contributed to his ultimate fate."

Now that Spector's disquisition was over, George Flint headed for the nearest vacant interview room where, Ibbs surmised, he might finally catch up on some much-needed sleep. Spector, who had the office to himself, lit a fresh cigarillo and stared out of the window. There was a haunted look on his face.

Martha, who had grown restless during the denouement, dragged Edmund Ibbs outside for a breath of air. It was going to be a beautiful day. She slipped her arm through the crook of his elbow. "Poor Ned," she said. "I love him to pieces, but he's such a dope, letting himself be tricked like that."

"Yes," Ibbs agreed, before biting his tongue.

"You're a smart one though, aren't you, Edmund? You were hot on Spector's heels every step of the way. I reckon if you'd had an hour or so longer, you'd have come up with the entire solution all by yourself. Oh, Edmund, you're blushing . . ."

"Am I? Oh, I'm sorry," said Ibbs, growing redder still.

Martha laughed. It was a hollow sound, with no real mirth in it. "Scandalous, isn't it, this whole thing? I'm glad it's over. Though I doubt I shall ever look at Ned the same way again."

Ibbs coughed awkwardly and said: "Well, yes, it's all been very . . ."

Fortunately, he was not obliged to finish the sentence. Martha stopped his burbling mouth with a kiss. A *real* kiss this time; no keys passed between their lips.

When they finally parted, Martha smiled. "I can't promise you much," she said. "I like to travel. Try new things. I can't promise I won't get bored with you, so please do try not to be boring. But if you're willing to risk it then so am I."

Was he willing to risk it? Draper had risked everything and lost. Surely, then, the odds were in Ibbs's favour?

At that moment, he forgot every single sliver of sage advice from the plenitude of world-weary romantics he had encountered in his short life. They would have told him to run a mile, to forget all about this strange, sad, and dangerous young woman who drugged policemen and wrote books of magic.

"I'm game if you are," he told her.

ONE WEEK LATER

Joseph Spector was just swallowing a mouthful of pea and ham pie when George Flint appeared in the doorway of the snug. "Flint! Come and sit down, there's a good fellow."

Spector was in his customary spot in The Black Pig, in a threadbare armchair beside the grate. Flint, as usual, was looking harried.

"Have you seen this morning's papers?"

"Afraid not. Have I missed something?"

"Sidney Draper. He's dead. They found him hanged in his cell."

Spector dabbed at his chin with a napkin. "Most unfortunate."

"They're marking it down as a suicide."

Spector shook his head sadly. "I'm afraid it was inevitable. And I suppose the henchman Branning has retracted the testimony he so willingly provided?"

"He has. He's completely button-lipped."

"I thought as much. It seems as though Titus Pilgrim has an arrow or two left in his quiver."

"But I just don't understand it," Flint said, with a sigh. "How could he have got to Draper in his cell?"

"You're on your own this time, my dear Flint. As the Pomegranate business shows, Titus Pilgrim can reach just about anybody, anywhere."

"I'll get him, Spector," said Flint. "Just you see if I don't."

"I know you will, old friend. Now what do you say to a drop of absinthe?"

George Flint left The Black Pig much more cheerful than when he arrived. So cheerful, in fact, that he failed to notice Edmund Ibbs when the young lawyer passed by him and ducked through the low doorway of the Elizabethan pub. Ibbs glanced around the barroom, blinking in the dingy half light. "Um . . . I'm looking for Joseph Spector," he said.

The barmaid pointed to a wooden door, and Ibbs headed through.

"Mr. Spector! I hope I'm not disturbing you."

The old conjuror beamed. "Far from it, Edmund! Come and sit down. What will you have to drink?"

"Just a beer please."

"One beer for my young friend," Spector called out the barmaid.

"This place is just how I pictured it," Ibbs observed.

"Marvellous, isn't it? Now, what brings you to this den of iniquity?"

"Well, I just wanted to speak to you about something."

"Yes?"

"Firstly, to share some good news. I rather think that Martha and I are going to be married."

"Goodness. Well, that *is* good news. If a little surprising, I must admit. Have you any idea when?"

"No, none at all. And we may not. It's just that things seem to be going that way, that's all. But really that's not why I came here. I came because I wanted to thank you again for everything you did for me, and I wanted to ask you one last favour."

"Yes? What's that?"

"Well, it's just that I've been practicing the Charlier cut, you see . . ." Ibbs fumbled in his jacket pocket and emerged with a deck of cards. But as he withdrew his hand, a small, gleaming object snagged on his sleeve and dropped to the ground.

Spector, quick as a flash, caught it before it hit the floor. He laid it on his palm and held it up to the light. "Well," he said.

"Oh! That's the bullet. You know, the one from Paolini's bullet catch trick. He gave it to me. As a . . . memento."

"Then you must keep it. If I didn't know better, I'd say that bullet was your lucky charm, Mr. Ibbs. It saw you through rather a lot of trouble."

"Or got me *into* a lot of trouble . . ."

"Well, that's one perspective. If this case has taught me anything, it's that it is worth retaining an open mind and a flexible perspective. But there must be more to your visit than the Charlier cut? I'm happy to provide a demonstration of course, but . . ."

Ibbs gave a grunt of laughter. "Is it that obvious?"

Spector leaned forward on his elbows. "What's on your mind?"

"It's about what happened to Paolini."

"You weren't satisfied with the official explanation of his death?"

Ibbs shook his head. "I just can't quite fathom it. The whole thing feels wrong somehow. It's been nagging at me day and night. I've been through it all in my mind so many times, and I just can't suss it out. But I know that your explanation is wrong."

Spector smiled thinly. "What makes you say that?"

"Because I opened the wardrobe myself. When I woke up in the dressing room with the gun in my hand. I couldn't believe what was happening, so I started searching the room for the killer."*

"I thought you might have done," said Spector. "But you were wise to keep it to yourself." Spector studied the young man very carefully, steepling his fingers. Then he continued in a matter-of-fact tone: "You're right, of course. The killer wasn't in the wardrobe. The killer wasn't even in the room at all. And it certainly wasn't Sidney Draper."

"Then who was it?"

"Can't you guess? Why do you think I fed my dear friend Flint such an unpalatable story?"

Ibbs's mouth dropped open. He had the answer at last. "It was Martha."

"I'm afraid it was. And she used a very clever method. One which was almost too good to reveal."

"I'm sorry," said Ibbs, "but I need a moment to digest this."

"Quite understandable. But it's important to note that she never intended to frame *you*. She originally meant to frame the reporter, Andrew Morgan."

"But why?"

---

*   *See page 125.*

"The answer was within your grasp the whole time, if you had but known it. Paolini himself announced it to us during his performance, before the unfortunate Miklos Varga made his stage debut. It was a trick in which you yourself participated."

"The bullet catch?"

"Right. But I want you to think about what Paolini *said*, as opposed to what he *did* during the trick. Can you remember?"

"He talked about dead magicians. Magicians who died during the bullet catch trick."

"Correct. His patter was in rather poor taste, I thought. But tell me, can you recall the names of any magicians he listed?"

"Well, there was Chung Ling Soo, obviously. He's the most famous one. And that woman from Germany. Madame . . . DeLinsky?"

"Right! But there was another name he mentioned, one which carried with it more than a hint of malice."

"That's right, it's coming back to me now. 'The Black Wizard' of somewhere or other, isn't that it? I've got it! Rusell Zanandra, that was the name!"

Spector was nodding and grinning. "'Rusell' with one 's,' I think you'll find. The spelling is important here. 'Rusell Zanandra,' spelled that way is an anagram of Lazarus Lennard. Zanandra was the stage name used by Martha's brother—evidently he had a penchant for anagrams."

Ibbs frowned. "But that can't be right. Didn't Paolini say the fellow was killed in Deadwood, South Dakota? Shot by an unfaithful wife, or something? That couldn't have been Martha's brother."

"You're right. It wasn't. Rusell Zanandra, also known as Lazarus Lennard, died here in England. A victim of the bullet catch trick. But as we now know, he was certainly not the charlatan or amateur that Paolini painted him to be. The opposite was true: *Paolini* was the impostor, who stole the great man's tricks! And imagine the gall of making a remark like that with Lennard's *sister* onstage beside him! Think about the character of Paolini. He could not resist gloating like this at every opportunity. And Martha had no choice but to stand by in silence. Scarcely a wonder, is it, that she killed him?"

Ibbs was silent a moment, then said: "But where did that 'Black Wizard of the West' business come from?"

"There *was* a fellow who went by that name. An American, whose fame never reached these shores. Instead he lives on as a kind of warning to the curious, as M. R. James might put it. His name was H. T. Sartell. A failure as a magician, and evidently as a husband. In actuality, Paolini's words onstage were: 'like Rusell Zanandra *or* the "Black Wizard of the West," a snake oil salesman shot dead in front of an audience by a scheming wife.'* They were not one and the same, as his speech implied, but distinct performers. The facts surrounding Zanandra's death are shrouded in mystery, but whether or not Paolini played an active part in it, he certainly did enough to debase the poor man's memory. And surely that was sufficient to instil a deep resentment in Martha. A resentment that could only be allayed by wiping Paolini off the face of the planet."

---

* *See page 51.*

"But why did she write the book? *The Master of Manipulation?* It doesn't make sense, if she was planning to kill him anyway."

Spector shrugged. "Another double bluff. She was aware that despite her efforts, her identity as author of the book would be revealed eventually. After all, Paolini knew full well where the tricks came from and who had access to them. The pool of suspects was bound to be limited, though the culprit could have been any of the backstage crew at the Pomegranate. And in the unlikely event that she found herself under suspicion of killing Paolini, investigators would inevitably ask the same question that you just have. Consequently, the fact that she had already put an end to Paolini's career *before* he was killed would seem to exonerate her from the murder charge. And so her revenge was twofold: she was able to enjoy his helplessness as his stolen book of tricks was shared with the world, before administering the lethal *coup de grace.*"

The old conjuror leaned forward conspiratorially. His thin face was now underlit by the candle, and looked positively demonic. "Listen close, Edmund. This is the first and only time I am going to tell this story.

"Martha came up with her plan while she and Paolini were touring the world. But she had to wait until they were back in England before she could go through with it. Fortunately for her, Paolini practically devised the scheme himself. Do you remember he mentioned obtaining English newspapers overseas?* Well, that's how he came across the Dean case. And it fascinated him. He became almost obsessed with it during the final weeks of his world

---

* *See page 83.*

tour. His imagination had latched onto Dominic Dean's murder. This, coupled with his close reading of the Sherlock Holmes canon, led him to devise an alternative solution to Dominic Dean's murder. That is what he was attempting to demonstrate.

"Fortunately, he left enough bread crumbs for me to trace his train of thought back to its origins. Namely, in a story of Conan Doyle's called 'The Problem of Thor Bridge.'

"In the story, a woman is shot dead on the eponymous bridge. Cold-blooded murder, or so it seems. In fact, the woman has rigged a device that will drag the weapon over the side of the bridge and down into the water. This will enable her to commit suicide in such a way that she *appears* to have been murdered, and in so doing to frame an innocent person for a nonexistent crime.

"That is the story that struck Paolini. He perceived a parallel between the woman on the bridge and the man on the Ferris wheel. In short, his theory was that Dominic Dean shot himself in an effort to frame his innocent wife.

"Now of course, you and I know that there are several arguments against this theory. Specifically, a stomach shot is a particularly agonising cause of death, and one which a man would be unlikely to inflict on himself. But it's not important whether *we* believe the theory. What matters is that *Paolini* believed it. He genuinely thought he had stumbled across the solution to an impossible problem. He thought Dominic Dean killed himself in an effort to frame his wife. That's what he was trying to prove. But his ego would not permit him to keep his ideas to himself; he confided in Martha. Of course he did. She was likely the only person who would listen. And that's when she worked out her own plan—to co-opt his fake murder scheme with her own *real* murder scheme."

Ibbs's head was spinning. "So who knocked me out?"

"Paolini."

"Why would he do that? It makes no sense."

"It makes sense when we take into account the character of Paolini. A man whose career was in its death throes and who was desperate to generate a sensation of some kind, no matter how outlandish it might prove to be. Remember, he anticipated the presence of Andrew Morgan, as he was hoping to get his name into the headlines once more. And it's safe to say that this little locked-room mystery is the reason he asked him to be at the theatre that night.

"Paolini was, if nothing else, an adept showman. His plan was for us to hear a gunshot and come running, which we did. His plan was for us to burst into the dressing room which, in a manner of speaking, we did. And his plan was for us to find his corpse. Which we did.

"However, *his* plan had a pronounced distinction from the way things actually turned out. You see, in *his* plan, he was merely playing dead. He engineered a locked-room situation with himself as the victim and you, Mr. Ibbs, as the murderer—a last-minute replacement for Morgan. He distracted you, then knocked you unconscious. His plan was to lie, so that when you awoke you found yourself in the same position as Carla Dean: an obvious murderer. He would wait until the police broke in, and then undergo a miraculous resurrection. Like Lazarus. He would gleefully explain how he had played everyone for fools. But of course, it didn't quite work out that way, did it?"

"So he was planning the locked-room business as a publicity stunt?"

"Yes. Naturally, it did not quite pan out the way he intended. First of all, the abrupt end to his show had sent Andrew Morgan, the reporter he had invited, scurrying off into the night. But *you* proved an able enough understudy, Mr. Ibbs. So Paolini decided to go ahead with his plan anyway. Perhaps it was Martha who urged him to do it—after all, her own plan would not work anywhere other than the Pomegranate, and she did not want to risk missing the opportunity. And while it was impossible for her to enter his dressing room, as you will soon see she did not need to."

"How come?"

Spector smiled thinly. "Here's the trick, Ibbs. I think you'll like it. But first, it's important to note that she needed to gain access to that central, unoccupied dressing room in order for her plan to work. The door connecting her own dressing room to the one in question is secured by an impermeable Chubb lock. But the opening and closing of this connecting door was really only a minor part of the illusion. The Chubb lock remains in perfect working order. Almost *too* good, in fact. That's what made me focus not on the lock but on the hinges. There are three hinges connecting the door to its frame, each with a metal pin holding it in place. These three hinge pins could be dealt with in a couple minutes; all it took was a bit of brute force. It would be quick and—most importantly—quiet. I've seen it done with the claw part of a hammer, sliding it onto the head of the hinge pin and simply levering it upward and out. It might be accompanied by a creak or a scrape of metal, but nothing too noisy or obtrusive. In other words, nothing that would be noticed by a passerby in the corridor. And, needless to say, no visible damage.

"With the hinge pins removed, the door could be eased out of its frame without troubling the lock. And when Martha was finished, it was simply a matter of returning to her dressing room and sliding those pins back into place, to be hammered in later. When we came to examine the door, our attention was focused solely on the lock. When, for all intents and purposes, the door could be opened *without* being unlocked."

"All right," said Ibbs, "so she got into the middle dressing room. I still don't understand how she killed Paolini and rigged that whole thing."

"No," said Spector, "but you will. Here's the next part of the trick: Benjamin Teasel, the fellow who owns the Pomegranate, is a tiresome old lecher and voyeur. He's a devil with the chorus girls and dancers. Why am I telling you this? Well, the fact is that Paolini's dressing room was previously occupied by eight chorus girls.* It's the largest dressing room in the building. Teasel is known to be a Peeping Tom,** and I think it highly likely he had created a minuscule peephole between that dressing room and the one beside it—which was usually kept vacant. In other words—a hole in the wall between dressing rooms."

"But there was no hole in that wall."

Spector smiled. "Yes, there was. A bullet hole."

---

*   *See page 83.*
**   *See page 79.*

"But wasn't that hole made when the bullet passed through Paolini and embedded in the door beyond?"

"That," said Spector, "is what we were intended to think. I have never seen evidence that such a peephole exists, but let us suppose that one existed between that central room and Paolini's, and that Martha knew about it. Perhaps she stumbled upon it for herself when she and Paolini performed at the Pomegranate in the past. She could use it to watch Paolini, and wait until he knocked you unconscious. Then all she had to do was attract his attention by either tapping on the wall or else simply calling out to him quietly. She drew him toward her, perhaps even inducing him to press his ear to the wall so that he might hear her better. Then she simply lined the barrel up to the peephole and fired, killing Paolini instantly with a close-range bullet wound."

Ibbs was fascinated, but he could not stop himself from asking a question: "Wait a moment, sir. So you're saying that hole in the wall was where the bullet went *in*, not where it came *out*?"

"Precisely. The walls of the dressing room were a rich claret colour,[*] so she did not need to worry about unsightly splatter giving the game away. But again, we let ourselves be guided by our assumptions. Because of an apparent bullet hole in the left-hand wall, we kept our attention on that part of the room. When, if we had taken the time to examine the *opposite* wall, we would likely have found telltale traces of blood that would have turned the whole business quite literally on its head."

---

[*]   *See page 82.*

"Then what about the position of the body? And how did the gun get into the room? How did it get in my *hand*?"

"All good questions—but easily answered. I would say that the whole thing—I mean the events which took place between the shooting of Paolini and the moment we entered the room—could be dealt with in roughly three minutes. Bearing in mind that it took us *five* to get into the blasted room, I think that sounds reasonable, don't you?

"Martha went back into her own dressing room, sealing the door behind her and creating the illusion of its impenetrability. Then she opened the window and handed the revolver out through the bars to . . . any guesses? Ned. Blindly obedient Ned must have been well-drilled in advance, for he performed almost perfectly. Incidentally, this was the *real* reason he was at the Pomegranate that night. Nothing to do with Toomey—that was just a convenient excuse. But if he had not been there, he would not have been sent up by Sidney Draper to cut that fateful rope. So, ironically enough, his role as accomplice in Martha's perfect crime led to his inadvertent scuppering of his *uncle's* perfect crime.

"Anyway, Ned headed along the alleyway to Paolini's window. You recall how everybody was convinced that the window was rusted shut? Though nobody actually tried it until *after* the crime. It had obviously been rusted shut at some point, so Winchester would not have had time to prise it open then and there. But he most likely did so earlier in the evening, perhaps with the aid of a crowbar and some oil. It was a vital part of the preparation. Maybe he did it while Paolini was performing. *Maybe* he even did it while his uncle was in the midst of murdering Miklos Varga. But it was vitally important that he was able to access Paolini's dressing room via the window, even though he could not have climbed in because of the bars.

"When he looked inside, he saw you unconscious and Paolini quite dead. There were three things he needed to accomplish in a very short space of time. First, to roll Paolini's corpse over, to reinforce the illusion that the bullet hole in the wall was a point of exit and not a point of entry. Second, to attach the weapon to your unconscious hand. And third, to seal the window so it had the appearance of being impermeable.

"I think he must have stowed one of those crooks in the alley. You know, the ones with the curved ends that they sometimes use in music hall comedy sketches? There was one lurking around backstage.* And after all, we know from his uncle that Ned had a knack for 'hook-a-duck,'** though of course this was a somewhat macabre variant. Perhaps hooking Paolini's corpse under the arm with the rod, he was able to use his own brute strength to force the dead man over onto his stomach. Step one—complete. Next came the somewhat trickier business of attaching the weapon to your hand. In many ways, this was the most demanding aspect of the whole crime, but it was certainly worth the effort. It bamboozled everyone—even me. You see, the aim of this rather unorthodox manoeuvre was not to try and convince us that you were the killer. No—rather like the Dean case and that wretched wheel, the plan was to frame you so perfectly that no one would possibly be

---

*   *See page 70.*
**   *See page 102.*

convinced of your guilt. But unlike Carla Dean, you really *were* innocent. No, the idea behind attaching the weapon to your hand was a subtle reinforcement of the notion that the killer could only have operated *inside* the dressing room. And it worked. Because, despite all the evidence to the contrary, none of us could reconcile the notion that the murderer was anywhere other than inside that room.

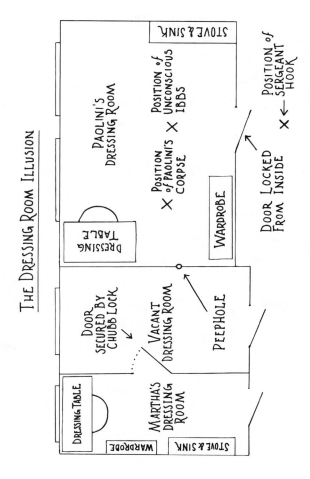

"So how did he do it? You've probably worked it out for yourself by now. He caught you by the wrist with that hook of his and hauled you up to the window like a ragdoll. You mentioned a pain in your arm which Flint was quick to ascribe to the pistol's 'kickback.'" In fact I believe this muscular injury was caused by Ned Winchester dragging you across the room by that arm. He reached in and attached the revolver to your hand with an adhesive he had brought with him. Then he simply let you fall back into the room beside your apparent victim.

"Lastly, sealing the window. This was easy enough thanks to the adhesive. A thin coating on the underside of the window frame before he closed it; that's all it took. When we finally got into the room, it was a while before we looked at the window. By that time, the adhesive had dried, sealing it up perfectly.

"But you know, there were two things missing from that dressing room. If not for them, I should never have seen through what truly was an excellent trick. The first was the glue. What Ned *should* have done was to drop the pot of adhesive into the room rather than taking it away with him. If he had done that, I doubt I should ever have got past the notion that the killer had to be inside the dressing room to complete this wicked business. So: no glue. That got me thinking.

"Next came the water. Previously, Paolini filled a glass from the tap. After the murder, I was scarcely able to coax a single drop.** I managed to trace this to a large dent in the corrugated water pipe

---

*   *See page 127.*
**   *See page 126.*

which ran along the right-hand wall. The dent had not been there earlier, and was most likely caused by the impact of a bullet. Do you see? The pipe on the *right*-hand wall bore a bullet mark. That could only mean the shot had come from an angle *opposite* to the one we were led to assume. The bullet itself had evidently ricocheted off the pipe and up into the ceiling. It had not passed out of the room at all. And it was that realisation which set me off along the trail that led me to the truth."

"I have one last question," said Ibbs.

"Please."

"Why are you protecting her? Why did you tell Scotland Yard that Draper was the one who killed Paolini?"

Spector shrugged. "Maybe it's because I never liked Paolini all that much. Maybe it's because I *do* like Martha. Maybe it's because I didn't want to see such a brilliant murder plot exposed—the magician in me wouldn't allow it. In fact, if Paolini had been the only one who died on the night in question, I should have been content to remove myself from the investigation altogether.

"Regardless, I knew that Draper's denials wouldn't stand up in a court of law. Perhaps he would not even have denied it. He might have enjoyed the notoriety. After all, you can only hang a man once. But as it happens, he will not face trial. He's dead. Suicide. So the records will show that he killed both Miklos Varga *and* Paul Zaibus, alias Professor Paolini."

"I see. . . ."

But Ibbs did not see. Evidently the young lawyer needed a bit more convincing. "When you're an old man like me," Spector said, "you'll realise that sometimes the truth is more painful than a convenient lie. And where's the harm? She's not a bad person, you know. Nor was Draper; not really. The one thing they had in common was their desperation, and the need to escape from circumstances which had entrapped them. But the underlying reason for Draper's crime was greed. The reason for Martha's was love. Love for her brother, and the need to do right by his memory. I think she'll make you a good wife. Provided, of course, that you stay on her good side."

Ibbs looked back at the old man. Spector's pale eyes gleamed.

ACKNOWLEDGEMENTS

This book is a tribute to the Golden Age of Detective Fiction. It couldn't have been written if not for the dazzling work of so many authors during the first half of the twentieth century. I am grateful to them all- particularly John Dickson Carr, Agatha Christie, Ellery Queen, Christianna Brand, Clayton Rawson and Hake Talbot.

I'd like to offer my thanks to Gabriele Crescenzi, Michael Dahl, Ana Teresa Pereira, Rob Reef and Dan Napolitano. Not only did they all read early drafts of *The Murder Wheel*, but they have been endless sources of encouragement and enthusiasm.

Thanks also to Martin Edwards, Jeff Marks, Douglas Greene, Gigi Pandian and Lenny Picker for continuing to champion vintage-style mysteries and locked rooms.

I am immensely grateful to the authors who provided such wonderful blurbs for *Death and the Conjuror*, which helped that book to reach a wider readership. Specifically, thank you to John Connolly, Charles Todd and Daniel Stashower, who set the ball rolling.

ACKNOWLEDGEMENTS

Thanks to Otto Penzler and Charles Perry at Mysterious Press for their wonderful support of the Spector stories, as well as their great work in bringing Golden Age mysteries to new generations of readers.

Thank you to the usual suspects: Michael Pritchard, Milan Gurung, Amy Louise Smith and Georgia Robinson, for their friendship and support during the writing of *The Murder Wheel*.

And last of all, thank you to the rich community of readers and bloggers who have embraced the Spector stories, and with whom I have enjoyed plenty of lively discussions. Here's to many more.